# HARD TO BE A GOD

# HARD
## TO BE A GOD

Arkady and Boris Strugatsky

Translated by Olena Bormashenko

CHICAGO
REVIEW
PRESS

Published by Chicago Review Press Incorporated
814 North Franklin Street
Chicago, IL 60610
ISBN 978-1-61374-828-2

*The publication was effected under the auspices of the Mikhail Prokhorov
Foundation TRANSCRIPT Programme to Support Translations of Russian
Literature.*

ИНСТИТУТ ПЕРЕВОДА

AD VERBUM

*Published with the support of the Institute for Literary Translation (Russia).*

**Library of Congress Cataloging-in-Publication Data**
Strugatskii, Arkadii, 1925–1991, author.
  [Trudno byt' bogom. English. 2014]
  Hard to be a god / Arkady and Boris Strugatsky ; translated by Olena
Bormashenko.
    pages ; cm
  ISBN 978-1-61374-828-2
  I. Strugatskii, Boris, 1933–2012, author. II. Bormashenko, Olena, translator.
III. Title.

PG3476.S78835T7813 2014
891.73'44—dc23
                        2014007355

Cover design: Sarah Olson
Cover image: Photo by S. Aksionov, © Sever Ltd.
Interior design: PerfecType, Nashville, TN

Printed in the United States of America

# Foreword

by Hari Kunzru

There are always schisms, even in medieval fantasy. Weird tales are weird in more than one way. One the one hand we have a rural tradition, sentimental, conservative, and wedded to absolute notions of good and evil. This is the English school of Tolkien and Lewis, in which Christ-lions and schoolchildren fight cosmopolitan witches and wizards with suspiciously foreign names. The nasty working classes of industrial Mordor threaten the exurban tranquility of the Shire, a place full of morally centered artisans and small tradesmen, destined, once the dwarves build the railway and the elves finally get out of their hot tubs and invent the Internet, to end up as commuters. Elsewhere Anglo-Saxon Potters and Weasleys, first cousins of the hobbits, take on effete Norman-French Malfoys and Voldemorts. Fantasy of this kind is intended as comfort and consolation, which is why it's often written for and marketed to children. One can retreat from the ambiguities of the real world into the green-wood, where the demarcation between right and wrong is clear. In the final pages, the reign of King John will come to an end and good King Richard will return, heralding a time of merriment and feasting.

In the English tradition, the city is conspicuous by its absence. But there's a countertradition, sexy and cynical, devoted to the romance of urban life, with its giddying complexity, its taverns and towers, its markets and locked doors and alleyways. In Viriconium or Lankhmar or King's Landing, there are thieves and rogues and sorcerers and beautiful women at high windows. In such fantastical cities, shadows abound and good doesn't always prevail. It's a type of romance that owes more to Paris (the city of Dumas's musketeers and the Baudelairean flaneur) than medieval chivalry or Icelandic sagas. So when *Hard to Be a God* deposits us in Arkanar, we may feel we know where we are. Don Rumata, swashbuckling swordsman, *bon viveur*, and wit, is no Bilbo Baggins, blushing when required to talk to a lady. And Arkanar is a far cry from Camelot or Gondor. Its citizens delight in hanging "suspicious bookworms" and the noble lord is clearly accustomed to using his blade against boors, footpads, and impertinent members of the lower orders.

However, this is no reactionary celebration of aristocratic derring-do. Rumata is really Anton, an emissary from a future Earth where Communism has triumphed, creating a rational, benevolent society that can only look on the filth and cruelty of this backward world with disgust. Rumata/Anton is an operative working on behalf of Earth historians, studying the feudal mores of the planet with a view to assisting them to "progress" along the straight and narrow path of history. Unlike their Yankee contemporaries (who always seem to be planting moonbases and generally making themselves at home on alien planets), the enlightened peoples of the Noon Universe don't intervene as imperialists. Anton isn't the probe-head of some future project of settlement or colonization. Instead he's a kind of human webcam, feeding video back to his home planet, even as he's embroiled in Arkanar's vicious court politics. Like his fellow operatives, he rails against the strict injunction not to intervene overtly in the planet's affairs. Faced with the brutality and excesses of the worthless, decadent aristocracy, he is sorely tempted to right some wrongs—and break some skulls. He is a god who must hide his divinity.

Confined by his rules of engagement, Anton sometimes seems less a god than a trickster—a semidivine Raven or Anansi or Coyote, mixed up in situations rather than standing transcendentally above them. He has special powers but a limited scope in which to use them. All the time he suffers the psychological torments of any operative who spends a long time in deep cover. What does his far distant home really mean to him? Will the mask of the aristocratic dandy begin to eat into his face?

It's a common observation that all science fiction novels say as much about the time of their composition as they do about the future. As they wrote *Hard to Be a God*, the Strugatsky brothers were working under considerable political pressure. Following Khrushchev's infamous visit to an exhibition of abstract art in 1962 ("dog shit" was one of his more printable responses) a wave of panicked ideological housecleaning swept through the Soviet Union's artistic establishment. For SF writers, as Boris Strugatsky remembers, this resulted in a reminder that the only truly orthodox subject

was "the collision of two worlds." At the time the brothers still harbored hopes that Communism could produce the
kind of enlightened civilization that forms the backdrop of
their Noon novels. But perhaps inevitably, their initial plans
for a Dumas-influenced swashbuckling tale about an earth-
man's adventures in a feudal world became a much darker
story about the fate of the intelligentsia under totalitarianism.
The spymaster villain Don Reba was originally called Rebia,
a none-too-subtle anagram of Beria, the infamous head of
Stalin's secret police, the NKVD. Reba's systematic destruction of the values of science and intellectual inquiry are thus
both a reminder of the purges of the 1930s and a coded plea
to Khrushchev not to follow in his predecessor's footsteps.
The resulting novel, part Boy's Own adventure and part dys-
topian political satire, is a sort of metafantasy, neither Dumas
nor Tolkien but a wry commentary on the medievalism of
the genre. In Russia, it has been wildly popular for almost
half a century. It's sure to find new fans in English.

# HARD TO BE A GOD

The sorrow that tortured me, the shame that overwhelmed me, the desperation that wracked my mind, all these I could then feel, but even now I can find no words to express them.

—Pierre Abelard

Now one thing I have to tell you. In this particular show you have to be armed to enforce your authority. But you're not to use your weapon under any circumstances. Under any circumstances. Is that quite clear?

—Ernest Hemingway

# Prologue

The black stock of Anka's crossbow was made of plastic, while the strings were chrome steel, operated by a single motion of a noiselessly sliding lever. Anton didn't trust newfangled technology; he had an old-fashioned arbalest in the style of Marshal Totz (King Pitz the First), overlaid with black copper, with a cable of ox sinew wound around a little wheel. And Pashka had taken a pneumatic rifle. Since he was lazy and lacked the mechanical aptitude to work crossbows, he thought they were childish.

They landed on the north shore, where the gnarled roots of the giant pines jutted out of the sandy yellow cliff. Anka let go of the rudder and looked around. The sun was already over the forest, and everything was blue, green, and yellow—the blue fog above the lake, the dark green pine trees, and the yellow shore on the other side. And the sky above it all was a pale, clear blue.

"There's nothing there," Pashka said.

The kids sat leaning over the side of the boat, looking into the water. "A huge pike," Anton said confidently.

"With fins *this* big?" Pashka asked.

Anton didn't reply. Anka also took a look, but saw only her own reflection.

"Be good to take a swim," said Pashka, plunging his arm into the water up to his elbow. "It's cold," he reported.

Anton clambered to the front and jumped onto the shore. The boat swayed. Anton grabbed its side and looked expectantly at Pashka. Then Pashka stood up, put the oar behind his neck like a yoke, and wriggling his lower body, sang:

> Grizzled seadog Tarkypark!
> Pal, you'd better stay awake.
> Careful, schools of deep-fried sharks
> Rush toward you through the lake.

Anton silently jerked the boat.

"Hey, hey!" Pashka shouted, grabbing at the sides.

"Why deep-fried?" Anka asked.

"Dunno," answered Pashka. They climbed out of the boat. "Sounds good, huh? Schools of deep-fried sharks!"

They hauled the boat onto the shore. Their feet sank into the damp sand, full of dried needles and pinecones. The boat was heavy and slippery, but they managed to drag it out all the way to the stern, then stopped, breathing hard.

"I crushed my foot," said Pashka, fixing his red bandanna. He always made sure that his bandanna was tied precisely over his right ear, in the fashion of the hook-nosed Irukanian pirates. "Life ain't worth a dime," he declared.

Anka was intently sucking on her finger.

"A splinter?" Anton asked.

"No. A scratch. One of you two has real claws . . ."

"Let me have a look."

She showed him.

"Yes," said Anton. "A wound. Well, what should we do?"

"Hoist the boat onto our shoulders and walk along the shore," Pashka suggested.

"So why did we get out?" Anton asked.

"Any idiot could manage in the boat," Pashka explained. "But on the shore, there are reeds—that's one. Cliffs—that's two. And ponds—that's three. And the ponds are full of carp, and catfish."

"Schools of deep-fried catfish," said Anton.

"You ever dive into a pond?"

"Sure."

"Never seen you do it. Must have missed it somehow."

"Lots of things you haven't seen."

Anka turned her back to them, raised her crossbow, and shot at a pine tree about twenty paces away. Bits of tree bark rained down.

"Nice," said Pashka, and immediately fired his rifle. He had aimed at Anka's bolt, but he missed. "Didn't hold my breath," he explained.

"And if you had?" asked Anton. He was looking at Anka.

Anka pulled the bowstring lever. She had excellent muscles—Anton enjoyed watching the little hard ball of her biceps roll under her tanned skin. She took very careful aim and fired another bolt. It pierced the tree trunk right below the first with a crack. "We shouldn't be doing that," she said, lowering her crossbow.

"Doing what?" Anton asked.

"Hurting the tree, that's what. Some kid was shooting at a tree with a bow yesterday, so I made him pull the arrows out with his teeth."

"Pashka," said Anton. "Go on, you have good teeth."

"One of my teeth makes me whistle," he retorted.

"Forget it," said Anka. "Let's do something."

"I don't feel like climbing cliffs," Anton said.

"Me neither. Let's go straight."

"Go where?" Pashka asked.

"Wherever."

"Well?" said Anton.

"That means the saiva," Pashka said. "Let's go to the Forgotten Highway. Remember, Toshka?"

"Of course!" Anton replied.

"You see, Anechka—" Pashka began.

"Don't you call me Anechka," Anka said sharply. She couldn't stand it when people called her anything other than Anka.

Anton took careful note of her preference. He quickly said, "The Forgotten Highway. No one drives on it. And it's not on the map. And we have no idea where it goes."

"And you've been there?"

"Once. But we didn't have the time to explore."

"A road from nowhere to nowhither," declared the recovered Pashka.

"That's amazing!" Anka said. Her eyes became like black slits. "Let's go. Will we make it by night?"

"Come on! We'll make it by noon."

They climbed up the cliff. When he got to the top, Pashka turned around. He saw the blue lake with the yellowish bald patches of the sandbars, the boat lying on the sand, and large ripples spreading in the calm, oily water by the shore—probably a splash from that same pike. And Pashka was filled with the vague elation he always felt when he and Anton had run away from boarding school and a day of total independence lay ahead—full of undiscovered places, wild strawberries, hot deserted meadows, gray lizards, and ice-cold water from unexpected springs. And as always, he wanted to whoop and leap up high in the air, and he immediately did so, and Anton looked at him, laughing, and Pashka saw that Anton's eyes expressed complete understanding. And Anka put two fingers in her mouth and gave a wild whistle, and they entered the forest.

It was a forest of sparse pines; their feet kept slipping on the fallen needles. The slanting rays of the sun fell between the straight trunks, and the ground was dappled with golden spots. It smelled of tar, the lake, and wild strawberries; unseen birds screeched somewhere in the sky.

Anka was walking in front, holding the crossbow underneath her arm, occasionally bending down to pick the blood-red wild strawberries, so shiny they looked varnished. Anton followed with the good old-fashioned arbalest of Marshal Totz on his shoulder. The quiver with the good old-fashioned bolts slapped heavily against his behind. He walked and glanced at Anka's neck—tanned, almost black, with protruding vertebrae. Once in a while he'd look around, searching for Pashka, but Pashka was nowhere to be found—except that from time to time, first to his right, then to his left, a red bandanna would flash in the sun. Anton pictured Pashka silently gliding between the pine trees, his rifle at the ready, his thin, predatory face with the peeling nose stretched out in front of him. Pashka was stealing through the saiva, and the saiva meant business. The saiva will call, my friend—and you have to respond in time, thought Anton. He was about to duck down, but Anka was in front of him and she might turn around. It'd be ridiculous.

Anka turned around and asked, "You left quietly?"

Anton shrugged. "Who leaves loudly?"

"Actually, I might have been noisy," Anka said anxiously. "I dropped a basin—then, suddenly, there were footsteps in the hall. Must have been old maid Katya—she's on duty today. I had to jump into the flower bed. What do you think, Toshka, what kind of flowers grow in there?"

Anton furrowed his brow. "Underneath your window? No idea. Why?"

"Very hardy flowers. 'No wind can bend them, no storm can fell them.' People have jumped in there for years, but they couldn't care less."

"That's interesting," Anton said with an air of deep thought. He remembered that underneath his window there was also a flower bed with flowers "no wind can bend, no storm can fell." But he had never paid any attention.

Anka stopped, waited for him, and offered him a handful of wild strawberries. Anton carefully took three berries. "Have some more," said Anka.

"Thanks," said Anton. "I like taking them one by one. Old maid Katya isn't too bad, right?"

"Depends on your point of view," said Anka. "When someone tells you every night that your feet are either dirty or dusty . . ." She stopped talking. It was wonderful walking alone in the forest with her like this, shoulder to shoulder, bare elbows touching, glancing over occasionally to take in how pretty she was, how agile, and how amazingly friendly. How her eyes were big and gray, with black eyelashes.

"Yeah," said Anton, stretching out his hand to brush aside a cobweb that gleamed in the sun. "I bet her feet are never dusty. If you're carried over puddles, you sure won't get covered in dust . . ."

"Who's been carrying her?"

"Henry from the weather station. You know, the big blond one."

"Really?"

"What's the big deal? Everyone knows that they're in love."

They stopped talking again. Anton took a look at Anka. Her eyes were like black slits. "Since when?" she asked.

"Oh, one moonlit night," Anton answered cautiously. "Just don't tell anyone."

Anka chuckled. "No one made you talk, Toshka," she said. "Want some wild strawberries?"

Anton mechanically scooped berries from her stained little palm and stuffed them into his mouth. I don't like gossips, he thought. I can't stand blabbermouths. He suddenly found an argument. "You'll be carried in someone's arms yourself someday," he said. "How would you like it if people started gossiping about it?"

"What makes you think I'm going to gossip?" Anka said, sounding distracted. "I don't like gossips myself."

"Listen, what are you up to?"

"Nothing in particular." Anka shrugged. A minute later she confided, "You know, I'm awfully sick of having to wash my feet twice every single night."

Poor old maid Katya, thought Anton. A fate worse than the saiva.

They came out onto the trail. It sloped down, and the forest kept getting darker and darker. It was overgrown with ferns and tall, damp grass. The pine trunks were covered in moss and the foam of white lichen. But the saiva meant business. A hoarse, utterly inhuman voice suddenly roared, "Stop! Drop your weapons—you, noble don, and you, doña!"

When the saiva calls, you have to respond in time. In a single precise motion, Anton knocked Anka into the ferns to the left, threw himself into the ferns to the right, then rolled over and lay in wait behind a rotten tree stump. The hoarse echo was still reverberating through the pine trunks, but the trail was already empty. There was silence.

Anton, lying on his side, was spinning the little wheel to draw the bowstrings. A shot rang out, and some debris fell on him. The raspy, inhuman voice informed them, "The don was struck in the heel!"

Anton moaned and grabbed his foot.

"Not in that one, the other one," the voice corrected.

You could hear Pashka giggle. Anton carefully peered out from behind the stump, but he couldn't see a thing in the thick green gloom.

At this instant, there was a piercing whistle and a sound like a tree falling. "Ow!" Pashka gave a strangled cry. "Mercy! Mercy! Don't kill me!"

Anton immediately jumped up. Pashka was backing up out of the ferns toward him. His arms were above his head. They heard Anka's voice: "Anton, do you see him?"

"I see him," Anton answered appreciatively. "Don't turn around!" he yelled at Pashka. "Hands behind your head!"

Pashka obediently put his hands behind his head and announced, "I'll never talk."

"What are we supposed to do with him, Toshka?" Anka asked.

"You'll see," said Anton, and took a comfortable seat on the stump, resting his crossbow on his knees. "Your name!" he barked in the voice of Hexa the Irukanian.

Pashka expressed contempt and defiance with his back. Anton fired. A heavy bolt pierced the branch above Pashka's head with a crack.

"Whoa!" said Anka.

"My name is Bon Locusta," Pashka admitted reluctantly. "And here, it seems, will he die—'for I only am left, and they seek my life.'"

"A well-known rapist and murderer," Anton explained. "But he does nothing for free. Who sent you?"

"I was sent by Don Satarina the Ruthless," Pashka lied.

Anton said scornfully, "This hand cut the thread of Don Satarina's foul life two years ago in the Territory of Heavy Swords."

"Should I stick a bolt in him?" offered Anka.

"I completely forgot," Pashka said hastily. "Actually, I was sent by Arata the Beautiful. He promised me a hundred gold pieces for your heads."

Anton slapped his knees. "What a liar!" he exclaimed. "Like Arata would ever get involved with a villain like you!"

"Maybe I should stick a bolt in him after all?" Anka asked bloodthirstily.

Anton laughed demonically.

"By the way," said Pashka, "your right heel has been shot off. It's time for you to bleed to death."

"No way!" Anton objected. "For one thing, I've been constantly chewing on white tree bark, and for another, two beautiful barbarians have already dressed my wounds."

The ferns rustled, and Anka came out onto the trail. Her cheek was scratched, and her knees were smeared with dirt and grass. "It's time to dump him into the swamp," she announced. "When an enemy doesn't surrender, he's destroyed."

Pashka lowered his arms. "You know, you don't play by the rules," he said to Anton. "You always make Hexa seem like a good man."

"A lot you know!" said Anton, coming out onto the trail as well. "The saiva means business, you dirty mercenary."

Anka gave Pashka back his rifle. "Do you always let loose at each other like that?" she asked enviously.

"Of course!" Pashka said in surprise. "What, are we supposed to yell '*Boom-boom*'? '*Bang-bang*'? The game needs an element of risk!"

Anton said nonchalantly, "For example, we often play William Tell."

"We take turns," Pashka caught on. "One day the apple's on my head, the next day it's on his."

Anka scrutinized them. "Oh yeah?" she said slowly. "I'd like to see that."

"We'd love to," Anton said slyly. "Too bad we don't have an apple."

Pashka was grinning widely. Then Anka tore the pirate bandanna off his head and quickly rolled it into a long bundle. "The apple is just a convention," she said. "Here's an excellent target. Go on, play William Tell."

Anton took the red bundle and examined it carefully. He looked at Anka—her eyes were like slits. And Pashka was enjoying himself—he was having fun. Anton handed him the bundle. "'At thirty paces I can manage to hit a card without fail,'" he recited evenly. "'I mean, of course, with a pistol that I am used to.'"

"'Really?'" said Anka. She then turned to Pashka: "'And you, my dear, could you hit a card at thirty paces?'"

Pashka was placing the bundle onto his head. "'Some day we will try,'" he said, smirking. "'In my time, I did not shoot badly.'"

Anton turned around and walked down the trail, counting the steps out loud: "Fifteen . . . sixteen . . . seventeen . . ."

Pashka said something—Anton didn't catch it—and Anka laughed loudly. A little too loudly.

"Thirty," Anton said and turned around.

At thirty paces, Pashka looked incredibly small. The red triangle of the bundle was perched on top of his head like a dunce cap. Pashka was smirking. He was still playing around. Anton bent down and started slowly drawing the bowstrings.

"Bless you, my father William!" Pashka called out. "And thank you for everything, no matter what happens."

Anton nocked the bolt and stood up. Pashka and Anka were looking at him. They were standing side by side. The trail was like a dark, damp corridor between tall green walls. Anton raised the crossbow. The weapon of Marshal Totz had become extraordinarily heavy. My hands are shaking, thought Anton. That's not good. He remembered how in the winter Pashka and he had spent a whole hour throwing snowballs at the cast iron pinecone on the fence post. They threw from twenty paces, from fifteen, and from ten—but they just couldn't hit it. And then, when they were already bored and were leaving, Pashka carelessly, without looking, threw the last snowball and hit it. Anton pressed the stock of the crossbow into his shoulder with all his strength. Anka is too close, he thought. He wanted to call to her to step away but realized that it'd be silly.

Higher. Even higher . . . Higher still . . . He was suddenly seized with the certainty that even if he turned his back to them, the heavy bolt would still sink right into the bridge of Pashka's nose, between his cheerful green eyes. He opened his eyes and looked at Pashka. Pashka was no longer grinning. And Anka was very slowly raising a hand with her fingers spread, and her face was tense and very grown-up. Then Anton raised the crossbow even higher and pressed the trigger. He didn't see where the bolt went.

"I missed," he said very loudly.

Walking on unbending legs, he started down the trail. Pashka wiped his face with the red bundle, shook it, unfolded it, and started tying it around his head. Anka bent down and picked up her crossbow. If she hits me over the head with that thing, Anton thought, I'll thank her. But Anka didn't even look at him.

She turned toward Pashka and asked, "Shall we go?"

"One second," Pashka said. He looked at Anton and silently tapped his forehead with a bent finger.

"And you really got scared," Anton said.

Pashka tapped his forehead with a finger again and followed Anka. Anton trudged behind them and tried to suppress his doubts.

What did I do wrong, exactly? he thought dully. Why are they so mad? Well, Pashka I understand—he got scared. Except I don't know who was more frightened, William the father or Tell the son. But what about Anka? She must have gotten scared for Pashka. But what could I have done? Look at me, trailing behind them like a cousin. I should just take off. I'll turn left here, there's an interesting swamp that direction. Maybe I'll catch an owl. But he didn't even slow down. That means it's for life, he thought. He had read that it very often happened like this.

They came out onto the abandoned road even sooner than expected. The sun was high; it was hot. The pine needles prickled under Anton's collar. The road was concrete, made of two rows of cracked, grayish-red slabs. Thick dry grass grew in the interstices. The side of the road was full of dusty burrs. Beetles were buzzing, and one of them insolently slammed right into Anton's forehead. It was quiet and languid.

"Look!" said Pashka.

A round tin disk, covered with peeling paint, hung in the middle of a rusty wire stretched across the road. It seemed to show a yellow rectangle on a red background.

"What is it?" Anka asked, without any particular interest.

"A road sign," Pashka said. "Says not to go there."

"Do not enter," Anton confirmed.

"Why is it here?" Anka asked.

"It means you can't go that way," Pashka said.

"So why the road?"

Pashka shrugged his shoulders. "It's a very old highway," he said.

"An anisotropic highway," declared Anton. Anka was standing with her back to him. "It only goes one way."

"The wisdom of our forefathers," Pashka said pensively. "You drive and drive for a hundred miles, then suddenly—boom!—a do-not-enter sign. You can't go straight, but there's no one to ask for directions."

"Imagine what could be beyond the sign!" said Anka. She looked around. They were surrounded by many miles of empty forest, and there was no one to ask what could be beyond the sign. "What if it doesn't even say do not enter?" she asked. "The paint is mostly peeled off . . ."

Then Anton took careful aim and fired. It would have been fantastic if the bolt had shot through the wire and the sign had fallen at Anka's feet. But the bolt hit the top of the sign, piercing the rusty tin, and the only thing that fell was dried paint.

"Idiot," said Anka, without turning around.

This was the first word she had addressed to Anton after the game of William Tell. Anton smiled crookedly. "'And enterprises of great pitch and moment,'" he recited. "'With this regard their currents turn awry, and lose the name of action.'"

Good old Pashka shouted, "Guys, a car has driven this way! Since the thunderstorm! Here's the flattened grass! And here . . ."

Lucky Pashka, thought Anton. He started examining the marks on the road and also saw the flattened grass and the black stripe left by the treads when the car had braked before a pothole.

"Aha!" said Pashka. "He came from past the sign!"

That was completely obvious, but Anton objected: "No way, he was going the other direction."

Pashka raised his astonished eyes at him. "Have you gone blind?"

"He was going the other direction," Anton repeated stubbornly. "Let's follow him."

"That's ridiculous!" Pashka was outraged. "For one thing, no respectable driver would go the wrong way past a do-not-enter sign. For another, just look: here's the pothole, here are the tracks of the brakes . . . So which way was he going?"

"Who cares about respectable! I'm not respectable myself, and I'm going past the sign."

Pashka exploded. "Do what you want!" he said, stuttering slightly. "Moron. The heat's gone to your head!"

Anton turned around and, staring fixedly in front of him, went past the sign. The only thing he wanted was to come across a blown-up bridge and to have to fight his way through to the other side. What do I care about some respectable guy! he thought. They can do what they want—Anka and her Pashenka. He remembered how Anka had cut Pavel down when he called her Anechka, and he felt a bit better. He looked back.

He saw Pashka right away: Bon Locusta, bent in two, following the receding tracks of the mysterious car. The rusty disk above the road swayed gently, and the blue sky flickered through the hole in the disk. And Anka was sitting by the roadside, her elbows propped on her knees and her chin on her clenched fists.

On their way back, it was already dusk. The boys were rowing, and Anka was at the rudder. A red moon was rising over the black forest, and frogs were croaking incessantly.

"We planned the outing so well," Anka said sadly. "You two!"

The boys were silent. Then Pashka asked quietly, "Toshka, what was there, beyond the sign?"

"A blown-up bridge," answered Anton. "And the skeleton of a fascist, chained to a machine gun." He thought a moment and added, "The machine gun had sunk into the ground."

"Hmm," Pashka said. "It happens. And guess what? I helped that guy fix his car."

# Chapter 1

When Rumata passed Holy Míca's grave—the seventh and last along the road—it was already completely dark. The much-ballyhooed Hamaharian stallion, received from Don Tameo in payment of a gambling debt, had turned out to be completely worthless. He had become sweaty and footsore, and moved in a wretched, wobbly trot. Rumata dug his knees into the horse's sides and whipped him between the ears with a glove, but he only dejectedly shook his head without moving any faster. Bushes stretched alongside the road, resembling clouds of solidified smoke in the gloom. The whine of mosquitoes was intolerable. Scattered stars trembled dimly in the murky sky. A mild wind was blowing in gusts, warm and cold at the same time, as was always the case in autumn in this seaside country, with its dusty, muggy days and chilly nights.

Rumata wrapped his cloak tighter and let go of his reins. He had no reason to hurry. There was still an hour until midnight, and the jagged black edge of the Hiccup Forest had already appeared above the horizon. Plowed fields flanked the road; swamps flickered beneath the stars, stinking of inorganic rust; barrows and rotting palisades from the time of the Invasion were visible in the dark. To his left, a grim glow was flaring up and dying down; a village must be burning, one of the innumerable indistinguishable places known as Deadtown, Gallowland, or Robberdale, though august decree had recently renamed them Beloved, Blessed, and Angelic. This country extended for hundreds of miles—from the shores of the Strait until the saiva of the Hiccup Forest—blanketed with mosquito clouds, torn apart by ravines, drowning in swamps, stricken by fevers, plagues, and foul-smelling head colds.

At the turn of the road, a dark figure materialized from the bushes. The stallion shied, throwing back his head. Rumata grabbed the reins, adjusted the lace on his right sleeve out of habit, and put his hand on the hilt of his sword before taking a good look.

The figure took off his hat. "Good evening, noble don," he said quietly. "I beg your pardon."

"What is it?" Rumata asked, listening hard.

There's no such thing as a silent ambush. Robbers give themselves away by the creak of their bowstrings, the gray storm troopers belch uncontrollably from the stale beer, the baronial militiamen breathe avidly through their noses and clatter their weapons, while the slave-hunting monks noisily scratch themselves. But the bushes were quiet. It seemed the man wasn't a bandit. Not that he looked much like a bandit—a short, thickset city resident in a modest cloak.

"May I run alongside you?" he asked, bowing.

"Certainly," said Rumata, lifting the reins. "You may hold the stirrup."

The man began to walk next to Rumata. His hat was in his hand, and a substantial bald patch shone on top of his head. Probably a steward, thought Rumata. Visiting the barons and cattle dealers, buying flax or hemp. A brave steward, though . . . Maybe he isn't a steward. Maybe he's a bookworm. A fugitive. An outcast. There are a lot of them on the night roads nowadays, more than there are stewards. Or maybe he's a spy.

"Who are you and where are you from?" Rumata asked.

"My name is Kiun," the man said sadly. "I'm coming from Arkanar."

"You're *running away* from Arkanar," Rumata said, bending down.

"I'm running away," the man agreed sadly.

Some eccentric, thought Rumata. Or maybe he really is a spy? I should test him . . . Actually, why should I? Who says I should? What right do I have to test him? No, I don't want to! Why can't I simply trust him? Here is a city dweller, clearly a bookworm, running for his life . . . He's lonely, he's scared, he's weak, he's looking for protection. He meets an aristocrat. Due to their arrogance and stupidity, aristocrats don't understand politics, but their swords are long and they don't like the grays. Why shouldn't Kiun the city dweller benefit from the disinterested protection of a stupid and arrogant aristocrat? That's it. I won't test him. I have no reason to test him. We'll talk, pass the time, part as friends . . .

"Kiun . . ." Rumata said. "I knew a Kiun once. A seller of potions and an alchemist from Tin Street. Are you a relative of his?"

"Unfortunately, I am," said Kiun. "Just a distant relative, but it's all the same to them . . . until the twelfth generation."

"And where are you running away to, Kiun?"

"Somewhere . . . The farther the better. Lots of people run away to Irukan. I'll try Irukan too."

"Well, well," Rumata said. "And you think that the noble don will help you across the border?"

Kiun was quiet.

"Or maybe you think that the noble don doesn't know who the alchemist Kiun from Tin Street is?"

Kiun stayed quiet.

What am I saying? thought Rumata. He stood up in his stirrups and shouted, imitating the town crier in the Royal Square, "Accused and convicted of terrible, unforgivable crimes against God, peace, and the Crown!"

Kiun was quiet.

"And what if the noble don adores Don Reba? What if he's wholeheartedly devoted to the gray word and the gray cause? Or do you think that's impossible?"

Kiun was quiet. The jagged shadow of a gallows appeared out of the darkness to the right of the road. A naked body, strung up by its feet, shone white beneath the crossbeam. Bah, it's not even working, thought Rumata. He reined his horse in, grabbed Kiun by the shoulder, and spun him around to face him.

"And what if the noble don decides to string you up right next to this tramp?" he said, peering into the white face with dark pits for eyes. "All by myself. Quickly and neatly. Why are you quiet, literate Kiun?"

Kiun was quiet. His teeth chattered, and he squirmed weakly in Rumata's grasp, like a crushed lizard. Then something suddenly fell into the roadside ditch with a splash, and immediately, as if to drown out the splash, he shouted frantically: "Then hang me! Hang me, traitor!"

Rumata took a deep breath and let Kiun go. "I was joking," he said. "Don't be scared."

"Lies, lies ..." Kiun mumbled, sobbing. "Lies everywhere!"

"Come on, don't be mad," Rumata said. "You'd better pick up what you threw in—it'll get wet."

Kiun waited a bit, rocking in place and blubbering, then he pointlessly patted his cloak with the palms of his hands and climbed into the ditch. Rumata waited, hunching wearily in his saddle. That's how it has to be, he thought; there's no other way.

Kiun climbed out of the ditch, hiding the bundle underneath his shirt.

"Books, of course," Rumata said.

Kiun shook his head. "No," he murmured. "Just one book. My book."

"And what are you writing about?"

"I'm afraid it wouldn't interest you, noble don."

Rumata sighed. "Take the stirrup," he said. "Let's go."

For a long time, they were silent.

"Listen, Kiun," said Rumata. "I was joking. Don't be scared of me."

"What a wonderful world," Kiun said. "What a merry world. Everybody jokes. And everybody's jokes are the same. Even noble Rumata's."

Rumata was surprised. "You know my name?"

"I do," Kiun said. "I recognized you by the circlet on your head. I was so glad to meet you on the road . . ."

Ah, of course, that's what he meant when he called me a traitor, thought Rumata. He said, "You see, I thought you were a spy. I always kill spies."

"A spy," repeated Kiun. "Yes, of course. In our times it's so easy and rewarding to be a spy. Our eagle, the noble Don Reba, is interested in what the king's subjects say and think. I wish I could be a spy. A rank-and-file informer at the Gray Joy Inn. How lovely, how respectable! At six o'clock I come to the bar and sit down at my table. The proprietor rushes toward me with my first pint. I can drink however much I want, the beer is paid for by Don Reba—or rather, it isn't paid for at all. I sit there, sip my beer, and listen. Sometimes I pretend to write down conversations, and the frightened little people hurry to me with offers of friendship and money. Their eyes express only the things I want: doglike devotion, fearful awe, and delightful impotent hatred. I can grope girls with impunity and fondle wives in front of their husbands—big burly men—and they'll only giggle obsequiously. What beautiful reasoning, noble don, is it not? I heard it from a fifteen-year-old boy, a student of the Patriotic School."

"And what did you tell him?" asked Rumata curiously.

"What could I tell him? He wouldn't have understood. So I told him that when Waga the Wheel's men catch an informant, they rip his belly open and fill his insides with pepper. And drunken soldiers stuff the informant into a sack and drown him in an outhouse. And this was gospel truth, but he didn't believe me. He said that wasn't covered in school. Then I took out some paper and wrote down our conversation. I needed it for my book, but he, poor thing, decided that it was for a report, and he wet himself from fright."

The lights of Skeleton Baco's inn flashed through the bushes ahead. Kiun stumbled and went quiet. "What's wrong?" asked Rumata.

"It's a gray patrol," muttered Kiun.

"So what?" said Rumata. "Listen to another bit of reasoning, worthy Kiun. We love and value these simple, rough boys, our gray fighting beasts. We need them. From now on, a commoner better keep his tongue in his mouth, unless he wants it to dangle out on the gallows!" He roared with laughter, because it was so well put—in the finest tradition of the gray barracks.

Kiun shuddered and drew his head into his shoulders.

"A commoner's tongue should know its place. God gave the commoner a tongue not for making fine speeches but for licking the boots of his master, who has been placed above him since time immemorial."

The saddled horses of the gray patrol were tied to the hitching post in front of the tavern. Husky, avid swearing came through the open window. There was a clatter of dice. In the door, blocking the way with his monstrous belly, stood Skeleton Baco himself, in a ragged leather jacket with the sleeves rolled up. In his hairy paw was a cleaver—clearly he had been chopping dog meat for the soup, gotten sweaty, and come out to catch his breath. A dejected-looking gray storm trooper was sitting on the front steps, his battle-ax between his knees. The ax handle was pulling his mug off to one side. He was clearly feeling the effects of drink. Noticing the rider, he pulled himself together and bellowed huskily, "S-Stop! Who goes there? You, no-obility!"

Rumata, jutting out his chin, rode past without a single look. ". . . and if a commoner's tongue licks the wrong boot," he said loudly, "then it should be removed altogether, for it is said: 'Thy tongue is my enemy.'"

Kiun, hiding behind the horse's croup, was taking long strides by his side. Out of the corner of his eye, Rumata saw his bald patch glistening with sweat.

"I said stop!" roared the storm trooper.

They could hear him stumbling down the stairs, rattling his ax, cursing God, Satan, and those noble scum in one breath.

About five men, thought Rumata. Drunk butchers. Piece of cake.

They passed the inn and turned toward the forest.

"I can walk faster if you like," Kiun said in an unnaturally steady voice.

"Nonsense!" Rumata said, reining in his stallion. "It'd be dull to ride so far without a single fight. Don't you ever want to fight, Kiun? It's all talk and talk . . ."

"No," said Kiun. "I never want to fight."

"That's just the trouble," Rumata muttered, turning the stallion around and slowly pulling on his gloves.

Two horsemen jumped out from beyond the bend, coming to a sudden halt when they saw him. "Hey you, noble don!" one of them shouted. "Come on, show us your traveling papers!"

"Boors!" Rumata said icily. "You're illiterate, what would you do with them?"

He nudged his stallion with his knees and trotted toward the storm troopers. They're chickening out, he thought. Hesitating. Come on, at least a couple of blows! No . . . no luck. How I'd like to let out some of the hatred that's accumulated over the past twenty-four hours, but it looks like I'll have no luck. Let us remain humane, forgive everyone, and be calm like the gods. Let them slaughter and desecrate, we'll be calm like the gods. The gods need not hurry, they have eternity ahead.

He rode right up to them. The storm troopers raised their axes uncertainly and backed up.

"*Well?*" said Rumata.

"What's this, eh?" said the first storm trooper in confusion. "Is this the noble Don Rumata, eh?"

The second storm trooper immediately turned his horse around and galloped away at full speed. The first one kept backing up, his ax lowered. "Beg your pardon, noble don," he was saying rapidly. "Didn't recognize you. Just a mistake. Affairs of state, mistakes do happen. The boys drank a bit much, they're burning with zeal . . ." He started to ride away sideways. "As you know, it's a difficult time . . . We're hunting down fugitive literates. We wouldn't like you to be displeased with us, noble don . . ."

Rumata turned his back to him.

"Have a good journey, noble don!" said the storm trooper with relief.

When he left, Rumata called softly. "Kiun!"

No one answered.

"Hey, Kiun!"

And again no one answered. Listening carefully, Rumata could make out the rustling of bushes through the whine of the mosquitoes. Kiun was hurrying west through the fields, toward the border with Irukan. And that's that, thought Rumata. That's it for that conversation. That's how it always is. A careful probing, a wary exchange of cryptic parables. Whole weeks are wasted in trite chatter with all sorts of scum, but when you meet a real man there's no time to talk. You have to protect him, save him, send him out of danger, and he leaves you without even knowing whether he was dealing with a friend or a capricious ass. And you don't learn much about him either. His wishes, his talents, what he lives for . . .

He thought of Arkanar in the evening: the solid stone houses on the main streets, the friendly lantern above the entrance to the tavern, the complacent, well-fed shopkeepers drinking beer at clean tables and arguing that the world isn't bad at all—the price of bread is falling, the price of armor is rising, conspiracies are quickly discovered, sorcerers and suspicious bookworms are hanged on the gallows, the king is, as usual, great and wise, while Don Reba is infinitely clever and always on his guard. "The things they come up with! The world is round! For all I care it's square, just don't stir things up!" "Literacy, literacy is the source of it all, my brothers! First they tell us money can't buy happiness, then they say peasants are people, too, and it only gets worse—offensive verses, then rioting." "Hang them all, my brothers! You know what I'd do? I'd ask them straight out: Can you read? Off to the gallows! Write verses? Off to the gallows! Know your multiplication tables? Off to the gallows, you know too much!" "Bina, honey, three more pints and a serving of rabbit stew!" Meanwhile, squat, red-faced young men, with heavy axes on their right shoulders, pound the cobblestones— *thump, thump, thump*—with their hobnailed boots. "My brothers! Here they come, our defenders! Would they let it happen? Not on your life! And my boy, my boy . . . he's on the right flank! Seems like only yesterday I was flogging him! Yes, my brothers, these are no troubled times! The throne is strong, prosperity reigns, there's inviolable peace and justice. Hurray for the gray troops! Hurray for Don Reba! Glory to the king! Oh, my brothers, how wonderful life has become!"

Meanwhile, the roads and trails of the dark plains of the Kingdom of Arkanar, lit by the glows of fires and the sparks of torches, are filled with hundreds of wretches running, walking, stumbling, avoiding outposts. They are tormented by mosquitoes, covered in sweat and dust, exhausted, frightened, and desperate, yet hard as steel in their convictions. They've been declared outside the law because they are able and willing to heal and teach their sick and ignorant race; because they, like the gods, use clay and stone to create another reality to beautify the life of a race that knows no beauty; because they penetrate the secrets of nature, hoping to put these secrets in the service of their inept race, which is still cowed by ancient superstitions . . . helpless, kind, impractical, far ahead of their time.

Rumata pulled off his glove and whipped his stallion hard between the ears. "Giddyup, lazybones!" he said in Russian.

It was already midnight when he entered the forest.

No one was quite sure where the strange name came from—the Hiccup Forest. The official version was that three hundred years ago, the troops of Imperial Marshal Totz—later the first king of Arkanar—were hacking their way through the saiva, pursuing the retreating hordes of copper-skinned barbarians, and during rest stops they boiled white tree bark to make a brew that caused uncontrollable hiccups. According to this legend, one day Marshal Totz was making the rounds of the camp and, wrinkling his aristocratic nose, declared, "This is truly insupportable! The whole forest has hiccups and reeks of home brew!" And this was allegedly the source of the strange name.

In any case, it wasn't quite an ordinary forest. It was full of gigantic trees with hard white trunks, which no longer existed elsewhere in the empire—not in the Duchy of Irukan, and definitely not in the Mercantile Republic of Soan, which had long since used up its timber on ships. It was said that there were many such forests beyond the North Red Ridge in the country of the barbarians, but lots of tales were told about the country of the barbarians.

A road had been cut through the forest two centuries ago. It led to the silver mines and by feudal right belonged to the Barons Pampa, descendants of one of the companions of Marshal Totz. This feudal right cost the kings of Arkanar twelve pounds of pure silver per year, and therefore each successive king, after ascending the throne, gathered an army and went to war with Castle Bau, the seat of the barons. The castle walls were strong, the barons were brave, and each campaign cost thirty pounds of silver. After the return of the defeated army, the king of Arkanar would once again confirm the feudal right of the Barons Pampa, along with their other privileges—picking their noses at the royal table, hunting to the west of Arkanar, and calling princes only by their names, without adding titles and ranks.

The Hiccup Forest was full of dark secrets. During the day, wagons of processed ore trundled south along the road, and at night the road was empty, because few men were brave enough to walk it by starlight. It was said that at night, the Sioux bird—a bird that has never been seen and cannot be seen, since it is no ordinary bird—cried out from the Father-Tree. It was said that huge hairy spiders jumped out of the branches onto the necks of horses and instantly gnawed through their veins, drowning in blood. It was said that the ancient beast Pekh roamed the forest—a creature, covered in scales, that sired offspring every twelve years and dragged behind him twelve tails oozing poisonous sweat. And someone had seen the naked boar Y, cursed by the Holy Míca, crossing the road in broad daylight, grumbling plaintively — a ferocious animal, invulnerable to iron but easily pierced by bone.

Here you could also meet a runaway slave with a tar brand between his shoulder blades — silent and ruthless, like the hairy bloodsucking spider. Or a stooped warlock, collecting secret mushrooms for his magic potions, which could be used to become invisible, turn into various animals, or acquire a second shadow. The night sentries of the fearsome Waga the Wheel also walked this road, as did the fugitives from the silver mines with their black hands and white, transparent faces. Medicine men gathered here for their nightly vigils, and Baron Pampa's rowdy huntsmen would skewer stolen oxen and roast them whole in the scattered clearings.

In the depths of the forest, a mile away from the road, beneath an enormous tree that had dried up of old age, stood a lopsided hut made out of enormous logs, surrounded by a blackened picket fence. It had been here since the beginning of time, its door was always shut, and there were crooked idols carved from whole tree trunks around its rotting porch. This hut was the most dangerous place in the Hiccup Forest. It was said that this was the very place to which the ancient Pekh would come every twelve years to deliver his offspring, after which he would immediately crawl beneath the hut and expire, so the hut's entire cellar was filled with black poison. And when the poison seeped out — that's when the end would come. It was said that on stormy nights, the idols dug themselves out of the ground, came out onto the road, and signaled to passersby. And it was also said that sometimes the windows shone with unnatural light, sounds resounded through the forest, and a column of smoke reached up from the chimney to the sky.

Not long ago, Irma Kukish, a sober simpleton from the farmstead of Plenitude (in common parlance, Stinkfield) foolishly wandered by the hut at night and peered into the windows. He came home completely incoherent, and after he recovered a little, said that the hut was full of bright light and that a man with his feet on the bench sat behind a crude table and guzzled from a barrel held in one hand. The man's face hung all the way down to his waist and was spotted all over. It was obvious that this was the Holy Míca himself, before his conversion to the faith, a polygamist, drunkard, and blasphemer. To look at him was to be afraid. A sickly sweet smell wafted out the window, and shadows moved across the trees. People gathered from all over to hear the idiot's story. And it all ended when the storm troopers came, bent his elbows to his shoulder blades, and hustled him off to the city of Arkanar. But people still talked about the hut, and it was now called nothing but the Drunken Lair.

Rumata made his way through the thicket of giant ferns, dismounted by the Drunken Lair's porch, and wound his reins around one of the idols. The hut was fully lit, the door open and hanging by a hinge, and Father Cabani was sitting behind the table in a state of utter dejection. The room was filled with a powerful odor of spirits, and a huge stein towered on the table between the gnawed bones and pieces of boiled turnips.

"Good evening, Father Cabani," Rumata said, stepping over the threshold.

"Greetings," Father Cabani answered, in a raspy voice that sounded like a battle horn.

Rumata came up to the table, spurs jingling. He threw his gloves on the bench and took another look at Father Cabani. Father Cabani was motionless, supporting his drooping face with his hand. His shaggy, graying eyebrows hung down over his cheeks like dry grass over a cliff. With every breath, the nostrils of his coarsely pored nose whistled out air saturated with undigested alcohol.

"I invented it myself!" he said suddenly, raising his right eyebrow with effort and turning a puffy eye toward Rumata. "I did it myself! Why did I do it?" He extracted his right hand from underneath his cheek and shook a hairy finger. "But it's not my fault. I invented it . . . and it's not my fault, eh! That's right—not my fault. Anyway, we don't invent a thing, that's all nonsense!"

Rumata unbuckled his belt and pulled his swords off over his head. "Now, now," he said.

"The box!" barked Father Cabani and stayed silent for a long time, making strange motions with his cheeks.

Rumata, without taking his eyes off him, threw his dusty-booted feet over the bench and sat, putting his swords down nearby.

"The box . . ." Father Cabani repeated in a deflated voice. "We only say we invent things. Actually, it was all invented a long time ago. A long time ago, someone invented it all, stuck it in a box, made a hole in the lid, and left. Left to go to sleep . . . then what? Father Cabani comes in, closes his eyes, sh-shoves his hand into the hole." Father Cabani looked at his hand. "He g-grabs it! Aha! An invention! This thing here is my invention, he says! And if you don't believe it, you're a fool. I shove my hand in—th-that's one! What is it? Barbed wire! What's it for? Protecting farmyards from the wolves . . . I shove my hand in— th-that's two! What is it? The handiest thing—a meat grinder. What's it for? Tender minced meat . . . good job! I shove my hand in—that's three! What is it? F-Flammable water! What's it for? Kindling damp wood . . . eh!"

Father Cabani went quiet and began to slump, as if someone had grabbed his neck and was pushing him forward. Rumata picked up the stein, looked inside, then poured a few drops onto the back of his hand. The drops were purple and smelled of fusel oil. Rumata carefully wiped his hand with a lace handkerchief. Oil stains appeared on it. Father Cabani's shaggy head touched the table and immediately jerked up.

"The man who put it in the box—he knew what it was all for. Barbed wire for the wolves? How silly of me—for the wolves. The *mines*, the mines should be ringed with this wire . . . so state criminals can't escape! But I don't want that! I'm a state criminal myself! Did they ask me? Sure they did! Barbed wire, they said? Barbed wire. For the wolves, they said? For the wolves. Well done, they said, good job! We'll use it to ring the mines . . . Don Reba did it himself. And he took my meat grinder. Good job, he said! What a mind you've got, he said! So now the Merry Tower makes tender minced meat . . . very effective, they say."

I know, thought Rumata. I know about all this. And how you yelled in Don Reba's office, how you begged and groveled at his feet: "Give it back, don't do it!" It was too late. Your meat grinder had started turning.

Father Cabani grabbed the stein and put it to his hairy maw. Gulping down the poisonous brew, he roared like the boar Y, then he shoved the stein onto the table and started to chew on a piece of turnip. Tears crept down his cheeks.

"Flammable water!" he finally announced in a strangled voice. "For kindling fires and merry magic tricks. What does it matter that it's flammable if you can drink it? Mix it with beer—what a beer you get! I won't allow it! I'll drink it myself . . . and I drink it. All day long I drink it. All night long. I'm all swollen. I fall down all the time. The other day,

Don Rumata, you won't believe it, I was near a mirror—
and I got scared. I look—Lord help me!—where's Father
Cabani? A sea creature like an octopus—with colored spots
all over. First red spots. Then blue spots. That's what comes
of inventing water for magic tricks."

Father Cabani tried to spit on the floor but hit the table
instead, then shuffled his feet beneath the bench out of habit,
as if rubbing it into the dirt. He suddenly asked, "What day
is it today?"

"The eve of Cata the Pious," said Rumata.

"And why is there no sun?"

"Because it's night."

"Night again," Father Cabani said dejectedly, and fell
face-first into the table scraps.

Rumata looked at him for a while, whistling through his
teeth. Then he stood up from the table and went into the
pantry. There, between the heap of turnips and the heap of
sawdust, gleamed the glass tubes of Father Cabani's massive
brewing apparatus—an amazing creation of a born engineer,
natural chemist, and master glassblower. Rumata circled the
"infernal machine" twice, then felt for a crowbar in the dark
and swung hard at it, aiming nowhere in particular. Clanking, jingling, gurgling sounds filled the pantry. The nauseat-
ing smell of sour home brew assaulted his nostrils.

Broken glass crunching beneath his heels, Rumata made
his way into a far corner and turned on an electric lamp.
There, underneath a pile of trash, was the compact field
synthesizer Midas in its strong silicate safe. Rumata cleared
away the trash, entered in the code, and lifted the lid of the
safe. Even in the white electric light, the synthesizer looked
peculiar in the midst of the scattered junk. Rumata dumped
a few shovels of sawdust into the receiving funnel, and the

synthesizer began to hum quietly, its display panel turning on automatically. Rumata shoved a rusty bucket underneath the output chute with the toe of his boot. And immediately — *clink, clink, clink!* — gold disks with the aristocratic profile of Pitz the Sixth, King of Arkanar, started pouring onto its battered tin bottom.

Rumata carried Father Cabani to a squeaky bunk, pulled his shoes off, and covered him with the hairless hide of some long-extinct animal. During this process, Father Cabani woke up for a minute. He could neither move nor think. He merely sang a couple of verses from the forbidden love song "I'm Like a Scarlet Flower in Your Little Hand," after which he started snoring loudly.

Rumata cleared the table, swept the floor, and cleaned the glass in the only window, which had turned black from dirt and the chemical experiments Father Cabani was performing on the windowsill. He found a full barrel of alcohol behind the rusty stove and emptied it into a rat hole. Then he watered the Hamaharian stallion, poured him some oats from his saddlebag, washed up, and sat down to wait, gazing at the oil lamp's smoking flame. He had lived this strange double life for five years and thought he was completely used to it, but from time to time, like right now, for example, it would suddenly occur to him that there was no organized brutality and approaching gray threat, only a performance of a bizarre theatrical production with him, Rumata, in the lead. That at any moment now, after a particularly felicitous line, there would be a burst of applause, and fans from the Institute of Experimental History would shout admiringly from

their boxes, "Not bad, Anton! Not bad! Good job, Toshka!"
He even looked around to check—but there was no crowded
hall, only blackened mossy walls made from bare logs and
caked in layers of soot.

In the yard, the Hamaharian stallion neighed quietly and
beat his hooves against the ground. Rumata heard a steady
low hum, achingly familiar but here utterly improbable.
He listened hard, his mouth half-open. The hum stopped,
and the flame above the lamp flickered then shone brighter.
Rumata started to get up, and at that moment a man stepped
into the room out of the darkness of the night: Don Condor,
Chief Justice and Keeper of the Great Seals of the Mercantile
Republic of Soan, Vice President of the Conference of the
Twelve Merchants, and Knight of the Imperial Order of the
Hand of Mercy.

Rumata jumped up, nearly knocking over the bench. He
was ready to rush toward him, hug him, kiss him on both
cheeks—but his legs observed the proper etiquette in spite of
himself and bent at the knees. His spurs jingled solemnly, his
right hand swept out an arc starting at his heart and ending
at his side, and his head bent down so that his chin sank into
the foamy lace ruff. Don Condor ripped off his plumed velvet
beret, hastily waved it in Rumata's direction, as if he were chasing off mosquitoes, flung it on the table, and undid the clasps
of his cloak at his neck with both hands. His cloak was still
slowly falling behind his back and he was already sitting on
the bench with legs apart, his left hand on his hip and his right
hand grasping the hilt of a gilded sword that he had stuck into
the rotten floorboards. He was small and skinny, with large
protuberant eyes in a pale, narrow face. He wore his black hair
the same way as Rumata—gathered by a massive gold circlet
with a large green stone above the bridge of his nose.

"Are you alone, Don Rumata?" he asked curtly.

"Yes, noble don," Rumata answered sadly.

Father Cabani suddenly said loudly and soberly, "Noble Don Reba! You're a hyena, that's all."

Don Condor didn't turn around. "I flew here," he said.

"Let us hope," said Rumata, "that nobody saw you."

"One legend more, one legend less," Don Condor said irritably. "I don't have time to travel on horseback. Whatever happened to Budach? Where did he go? Do sit down, Don Rumata, I beg you! My neck hurts."

Rumata obediently sat on the bench. "Budach has disappeared," he said. "I waited for him in the Territory of Heavy Swords. But only a one-eyed ragamuffin showed up, who gave the password and handed me a bag of books. I waited for another two days, then got in touch with Don Gug, who informed me that he had accompanied Budach all the way to the border, and that from then on Budach was escorted by a certain noble don who can be trusted because he gambled away body and soul to Don Gug at cards. Therefore Budach must have disappeared somewhere in Arkanar. That's all that I know."

"It's not a whole lot," said Don Condor.

"Budach is not the point," Rumata objected. "If he's alive, I'll find him and save him. I know how to do that. That's not what I wanted to talk to you about. I want to once again draw your attention to the fact that the situation in Arkanar is not within the scope of basis theory."

A sour expression appeared on Don Condor's face. "No, you have to hear me out," Rumata said firmly. "I have the feeling that I'll never explain myself over the radio. Everything in Arkanar has changed! Some new, systematic factor has appeared. And it looks like Don Reba is intentionally inciting all the grayness in the kingdom against learned people. Everything that's even slightly above the average gray level is now in danger. Hear me out, Don Condor—these aren't emotions, these are facts! If you're smart, educated, a skeptic, if you say anything unusual—even if you simply don't drink wine!—you're in danger. Any shopkeeper has the right to hound you, even until death. Hundreds and thousands of people are declared outside the law. They are caught by troopers and strung up along the roads. Naked, upside down. Yesterday, they beat an old man with their boots after learning that he was literate. I hear they trampled him for two hours, the morons, with their sweaty animal mugs . . ." Rumata regained control of himself and ended calmly: "In short, there will soon be no literate people left in Arkanar. Like in the Region of the Holy Order after the Barkan slaughter."

Don Condor stared at him intently, pursing his lips. "I don't like how you sound, Anton," he said in Russian.

"I don't like a lot of things, Alexander Vasilievich," said Rumata. "I don't like that we've tied our hands and feet with the very formulation of the problem. I don't like that it's called the Problem of Nonviolent Impact. Because under my conditions, that means a scientifically justified inaction. I'm aware of all your objections! And I'm aware of the theory. But here there are no theories, here there are typical fascist practices, here animals are murdering humans every minute! Here everything is pointless. Knowledge isn't enough, and gold is worthless, because it comes too late."

"Anton," said Don Condor. "Don't lose your head. I believe that the situation in Arkanar is absolutely exceptional, but I'm convinced that you don't have a single constructive suggestion."

"Yes," Rumata agreed, "I don't have any constructive suggestions. But it's very hard for me to control myself."

"Anton," Don Condor said. "There are two hundred and fifty of us on this entire planet. Everybody controls themselves, and everybody finds it very hard. The most experienced of us have lived here for twenty-two years. They came here as nothing more than observers. They were completely forbidden to do anything whatsoever. Imagine that for a moment: forbidden to do anything. They wouldn't even have had the right to save Budach. Even if Budach was being trampled before their eyes."

"Don't talk to me as if I were a child," Rumata said.

"You're impatient like a child," Don Condor declared. "And we must be very patient."

Rumata smiled bitterly. "And while we watch and wait," he said, "calculating and planning, animals will be destroying humans every minute of every day."

"Anton," Don Condor said, "the universe has thousands of planets where we haven't come yet, where history is taking its course."

"But we've come here already!"

"Yes, we have. But we've come here to help these people, not to satisfy our righteous rage. If you're weak, leave. Go home. After all, you really aren't a child, and you knew what you'd encounter here."

Rumata stayed silent. Don Condor, slumping and seeming instantly older, walked up and down the table, dragging his sword by the hilt behind him like a stick, sadly nodding his head. "I understand," he said. "I've gone through it myself. There was a time when this feeling of helplessness and my own culpability seemed to be the worst thing. Some of us, the weakest ones, went crazy from it, were sent back to Earth, and are now being treated. It took me fifteen years, dear boy, to understand what the worst thing really is. The worst thing is to lose your humanity, Anton. To sully your soul, to become hardened. We're gods here, Anton, and we need to be wiser than the gods from the legends the locals have created in their image and likeness as best they could. And yet we walk along the edge of a swamp. One wrong step—and down you go in the dirt, and you won't be able to wash it off your whole life. Goran the Irukanian, in his *History of the Coming*, wrote, 'When God, after descending from the heavens, appeared to the people from the Pitanian marshes, his feet were covered in mud.'"

"For which Goran was burned," Rumata said grimly.

"Yes, he was burned," Don Condor said, returning to his seat. "But that was said about us. I've been here for fifteen years. My dear boy, I've even stopped having dreams about Earth. One day, rummaging through my papers, I found a picture of a woman and for a long time couldn't figure out who she was. I occasionally realize with terror that I've long stopped being an employee of the Institute, that I'm now an exhibit in the Institute's museum, the chief justice of a feudal mercantile republic, and that there's a room in the museum in which I belong. That's the worst thing—to lose yourself in the role. Inside each one of us, the noble bastard struggles with the communard. And everything around us helps the bastard, while the communard is all alone—the Earth is thousands and thousands of parsecs away." Don Condor paused, stroking his knees. "That's how it is, Anton," he said in a firmer voice. "We must remain communards."

He doesn't understand. And how could he? He's lucky, he doesn't know what gray terror is, what Don Reba is. Everything he's witnessed in his fifteen years of work on this planet has in one way or another fit into the framework of basis theory. And when I tell him about fascism, about the gray storm troopers, about the incitement of the petty bourgeoisie, he interprets it as emotional expressions. "Don't abuse terminology, Anton! Terminological confusion brings about dangerous consequences." He simply can't grasp the fact that in Arkanar, typical medieval brutality belongs to a happy past. For him, Don Reba is something like the Duke of Richelieu, a shrewd and farsighted politician, defending absolutism from feudal excesses. I'm the only one on this whole planet who's aware of the terrible shadow creeping over the country, but even I can't figure out whose shadow it is or where it's coming from. And how can I possibly convince him, when I can see in his eyes that he's almost ready to send me back to Earth for treatment?

"How's honorable Sinda?" Rumata asked.

Don Condor stopped eyeing him suspiciously and grumbled, "He's doing well, thank you." Then he said, "To conclude, we must be firmly aware of the fact that neither you nor I nor any of us will see the tangible fruits of our labors. We're not physicists, we're historians. For us, time isn't measured in seconds but in centuries, and our work isn't even sowing, it's preparing the ground for sowing. Because occasionally we do get . . . enthusiasts, blast them—sprinters who can't go the distance."

Rumata gave a crooked smile and started pointlessly fiddling with his boots. Sprinters. Yes, there've been sprinters.

Ten years before, Stephan Orlovsky, also known as Don Capata, the commander of a company of His Imperial Majesty's crossbowmen, ordered his soldiers to open fire on the executioners at a public torture of eighteen Estorian witches; he cut down the judge and two court bailiffs and was lanced by the Imperial Guard. Writhing in agonies of death, he shouted, "But you're human! Get them, get them!"—but few heard him over the roar of the crowd: "Fire! More fire!"

Approximately at the same time, in another hemisphere, Carl Rosenblum, one of the leading experts on the peasant wars in France and Germany, also known as the wool-seller Pani-Pa, led a revolt of Murissian peasants, stormed two cities, and was killed by an arrow to the back of the head while trying to stop the looting. He was still alive when they came for him in the helicopter, but he couldn't speak and only looked on in guilt and bewilderment with his big blue eyes, which constantly streamed tears . . .

And shortly before Rumata's arrival, the magnificently placed confidant of the Caisan tyrant (Jeremy Tafnat, a specialist in the history of agrarian reforms) suddenly staged a palace coup, usurped power, and for two months attempted to start a golden age. He stubbornly refused to reply to furious queries from his neighbors and from Earth, earned the reputation of a lunatic, managed to avoid eight assassination attempts, and was finally kidnapped by an emergency team of Institute workers and transferred by submarine to an island base by the planet's southern pole.

"Just think!" muttered Rumata. "And all of Earth still imagines that the hardest problems are in null-physics."

Don Condor looked up. "Finally!" he said quietly.

There was a clattering of hooves, the Hamaharian stallion let out an angry, shrill neigh, and they heard energetic swearing with a strong Irukanian accent. In the doorway appeared Don Gug, the Chamberlain of His Grace the Duke of Irukan, fat, ruddy, with a dashing upturned mustache, a smile from ear to ear, and merry little eyes underneath the chestnut curls of his wig. And once again, Rumata was about to jump up and hug him, because this was actually Pashka, but Don Gug suddenly assumed a formal posture, an expression of cloying sweetness appearing on his plump-cheeked face. He bent slightly at the waist, pressed his hat to his chest, and pursed his lips. Rumata briefly glanced at Alexander Vasilievich—but Alexander Vasilievich had disappeared. On the bench sat the Chief Justice and Keeper of the Great Seals, his legs apart, his left hand on his hip, and his right hand holding the hilt of his gilded sword.

"You're very late, Don Gug," he said in an unpleasant voice.

"A thousand apologies!" cried Don Gug, smoothly approaching the table. "I swear by the rickets of my duke, there were completely unforeseen circumstances! I was stopped four times by the patrols of His Majesty the King of Arkanar, and I got into two fights with various boors." He gracefully lifted his left hand, wrapped in a bloody rag. "By the way, noble dons, whose helicopter is that behind the house?"

"That's my helicopter," Don Condor said crossly. "I don't have time for roadside brawls."

Don Gug smiled pleasantly, sat down on the bench, and said, "Well, noble dons, we're forced to acknowledge that the highly learned Doctor Budach mysteriously disappeared somewhere between the Irukanian border and the Territory of Heavy Swords—"

Father Cabani suddenly tossed in his bed. "Don Reba," he said thickly, without waking up.

"Leave Budach to me," Rumata said in despair, "and try to understand what I'm saying . . ."

# Chapter 2

Rumata started and opened his eyes. It was already light out. There was a commotion in the street underneath his window. Someone, probably a military man, was shouting, "Scum! You'll lick this dirt off with your tongue!" (Good morning, thought Rumata.) "Silence! By Holy Míca's back, you'll make me lose my temper!" Another voice, rough and hoarse, mumbled that this was the sort of street where a man ought to watch his step. "In the morning it rained, and God knows when they paved it last . . ." "He dares tell me what to do!" "You should let me go, noble don, don't hold on to my shirt . . ." "He dares order me around!" There was a ringing crack. This was apparently the second slap—the first had woken Rumata up. "You shouldn't hit me, noble don," someone mumbled below.

A familiar voice—who could it be? Probably Don Tameo. I should let him win back his Hamaharian nag today. I wonder if I'll ever know much about horses. Although we, the Rumatas of Estor, have never known much about horses, we're experts in military camels. Good thing there are almost no camels in Arkanar. Rumata stretched, cracking his back, groped for a twisted silk cord by his head, and pulled on it a few times. Bells started jangling in the depths of the house. The boy is gawking at the scene outside, of course, thought Rumata. I could get up and dress myself, but that'll only breed rumors.

He listened to the profanity outside the window. What a powerful language! It has incredible entropy. I hope Don Tameo doesn't kill him. In recent years, certain enthusiasts in the Guard had announced that they reserved only one sword for noble battle, and used their other blades specifically for street trash—which, thanks to Don Reba, had really proliferated in glorious Arkanar. Although Don Tameo isn't one of those enthusiasts, Rumata thought. Our Don Tameo is a bit of a coward, and a well-known politician too.

How rotten when the day starts with Don Tameo. Rumata sat up and hugged his knees under his splendid torn blanket. That's the kind of thing that gives you a feeling of leaden hopelessness and makes you want to mope around and ponder how you are weak and helpless in the face of circumstances. This didn't occur to us on Earth. Over there, we are healthy, confident men who have gone through psychological conditioning and are ready for anything. We have excellent nerves; we know how not to flinch when faced with beatings and executions. We have amazing self-control; we're capable of putting up with the blathering of the most hopeless idiots. We've forgotten how to be fastidious—we

*a kind, wonderful man; to the east is Pashka, with whom you shared a school desk for seven years, a merry, loyal friend. You're just feeling depressed, Toshka. It's too bad, of course; we thought you were hardier, but who hasn't felt this way? The work is hellish, I understand. You'll go back to Earth, have a rest, do some theoretical work, and then we'll see.*

Alexander Vasilievich, by the way, is a true dogmatist. If basis theory doesn't allow for the grays (*In my fifteen years of work, dear boy, I haven't noticed such deviations from theory . . .*), I must be imagining them. Since I'm imagining things, I must be having a nervous breakdown, and I should be forced to take a vacation. *Well, all right, I promise, I'll take a look for myself and give you my opinion. But in the meantime, Don Rumata, I beg you, nothing extreme.* And Pavel, childhood friend, a polymath, a scholar, a treasure trove of information—he dives headfirst into the history of the two planets and gives a trivial proof that the gray movement is nothing more than a commonplace rebellion of the city residents against the barony. *Although one of these days I'll come see you, take a look. To be honest, I feel kind of uncomfortable about Budach.* And thank you for that! That'll do! I'll busy myself with Budach, since I'm not good for much else.

The highly learned Doctor Budach. A native of Irukan, a master physician, on whom the Duke of Irukan had almost conferred a title but instead changed his mind and imprisoned in a tower. The biggest authority on healing with poisons in the empire. The author of the widely disseminated treatise *About Grasses and Other Cereals, Which Can Mysteriously Cause Sorrow, Joy, and Calmness, as well as the Saliva and Juices of Reptiles, Spiders, and the Naked Boar Y, Which Also Have These and Many Other Properties.* Doubtlessly a remarkable man, a true intellectual—a dedicated humanist with no interest in money, all his property a bag of books. So who could have wanted you, Doctor Budach, in a twilit, ignorant country, mired in a bloody quagmire of avarice and conspiracy?

Let us assume that you're alive and in Arkanar. It's possible, of course, that you've been captured by barbarian raiders who've come down from the North Red Ridge. In that case, Don Condor is planning to get in touch with our friend Shushtuletidovodus, who specializes in the history of primitive cultures and is currently serving as a shaman-epileptic under a chief with a forty-five-syllable name. But if you really are in Arkanar, then, first of all, you might have been captured by the night bandits of Waga the Wheel. And not even captured, but taken along, because their main prey would have been your companion, the bankrupt noble don. Either way, they wouldn't kill you; Waga the Wheel is too greedy for that.

You might have also fallen into the clutches of some idiot baron, without any malicious intent on his part, just out of boredom and a hypertrophied sense of hospitality. He might have wanted to feast with a noble companion, so he stationed his militia along the road and dragged your companion into the castle. And you'll be sitting in stinky servants' quarters until the dons drink themselves into a stupor and part ways. In this case, you are also in no danger.

But there are also the remnants of the recently defeated peasant army of Don Ksi and Perta the Spine holed up somewhere in Rotland, who are surreptitiously being fed by our eagle Don Reba himself, in case of the entirely possible complications with the barons. These men know no mercy—but it's better not to even think about that. There's also Don Satarina, an extremely blue-blooded imperial aristocrat, 102 years old and completely senile. He has a blood feud with the Dukes of Irukan, and from time to time gets excited into activity and begins to capture everything crossing the border from Irukan. He's very dangerous, because when he issues orders during attacks of cholecystitis, the cemetery guards can't drag the corpses out of his dungeons fast enough.

And finally, the main possibility. Not the main possibility because it's the most dangerous, but because it's the likeliest. Don Reba's gray patrols. The storm troopers on the main roads. You might have fallen into their hands by accident, in which case we have to rely on the judgment and cool head of your companion. But what if Don Reba is actually interested in *you*? Don Reba can have such surprising interests . . . His spies may have reported that you'll be passing through Arkanar, and a detachment under the command of a diligent gray officer—a noble bastard from the inferior gentry—may have been sent to meet you, and now you're imprisoned in a stone cell underneath the Merry Tower.

Rumata gave the cord another impatient tug. The bedroom door opened with a hideous squeak, and in came a page, skinny and gloomy. His name was Uno, and his fate could have served as the subject of a ballad. He bowed at the threshold, shuffling feet in battered shoes, approached the bed, and put a tray containing letters, coffee, and a wad of chewing bark—for cleaning and strengthening the teeth—on the table.

Rumata looked at him crossly. "Tell me, please, are you ever going to oil the hinges?"

The boy stayed quiet, staring at the floor.

Rumata kicked off his blanket, sat up, and reached for the tray. "Have you bathed today?" he asked.

The boy shifted from one foot to the other and, without answering, walked around the room gathering the scattered clothes.

"Didn't I just ask you whether you've bathed today?" Rumata asked, opening his first letter.

"Water won't wash my sins away," the boy grumbled. "What am I, a noble, to be bathing?"

"What have I told you about germs?" said Rumata.

The boy put the green pants on the back of the chair and made a circular motion with his thumb to ward off the devil. "I prayed three times last night," he said. "What else can I do?"

"You goose," Rumata said, and started reading the letter.

The letter was from Doña Ocana, a lady-in-waiting and the new favorite of Don Reba. She proposed that Rumata visit her tonight, "pining tenderly." The postscript explained in plain language just what she expected from this meeting. Rumata couldn't help it—he blushed. He furtively glanced at the boy, muttering, "Well, really . . ." This had to be considered. To go would be repugnant; not to go would be foolish—Doña Ocana knew a lot. He drank his coffee in one gulp and put the chewing bark into his mouth.

The next envelope was made of thick paper and the sealing wax was smudged: it was clear that the letter had been opened. It was from Don Ripat, a resolute social climber, the lieutenant of a gray company of haberdashers. He inquired about Rumata's health, expressed confidence in the victory of the gray cause, and begged permission to defer paying a debt, citing exceptional circumstances. "All right, all right . . ." mumbled Rumata. He put the letter away, picked the envelope up again, and examined it with interest. Yes, they had gotten more subtle. Noticeably more subtle.

The third letter challenged him to a sword fight over Doña Pifa but agreed to withdraw the challenge if Don Rumata would be so good as to furnish proof that he, the noble Don Rumata, did not and had never had a relationship with Doña Pifa. This was a form letter; the body of the text had been written by a calligrapher, and the names and dates were crookedly filled in and rife with spelling errors.

Rumata flung the letter away and scratched his mosquito-bitten left arm. "All right, let's wash up," he ordered.

The boy disappeared through the door and came back shortly, walking backward and dragging a wooden tub full of water along the floor. Then he rushed out the door once again and brought back an empty tub and a pitcher.

Rumata jumped to the floor, pulled his tattered, elaborately hand-embroidered nightshirt over his head, and drew the swords hanging by the head of the bed from their scabbards with a clatter. The boy cautiously hid behind the chair. After practicing thrusts and parries for about ten minutes, Rumata threw his swords at the wall, bent over the empty tub, and gave the order: "Pour!" Not having soap was bad, but Rumata was used to it. The boy poured pitcher after pitcher on his back, neck, and head and complained, "Everyone else does things properly, only we have nonsense like this. Who's ever heard of using two vessels to bathe? The master's stuck some kind of pot in the outhouse . . . Every single day a clean towel. Hasn't even prayed yet, and master's already hopping around naked with swords . . ."

Rubbing himself down with the towel, Rumata said didactically, "I'm at court, not some lousy baron. A courtier should be clean and sweet-smelling."

"As if His Majesty has nothing better to do than smell people," the boy objected. "Everyone knows that His

Majesty is praying day and night for us sinners. And Don Reba never bathes at all. I heard it myself—His Lordship's footman said so."

"All right, quit grumbling," Rumata said, pulling on his nylon undershirt.

The boy looked at this undershirt with disapproval. The garment had long been the subject of rumors among the servants of Arkanar. But Rumata couldn't do anything about this because of his natural human squeamishness. As he was pulling on his underpants, the boy turned his head away and moved his lips as if warding off the devil.

It really would be good to bring underwear into style, thought Rumata. However, the only natural way to do so would involve the ladies, and in this respect Rumata happened to be unforgivably picky for an operative. An empty-headed ladies' man, who knew the ways of the capital and who had been sent to the provinces because of a duel for love, should have had at least twenty mistresses. Rumata made heroic efforts to maintain his reputation. Half of his agents, instead of doing their work, spread despicable rumors about him, calculated to excite the envy and admiration of the Arkanarian youth in the Guard. Dozens of frustrated ladies, at whose houses Rumata lingered on purpose, reading poetry late into the night (the third watch, a fraternal kiss on the cheek, and a leap from the balcony into the arms of his acquaintance, the commander of the watch), eagerly vied with each other in telling stories about the true metropolitan style of the ladies' man from the capital. Rumata managed to support himself only through the vanity of these silly and disgustingly debauched women, but the underwear conundrum remained unsolved.

It had been so much simpler with the handkerchiefs! At his very first ball, Rumata extracted an elegant lace handkerchief from his sleeve and dabbed his lips with it. At the next ball, dashing guardsmen were already wiping their sweaty faces with pieces of embroidered and monogrammed cloth of various sizes and colors. And in a month, there was a spate of dandies sporting entire bedsheets draped over an arm, the tails of which dragged elegantly across the floor.

Rumata pulled on his green pants and a white cambric shirt with a faded collar. "Is anybody waiting?" he asked.

"The barber is waiting," the boy replied. "And there are also two dons sitting in the living room, Don Tameo and Don Sera. They ordered wine and are playing dice. They are waiting to have breakfast with my master."

"Go call the barber. And tell the noble dons that I'll be there soon. And don't be rude, speak courteously . . ."

Breakfast wasn't too filling and would leave room for a quick lunch. They were served roasted meat, strongly seasoned with spices, and dog ears marinated in vinegar. They drank sparkling Irukanian wine, thick brown Estorian wine, and white Soanian wine. Dexterously carving a leg of lamb with two daggers, Don Tameo complained about the insolence of the lower classes. "I intend to submit a memorandum to His Majesty himself," he declared. "The gentry demands that the peasants and the craftsmen rabble be forbidden to show their faces in public spaces and the streets. Let them use the courtyards and back alleys. And in those instances where the appearance of a peasant in the street is unavoidable—for example, during the delivery of bread, meat, and wine into a noble house—let them apply for a special permit from the Ministry of the Defense of the Crown."

"What a brain!" Don Sera said delightedly, spraying spittle and meat juice. "And yesterday at court . . ." And he told the latest story: Don Reba's flame, the lady-in-waiting Ocana, had carelessly stepped on the king's injured foot. His Majesty became furious and, turning toward Don Reba, ordered him to punish the offender. To which Don Reba, without batting an eyelash, replied, "It will be done, Your Majesty. This very night!" "I laughed so hard," said Don Sera, shaking his head, "that two hooks flew off my waistcoat."

Protoplasm, thought Rumata. Nothing but a gluttonous, breeding protoplasm. "Yes, noble dons," he said. "Don Reba is the cleverest of men."

"Oh my, yes!" said Don Sera. "What a man! What a brain!"

"An eminent personality," Don Tameo said significantly, with a great show of feeling.

"It's strange to even think now," Rumata continued with a friendly smile, "what people said about him only a year ago. Do you remember, Don Tameo, how you wittily mocked his crooked legs?"

Don Tameo choked and drained a glass of Irukanian wine in one gulp. "I don't recall," he mumbled. "I'm no comedian . . ."

"You did, you did," Don Sera said, shaking his head reproachfully.

"That's right!" Rumata exclaimed. "You were present for this conversation, Don Sera! I remember, Don Tameo's witticisms made you laugh so hard that some piece of your clothing snapped off."

Don Sera turned purple and started stammering elaborate excuses, lying the whole time. The now glum Don Tameo applied himself to the strong Estorian wine. And since, in his own words, he had "started in the morning the day before yesterday and hadn't yet been able to stop," when they left the house, he had to be supported from both sides.

The day was bright and sunny. Common folk thronged in the streets and alleys searching for things to gawk at, boys shrieked and whistled as they flung mud, pretty towns-women in bonnets peered out of the windows, and bustling servant girls looked at them bashfully with moist eyes. The general mood gradually started to improve. Don Sera very adroitly knocked down some peasant, and he almost died laughing as he watched the man flounder in a puddle. Don Tameo suddenly discovered that he had put his sword slings on backward, shouted "Stop!" and started spinning in place, trying to rotate inside the slings. Something flew off Don Sera's waistcoat again.

Rumata caught a passing servant girl by her little pink ear and asked her to help Don Tameo put himself in order. A crowd of gawkers immediately gathered around the noble dons, giving the servant girl advice from which she turned completely crimson, while Don Sera's waistcoat kept raining clasps, buttons, and buckles. When they finally moved on, Don Tameo began composing an addendum to his memo-randum for all to hear, in which he indicated the need for the "noninclusion of pretty persons of the female persuasion to the category of peasants and commoners."

This was when their way was blocked by a cart full of clay pots. Don Sera drew both swords and declared that going around some stinking pots was beneath the noble dons' dig-nity, and that he would make his way through the cart. But as he was taking aim, trying to gauge where the wall of the house ended and the pots began, Rumata grabbed one of the wheels of the cart and turned it around, clearing the way. The gawkers, who had been watching the goings-on with delight, shouted a triple hurray for Rumata. The noble dons were about to move on, but a fat, gray-haired shopkeeper leaned out of a third-floor window and started to expound about the misdeeds of the courtiers, which "our eagle Don Reba will soon put an end to." They had to stay and pass him the entire load of pots through his window. Rumata threw two gold coins with the profile of Pitz the Sixth into the last pot and handed it to the stunned owner of the cart.

"How much did you give him?" Don Tameo asked when they moved on.

"Not much," Rumata replied offhandedly. "Two gold pieces."

"By Holy Míca's back!" exclaimed Don Tameo. "You are rich! Would you like me to sell you my Hamaharian stallion?"

"I'd rather win it in a game of dice," Rumata said.

"You're right!" Don Sera said and stopped. "Why don't we play a game of dice?"

"Right here?" Rumata asked.

"Well, why not?" asked Don Sera. "I see no reason three noble dons shouldn't play a game of dice wherever they like!"

At this point, Don Tameo suddenly fell down. Don Sera tripped over his feet and also fell down. "I completely forgot," Don Sera said. "It's time for us to report for guard duty."

Rumata got them up and guided them, holding them by the elbows. He stopped by the gigantic, gloomy house of Don Satarina. "Why don't we visit the aged don?" he asked.

"I see absolutely no reason why three noble dons shouldn't visit the aged Don Satarina," said Don Sera.

Don Tameo opened his eyes. "As servants of the king," he proclaimed, "we must do our utmost to look to the future.

D-Don Satarina is a relic of the past. Onward, noble dons! I must be at my post."

"Onward," Rumata agreed.

Don Tameo dropped his head on his chest and didn't lift it up again. Don Sera, using his fingers to count, was reciting his amorous conquests. In this way, they got to the palace. In the guardroom, Rumata put Don Tameo down on a bench with relief, and Don Sera sat down at the table, carelessly pushed away a stack of orders signed by the king, and declared that it was finally time to drink some cold Irukanian wine. "Let the owner roll up a barrel," he ordered, "and let those girls come over here"—he indicated the guards who were playing cards at the other table. The commander of the guard, a lieutenant of the company, came by. He spent a long time looking closely at Don Tameo and examining Don Sera; and when Don Sera asked him "Why have all the flowers withered in the mysterious garden of love?" decided that he probably shouldn't send them to their posts. Let them lie about for now.

Don Rumata lost a gold piece to the lieutenant and talked to him about the new uniform sword slings and methods of sword-sharpening. Rumata mentioned in passing that he was planning to pay a visit to Don Satarina, who owned some antique grinding stones, and expressed deep disappointment upon hearing that the venerable noble had lost the last of his marbles: a month ago, he released all his prisoners, let go of his entire militia, and donated his considerable arsenal of implements of torture to the treasury. The 102-year-old man had declared that he intended to devote the rest of his life to good works, and now probably wouldn't last long.

After saying good-bye to the lieutenant, Rumata left the palace and headed to the port. He walked along, skirting puddles and jumping over potholes full of scummy water, unceremoniously elbowing gawking commoners aside, winking at girls, who were apparently irresistibly struck by his appearance, bowing to ladies carried in chairs, exchanging friendly greetings with familiar noblemen, and pointedly ignoring the gray storm troopers.

He made a small detour by the Patriotic School. This school had been established two years ago through the efforts of Don Reba, for the purpose of preparing young oafs from the inferior gentry and merchant classes to become military and administrative personnel. It was a stone building of modern construction, without any columns or bas-reliefs, with thick walls, narrow windows that resembled embrasures, and semicircular towers flanking the main entrance. If necessary, the building could withstand an attack.

Rumata went up the narrow stairs to the second floor and, jingling his spurs on the stone, walked past the classes toward the office of the school procurator. Droning voices and choruses of shouts came from the classrooms. "Who is the king? His August Majesty. Who are the ministers? Faithful servants, knowing no doubts . . ." ". . . and God, our creator, said 'I shall curse you,' and curse them he did . . ." ". . . and if the horn sounds twice, scatter into pairs in chain formation, lowering your pikes at the same time . . ." "When the tortured faints, do not get carried away—the torture must cease . . ."

This is school, thought Rumata. The source of all wisdom. The pillar of the culture.

He pushed open the low, vaulted door without knocking and entered the office, which was dark and ice-cold, like a cellar. A tall man rushed out to greet him from behind a giant desk piled high with papers and canes for punishment—he was bald, with sunken eyes, dressed in a tight-fitting, narrow gray uniform with the insignia of the Ministry of the Defense of the Crown. This was the procurator of the Patriotic School, the highly learned Father Kin—a sadist and murderer who had become a monk, the author of *A Treatise on Denunciation*, which had attracted the attention of Don Reba.

Answering the flowery greeting with a curt nod, Rumata sat down in a chair and crossed his legs. Father Kin remained standing, bent in an attitude of deferential attention. "Well, how's it going?" Rumata asked affably. "Slaughtering some literates, educating others?"

Father Kin showed his teeth in a grin. "A literate is not the enemy of the king," he said. "The enemy of the king is the literate dreamer, the literate skeptic, the literate nonbeliever! Whereas here we—"

"All right, all right," said Rumata. "I believe you. What have you been scribbling? I read your treatise—a useful book, but a stupid one. How did that happen? Shame on you. Some procurator!"

"I do not endeavor to impress with my mind," Father Kin answered with dignity. "All I have sought is to be of service to the state. We do not need smart people. We need loyal people. And we—"

"All right, all right," Rumata said again. "I believe you. So are you writing anything new or not?"

"I'm planning to submit an essay to the ministry about a new state, modeled on the Region of the Holy Order."

"What's this?" Rumata said in surprise. "You want us all to become monks?"

Father Kin clasped his hands and leaned forward. "Allow me to explain, noble don," he said fervently, licking his lips.

"It's not about that at all! It's about the basic tenets of the new state. The tenets are simple, and there are only three of them: blind faith in the infallibility of the laws, unquestioning obedience to these laws, and also everyone vigilantly watching everyone else."

"Hmm," said Rumata. "But why?"

"What do you mean, why?"

"You really are stupid," Rumata said. "All right, I believe you. Where was I? Oh yes! Tomorrow you will get two new instructors. Their names are Father Tarra, a very venerable old man who works in, what's it called . . . cosmography, and Brother Nanin, also a trustworthy man, who is knowledgeable about history. These are my people, so treat them with respect. Here's money for the pledge." He threw a clinking pouch onto the desk. "Your share is five gold pieces. Understood?"

"Yes, noble don," Father Kin said.

Rumata yawned and looked around. "Well, I'm glad you understood," he said. "For some reason, my father was very fond of these people and left me instructions to set them up in life. You're a learned man—can you explain to me why a noble don would have such affection for a literate?"

"Maybe some special services?" proposed Father Kin.

"What are you talking about?" Rumata asked suspiciously. "On the other hand, why not? Yes . . . a pretty daughter or sister . . . You have no wine here, of course?"

Father Kin spread his hands apologetically.

Rumata picked up one of the papers off the desk and held it in front of his eyes for some time. "'Refacilitation . . .'" he read out loud. "What wisdom!" He dropped the page onto the floor and got up. "Make sure that your pack of scholars doesn't bother them. I'll pay a visit sometime, and if I find out . . ." He put his fist underneath Father Kin's nose. "All right, all right, don't be scared, I won't do anything."

Father Kin giggled deferentially. Rumata nodded to him and headed for the door, scraping the floor with his spurs.

On the Street of Overwhelming Gratitude he went into a weapons shop, bought new scabbard rings, tried out a couple of daggers (threw them at the wall, weighed them in his hand—didn't like them), then sat down on the counter and had a conversation with Father Hauk, the owner. Father Hauk had sad, gentle eyes and small, pale hands stained with ink. Rumata debated with him a little about the merits of the poems of Zuren, listened to an interesting commentary on the line "As a wilted leaf falls on my soul . . ." and asked him to read him something new. Then, as he was leaving, having sighed with the author over the inexpressibly sad verses, he recited "To be or not to be?" in his translation into Irukanian.

"Holy Míca!" cried the inflamed Father Hauk. "Whose poetry is this?"

"Mine," said Rumata, and left.

He went into the Gray Joy, drank a glass of sour Arkanarian brew, patted the hostess's cheek, and deftly used one of his swords to flip the table of the usual informer, who was gawking at him with empty eyes. Then he walked over to a far corner and tracked down a shabby bearded man with an inkwell around his neck. "Hello, Brother Nanin," he said. "How many petitions have you written today?"

Brother Nanin smiled shyly, showing small, decayed teeth. "There aren't many petitions written nowadays, noble don," he said. "Some people think that asking is pointless, while others expect that in the near future they'll be able to take without asking."

Rumata leaned down to his ear and explained that he'd arranged things with the Patriotic School. "Here are two gold pieces," he concluded. "Buy some clothes, get yourself in order. And try to be more careful—at least for the first couple of days. Father Kin is a dangerous man."

"I'll read him my *Treatise on Rumors*," said Brother Nanin cheerfully. "Thank you, noble don."

"What won't a man do in memory of his father!" said Rumata. "Now tell me where to find Father Tarra."

Brother Nanin stopped smiling and started blinking in confusion. "There was a fight here yesterday," he said. "And Father Tarra had a bit too much to drink. And then he's a redhead . . . They broke his rib."

Rumata grunted in vexation. "What rotten luck!" he said. "Why do you all drink so much?"

"Sometimes it's hard to resist," Brother Nanin said sadly.

"True," said Rumata. "Well, here are two more gold pieces. Take good care of him."

Brother Nanin caught Rumata's hand and bent down toward it. Rumata stepped back. "Now, now," he said. "That's not one of your best jokes, Brother Nanin. Good-bye."

The port smelled like nowhere else in Arkanar. It smelled of saltwater, rotten pond scum, spices, tar, smoke, and old salted meat; the taverns reeked of cooking, fried fish, and stale beer. The humid air was thick with swearing in many languages. Thousands of strange-looking people thronged on the piers, in the narrow alleys between the warehouses, and by the taverns: disheveled sailors, pompous merchants, sullen fishermen, dealers in slaves, dealers in women, painted girls, drunken soldiers, some dubious individuals hung with weapons, and outlandish vagrants with gold bracelets on their dirty paws. Everyone was agitated and angry. By the order of Don Reba, it had already been three days since a single ship, or a single canoe, had been allowed to leave port. Gray troopers were toying with their rusty butcher's axes by the docks—spitting occasionally, brazenly and gloatingly glancing at the crowd. On the detained ships, big-boned, copper-skinned people dressed in furry animal skins and copper caps were crouching in groups of five or six—barbarian mercenaries, worthless in close combat but terrifying like this, at a distance, due to their enormously long blowpipes that fired poison darts. And beyond the forest of masts, motionless on the open sea, loomed the long war galleys of the Royal Navy. From time to time they emitted red jets of flame and smoke, making the sea blaze up—burning petroleum for intimidation.

Rumata passed the customs office, where sullen sea dogs huddled in front of the locked doors, vainly waiting for permission to set sail, and pushed his way through the clamorous crowd, from which you could buy just about anything, from slave women and black pearls to drugs and trained spiders. He came out by the piers, looked askance at the row of bloated corpses in sailor's jackets laid out in the sun for public display, and taking a detour through a junk-filled vacant lot, entered the reeking alleyways on the outskirts of the port. It was quieter here. Half-naked girls dozed in the doors of the squalid dens, a drunken soldier with his pockets inside out was lying facedown and bleeding at an intersection, and suspicious figures with the pale faces of the night crept along the walls.

This was the first time Rumata had been here during the day, and initially he was surprised that he didn't attract attention; the bleary eyes of all the passersby looked either past him or seemingly through him, although they did move aside and give way. But as he was rounding a corner, he happened to turn around and had time to notice a dozen varied heads—male and female, long-haired and bald—instantly retracting into doorways, windows, and alleys. Then he became cognizant of the strange atmosphere of this vile place, an atmosphere not of hostility or danger but of some unsavory, greedy interest.

Pushing a door open with his shoulder, he entered one of the dens, where an old man with the face of a mummy was dozing behind a counter in a gloomy little hall. The tables were empty. Rumata silently approached the counter and was about to flick the old man's long nose when he suddenly realized that the sleeping old man wasn't sleeping at all but was examining him carefully through his half-closed eyelids. Rumata threw a coin on the counter, and the old man's eyes immediately shot open. "What would the noble don like?" he asked briskly. "Weed? Snuff? Girls?"

"Drop it," said Rumata. "You know exactly why I come here."

"Why, it's the noble Don Rumata," exclaimed the old man in a tone of extraordinary surprise. "I did think something looked familiar . . ."

After saying this he lowered his eyelids again. Everything was clear. Rumata walked around the counter and squeezed through a narrow door into a tiny adjacent room. Here it was cramped and dark, and the stuffy air had a sour reek. A wizened old man in a flat black cap stood behind a tall desk in the middle of the room, bent over some papers. An oil lamp flickered on the desk, and the only things visible in the gloom were the faces of the people sitting motionless by the walls. Rumata, keeping a hand on his swords, also groped for a stool by the wall and sat down. This place had its own laws and its own etiquette. No one paid any attention to the newcomer; if a man came here, then that was how it should be, and if it wasn't how it should be, he would disappear in the blink of an eye. And you'd never find him, even if you searched the world over. The wizened old man diligently scratched his stylus against the paper; the people by the wall sat motionless. From time to time, one or another of them would sigh deeply. Unseen flytrap lizards ran up and down the walls with a light pitter-patter.

The motionless people by the walls were the chiefs of the robber bands; Rumata had long known some of them by sight. These dull beasts weren't worth much in and of themselves. Their psychology was no more complicated than that of the average shopkeeper. They were ignorant, merciless, and had a way with knives and short cudgels. The man behind the desk, on the other hand . . .

His name was Waga the Wheel, and he was the all-powerful, uncontested head of all the criminal forces of the Land Beyond the Strait, which stretched from the Pitanian marshes to the west of Irukan to the maritime borders of the Mercantile Republic of Soan. He had been damned by all three official churches of the empire for his excessive pride, for he called himself the younger brother of the reigning monarch of Arkanar. He had at his disposal a night army numbering in the tens of thousands of men and a fortune totaling hundreds of thousands of gold pieces, and his agents had penetrated the inner sanctums of the state apparatus. During the last twenty years, he had been executed four times, each time attracting a large crowd of people; the official story was that he was currently languishing in three of the darkest dungeons of the empire at the same time, and Don Reba had repeatedly issued decrees "concerning the outrageous spread of legends by state criminals and other malefactors about the so-called Waga the Wheel, who in reality does not exist and is therefore legendary." The same Don Reba had, according to rumors, summoned several barons with strong militias and offered them a reward: five hundred gold pieces for Waga dead and seven thousand for Waga alive. In his time, Rumata himself had spent a considerable amount of gold and effort to make the acquaintance of this person. Waga inspired an extreme disgust in him but was occasionally immensely useful—literally irreplaceable. Furthermore, Waga really interested Rumata as a scientific specimen. This was a most curious exhibit in his collection of medieval monsters, a personage who apparently had absolutely no past.

Waga finally put down the stylus, stood up, and rasped out, "Here's how it is, my children. Two and a half thousand gold pieces over three days. And only one thousand nine hundred and ninety-six in expenses. Five hundred and four little round gold pieces over three days. Not bad, my children, not bad."

No one moved. Waga walked away from the desk, sat down in a corner, and vigorously rubbed his dry palms together.

"I have happy news for you, my children," he said. "Good times are coming, abundant times . . . But we'll have to work hard. Oh, so hard! My elder brother, the king of Arkanar, has decided to exterminate all the learned men in our kingdom. Well, he knows best. And anyway, who are we to argue with his august decisions? However, we can and must capitalize on this decision. And since we're his loyal subjects, we shall serve him. But since we're his subjects of the night, we will not neglect to take our small share. He will not notice and will not be angry with us. What did you say?"

No one moved.

"I thought that Piga sighed. Is that true, Piga, my son?"

Someone fidgeted and cleared his throat in the dark. "I didn't sigh, Waga," said a coarse voice. "Why would I—"

"You wouldn't, Piga, you wouldn't! That's right! Now is the time to listen to me with bated breath. You will all leave here and begin difficult labors, and then you will have no one to advise you. My elder brother, His Majesty, through the mouth of his minister Don Reba, promised us a considerable sum for the heads of certain escaped fugitive learned men. We must deliver these heads to him and make the old man happy. On the other hand, certain learned men wish to hide from my elder brother's wrath and will spare no expense in doing so. In the name of mercy, and in order to relieve my elder brother's soul from the burden of additional villainies, we will help these people. However, if his majesty also needs these heads in the future, he will receive them. For a good price, a very good price . . ."

Waga stopped talking and bowed his head. An old man's slow tears suddenly started flowing down his cheeks.

"I'm getting old, my children," he said with a sob. "My hands tremble, my legs buckle beneath me, and my memory is beginning to fail me. I'd forgotten, completely forgotten, that a noble don has been languishing amongst us in this stuffy, cramped little room, and that he cares nothing for our financial affairs. I will go now. I will go and rest. In the meantime, my children, let us apologize to the noble don."

He stood up and bowed with a groan. The others also stood up and also bowed, but with obvious hesitation and even fear. Rumata could practically hear the whirring of their dull, primitive brains as they vainly attempted to keep up with the meaning of the words and deeds of this hunched old man.

Of course, it was a very simple matter: the outlaw had taken advantage of an extra opportunity to bring to Don Reba's attention the fact that in the ongoing massacre, the night army intended to work together with the gray forces. And now, when the time had come to give specific instructions, to name the names and dates of the campaigns, the presence of the noble don became irksome, to say the least, and he, the noble don, was invited to quickly state his business and clear out of there. A dark old man. A terrifying old man. And why is he in the city? thought Rumata. Waga can't stand the city.

"You're right, honorable Waga," Rumata said. "I must be on my way. However, I'm the one who should be apologizing, since I've come to trouble you about a completely trivial matter." He stayed seated, and everyone who was listening to him remained standing. "I happen to need your advice. You may sit down."

Waga bowed again and sat down.

"The case is as follows," Rumata continued. "Three days ago, I was supposed to meet a friend of mine, a noble don from Irukan, in the Territory of Heavy Swords. But we never met. He's disappeared. I know for a fact that he had safely crossed the border from Irukan. Perhaps you know what has become of him?"

Waga didn't respond for some time. The bandits wheezed and sighed. Then Waga cleared his throat. "No, noble don," he said. "We know nothing of this matter."

Rumata immediately stood up. "Thank you, honorable Waga," he said. He stepped into the center of the room and put a pouch with ten gold pieces onto the desk. "Before I leave, I have a favor to ask: if you do find anything out, let me know." He touched his hat. "Good-bye."

When he was almost out the door, he stopped and casually said over his shoulder, "You had been saying something about learned men. Something just occurred to me. I have the feeling that by the king's efforts, in another month it will be impossible to find a single decent bookworm in Arkanar. And I made a vow to establish a university back home after being healed from the black plague. If you'd be so kind, whenever you get ahold of some bookworms, let me know first, and only then tell Don Reba. It's possible that I'll select one or two for the university."

"It'll cost you," said Waga in a honeyed voice. "The product is rare, flies off the shelf."

"My honor is worth more," Rumata said haughtily and left.

# Chapter 3

It would be very interesting, thought Rumata, to catch this Waga and take him back to Earth. Technically, it wouldn't be difficult. We could do it right now. What would he do on Earth? Rumata tried to imagine it. Take a bright, air-conditioned room with mirrored walls that smells like pine needles or the sea, and toss a huge hairy spider inside it. The spider presses down to the gleaming floor, looks around frantically with its beady eyes, and then—what else can it do?—scurries sideways into the darkest corner and crouches down, menacingly displaying its poisonous mandibles.

Of course, first of all Waga would search for the resentful people. And of course, the stupidest of the resentful would seem to him too clean and unsuitable for use. You know, the old man might sicken. He'd probably even waste away.

Although who can tell? That's the thing—the psychology of these monsters is very much a dark forest. Holy Míca! Making sense of it is much more difficult than making sense of the psychology of a nonhumanoid civilization. All of the actions of these men can be explained, but they are fiendishly difficult to predict.

Yes, maybe he'd die from melancholy. Or maybe he'd look around, adapt, figure out how things stand, and get a job as a ranger in some national park. After all, it can't be the case that he doesn't have a single small, harmless hobby—which only gets in his way here, but there could become the meaning of his life. I think he likes cats. He keeps a whole herd of them, they say, in his lair, and he has a special keeper for them. And he even pays this keeper, although he's stingy and could have simply threatened him. But what he'd do on Earth with his monstrous lust for power—that's hard to know.

Rumata stopped in front of a tavern and was about to go in, but then realized that his coin purse was missing. He stood in front of the door in complete confusion (he just couldn't get used to such occurrences, although this wasn't the first time) and spent a long time digging through his pockets. There had been three pouches, with ten gold pieces in each. He gave one to the procurator, Father Kin, and another to Waga. The third one had disappeared. His pockets were empty, all gold buckles had been carefully cut off his left pant leg, and the dagger had disappeared from his belt.

Then he noticed two storm troopers standing nearby, gawking at him and grinning stupidly. The employee of the Institute couldn't care less, but the noble Don Rumata of Estor went berserk. For a second he lost control of himself. He took a step toward the storm troopers, and unconsciously raised his hand, clenching it into a fist. Apparently, his face had become horrifying, because the mockers shied away, grins frozen as if they'd been paralyzed, and hurriedly ducked into the tavern.

Then he became frightened. He had only been this scared once in his life, when he—at the time still the second pilot of a passenger starship—felt his first attack of malaria. God knows where this disease had come from, and after two hours filled with surprised jokes and quips he was already cured, but he had never forgotten the shock that he, a perfectly healthy man who had never been sick, felt at the thought that something had gone wrong inside him, that he had become defective and had somehow lost unilateral authority over his body.

But I didn't mean to, he thought. I wasn't even considering it. They weren't even doing much—OK, so they were standing around, so they were grinning. Grinning very foolishly, but I probably did look completely ridiculous digging through my pockets. I was this close to cutting them down, he suddenly realized. If they hadn't cleared out, I would have cut them down. He remembered that on a recent bet, he had split a dummy dressed in Soanian double armor from top to bottom with a single sword stroke, and he felt the skin on his back crawl. They would have been lying here like pig carcasses, and I'd be standing here with a sword in my hand and wouldn't have known what to do. Some god! Turning into a savage . . .

He suddenly noticed that all his muscles ached, as if after hard labor. Now, now, calm down, he told himself. Nothing happened. It's over. Just an outburst. A momentary outburst, and it's all over. After all, I'm human, and humans are still animals. It's just my nerves. My nerves and the tension of the last couple of days . . . But mostly, it's the feeling of a shadow creeping over us. I can't tell whose shadow, or where it's coming from, but it's creeping over us, inexorably so.

This inexorability was palpable everywhere. It was palpable in the fact that the storm troopers, who had until very recently cowardly stuck close to their barracks, now strolled freely with their axes in plain sight in the middle of the street—a place where previously only noble dons were allowed to walk. And in the fact that all of the city's street singers, storytellers, dancers, and acrobats had disappeared. And in the fact that the residents had stopped singing political ditties, had become very serious, and knew exactly what was needed for the good of the state. And in the sudden and inexplicable port closure. And in the fact that "angry mobs" had sacked and burned all the curiosity shops—the only places in the kingdom where it had been possible to buy or borrow books in all the languages of the empire, and in the ancient and now dead languages of the native people of the Land Beyond the Strait. And in the fact that the jewel of the city, the gleaming tower of the astrological observatory, now protruded into the sky like a black rotten tooth, burned down in an "accidental fire." And in the fact that over the last two years, the consumption of alcohol had grown four-fold—in Arkanar, legendary for its rampant alcoholism since ancient times! And in the fact that the eternally oppressed, persecuted peasants had totally burrowed underground in their villages of Sweet Smells, Heavenly Shrubs, and Celestial Kisses, and didn't even dare leave their mud huts for the necessary field labor. And finally, in the fact that the old vulture Waga the Wheel had moved to the city, sensing a big haul. Somewhere in the bowels of the palace, in luxurious apartments, sits a gouty king who hasn't seen the sun for twenty years for fear of everything in the world. His own great-grandfather's son, he giggles half-wittedly and signs one horrifying order after another, dooming to an agonizing death the most honest and selfless people. Somewhere over there, a monstrous abscess has matured and any day now will rupture . . .

Rumata slipped on a piece of cantaloupe and looked up. He was on the Street of Overwhelming Gratitude, in the domain of respectable merchants, money changers, and master jewelers. The street was lined with solid old-fashioned houses that had benches and storage sheds, the sidewalk here was wide, and the road was paved with granite blocks. The people he usually encountered here were noblemen and the rich, but right now a dense crowd of excited commoners was pouring toward Rumata. They carefully walked around him, glanced at him obsequiously, and many bowed just in case. The upper-story windows were full of fat faces, whose curiosity had been piqued and was now satisfied. Someone in front was shouting peremptorily: "Go on, keep walking! Break it up! Go on, quick!"

The people in the crowd were talking to each other: "That's the worst kind, they're the real dangerous ones. They seem so quiet, well mannered, respectable—a merchant like any other—but there's bitter poison inside!"

"What they did to him, the poor devil . . . I'm used to everything, but believe it or not, it made me sick to watch."

"And they're none the worse for it. What boys! It warms my heart. They won't let us down."

"Maybe we shouldn't do it like this? After all, he's a man, a living creature. All right, so he's a sinner—then punish him, teach him, but why this?"

"Hey, stop that, you! Be quiet, you. First, there are people around . . ."

"Master, master! The broadcloth's good, and they'll sell it to us without raising the price if you push 'em. Although we better hurry up or Pakin's guys will beat us to it again."

"My son, you must not doubt. You must have faith. If the authorities are taking steps, they know what they are doing."

They got another one, thought Rumata. He wanted to change course and walk around the place from which the crowd streamed, where they were shouting to keep walking and break it up. But he didn't change course. He only ran his hand through his hair, so that a stray strand wouldn't cover the stone on his circlet. The stone wasn't a stone but a camera lens, and the circlet wasn't a circlet but a radio transmitter. Historians on Earth saw and heard everything that the 250 operatives saw and heard on the nine continents of the planet. And therefore, the operatives were required to keep their eyes and ears open.

Jutting out his chin and splaying his swords in order to take up as much room as possible, he headed right at the people in the middle of the street, and everyone going the opposite direction hastily jumped aside and gave way. Four stocky porters with painted faces were carrying a silver-hued sedan chair through the streets. A beautiful cold little face with mascaraed eyelashes peered out from behind the curtain. Rumata tore off his hat and bowed. This was Doña Ocana, the current favorite of our eagle Don Reba. When she saw the magnificent suitor, she smiled languidly and meaningfully at him. It was possible to immediately name two dozen noble dons who, after receiving such a smile, would have rushed to their wives and mistresses with the joyful news: "All the others better beware, I'll buy and sell them all, I'll show them who's boss!" Such smiles were rare and often invaluable. Rumata stopped, following the chair with his eyes. I should make up my mind, he thought. I should finally make up my mind. He shuddered at the thought of what it would cost him. But I should do it! I really should . . .

My mind's made up, he thought. There's no other way. I'll do it tonight. He reached the weapons shop he had gone into that morning to check the price of daggers and listen to poetry, and stopped again. So that's what it was. That means it was your turn, my good Father Hauk.

The crowd had already dispersed. The shop's door was torn from its hinges and the windows were broken. A huge storm trooper in a gray shirt stood in the doorway, his foot planted on the doorjamb. Another storm trooper, a scrawnier one, squatted by the wall. The wind was blowing crumpled sheets covered with writing along the pavement.

The huge storm trooper stuck his finger in his mouth, sucked on it, then took it out and examined it carefully. The finger was covered in blood. The storm trooper caught Rumata's eye and rasped affably, "Bit worse than a ferret, the bastard!"

The second storm trooper quickly snickered. A shrimpy, pale kid, uncertain-looking, with a pimply mug—it was immediately obvious that he was a rookie, a tadpole, a cub . . .

"What's going on here?" Rumata inquired.

"Got a concealed bookworm," the cub said nervously.

The giant started sucking on his finger again, without changing his attitude.

"At attention!" Rumata ordered quietly.

The cub quickly jumped up and picked up his ax. The giant thought about it but did put his foot down and stand up fairly straight.

"So who was the bookworm?" Rumata asked.

"I don't know," the cub said. "It was the order of Father Zupic."

"Well, what happened? You took him?"

"That's right! We took him!"

"That's good," said Rumata. That really wasn't bad. There was still time. Nothing is more precious than time, he thought. An hour buys a life; a day is invaluable. "And what did you do with him? Stick him in the tower?"

"Huh?" the cub asked in confusion.

"I'm asking, is he now in the tower?"

The pimply mug spread into an uncertain grin. The giant roared with laughter. Rumata rapidly turned around. There, on the other side of the street, Father Hauk's corpse hung like a sack of rags from the crossbeam of a gate. A few ragged urchins, mouths wide open, gawked at him from the yard.

"It isn't everyone who gets sent to the tower nowadays," the giant rasped out amiably behind him. "We do things quick nowadays. A knot by the ear—and off you go."

The cub giggled again. Rumata glanced at him blindly, and slowly crossed the street. The sad poet's face was black and unrecognizable. Rumata looked down. Only the hands were recognizable, with their long, weak fingers, stained with ink.

> Nowadays we don't pass away,
> We're led away into darkness.
> And even if anyone dares to
> Wish that it were otherwise,
> Powerless and incompetent,
> He lowers his weak hands,
> Not knowing where the dragon's heart is.
> And whether the dragon has one.

Rumata turned around and walked away. My good, weak Hauk . . . The dragon does have a heart. And we know where it is. And that's the most frightening thing, my quiet, helpless friend. We know where it is, but we can't destroy it without spilling the blood of thousands of frightened, hypnotized, blind people who know no doubts. And there are so many of them, hopelessly many—ignorant, isolated, embittered by perpetual thankless labor, downtrodden, not yet able to rise above the thought of an extra penny. And they cannot yet be taught, united, guided, saved from themselves. Far too early, centuries earlier than it should have, the gray muck has risen in Arkanar. It won't meet with resistance, and all that's left is to save those few there is still time to save. Budach, Tarra, Nanin, maybe another dozen, maybe another two dozen.

But the very thought that thousands of others—maybe less talented but also honest and truly noble people—were fatally doomed caused an icy chill in his chest and an awareness of his own vileness. Sometimes this awareness became so acute that his mind would become clouded, and Rumata could almost see the backs of the gray bastards illuminated by lilac flashes of gunfire, and Don Reba's eternally insignificant, pale visage contorted with animal terror, and the Merry Tower collapsing on itself. Yes, that'd be sweet. That would be actual work. An actual macroscopic impact. But then . . . Yes, they were right at the Institute. Then the inevitable. Bloody chaos in the country. The surfacing of Waga's night army, ten thousand thugs excommunicated by every church—rapists, murderers, and sadists; hordes of copper-skinned barbarians descending from the mountains and destroying everything that moves, from newborns to the aged; huge crowds of peasants and townspeople, blind with terror, fleeing to the forests, mountains, and deserts; and your supporters—merry men, brave men!—ripping open each other's bellies in a brutal struggle for power and for the right to control the machine gun after your inevitable violent death. And this absurd death—from

a cup of wine served by your best friend, or from a crossbow bolt whistling toward your back from behind a curtain.
And the horrified face of the one who will be sent from Earth
to replace you, and who will find a country depopulated,
drenched in blood, still burning, in which everything, everything, everything will need to be started over again.

When Rumata kicked open the door of his house and
entered the magnificent, dilapidated entrance hall, he was as
gloomy as a storm cloud. Muga, the gray-haired, hunched
servant of forty years' experience, cowered at the sight of
him and only watched, drawing his head further into his
shoulders, as his savage young master tore off his hat, coat,
and gloves, hurled his swords onto the bench, and climbed to
his chambers. Uno waited for him in the living room.

"Order dinner," growled Rumata. "To my study."

"Someone's waiting for my master in there," Uno
reported gloomily.

"Who?"

"Some common girl. Or maybe a doña. She speaks like a
commoner—so gentle, but she's dressed like a noblewoman
. . . pretty."

Kira, thought Rumata with tenderness and relief. Oh,
how wonderful! As if she sensed it, my little one. He stood
still, his eyes closed, gathering his thoughts.

"Should I turn her out?" the boy asked briskly.

"You dummy," said Rumata. "Don't you dare! Where is
she?"

"In master's study, of course," the boy said with an inept
smile.

Rumata hurriedly headed there. "Order dinner for two,"
he instructed along the way. "And listen: don't let anyone in!
Not the king, not the devil, not Don Reba himself."

She was in his study, sitting with her feet up on a chair, her chin propped up on her fist, absentmindedly flipping through the *Treatise on Rumors*. When Rumata walked in, she started, but he didn't let her get up. He ran up to her, hugged her, and stuck his nose into her thick, fragrant tresses, muttering, "It's so good to see you, Kira! It's so good to see you."

There was nothing extraordinary about her. She was just a girl, eighteen years of age, snub-nosed, her father an assistant to the court clerk, her brother a sergeant in the storm troopers. And she was late getting married, because she was a redhead, and Arkanar didn't think much of redheads. For that same reason, she was surprisingly quiet and shy, and she had nothing in common with the loudmouthed, voluptuous women who were so appreciated in every class of this society. Nor was she like the languid court beauties, who found out a woman's lot too early and for life. But she knew how to love the way they now loved on Earth—calmly and unconditionally.

"Why were you crying?" Rumata asked.

"Why are you so angry?"

"No, tell me why you were crying."

"I'll tell you later. Your eyes are so very tired. What happened?"

"Later. Who upset you?"

"No one upset me," Kira said. "Can you take me away from here?"

"Definitely."

"When are we leaving?"

"I don't know, little one. But we're definitely going to leave."

"Far away?"

"Very far away."

"To the metropole?" she asked.

"Yes . . . to the metropole. To my country."

"Is it nice there?"

"It's wondrously nice. No one ever cries there."

"That's impossible."

"Of course," Rumata admitted. "But *you'll* never cry there."

"And what are the people there like?"

"Like me."

"All of them?"

"Not all of them. Some are much better."

"That's definitely impossible."

"That's not only possible," he replied, "it's true!"

"Why is it so easy to believe you? My father doesn't believe anyone. My brother says that all people are swine, the only difference is that some are filthy and others are not. But I don't believe them, and you I always believe."

"I love you."

"Wait . . . Rumata. Take your circlet off. You said it's a sin . . ."

Rumata laughed happily, pulled the circlet off, put it on the table, and covered it with a book. "It's the eye of God," he said. "Let it be closed." He lifted her up in his arms. "It's very sinful, but when I'm with you, I don't need God. Right?"

"Right," she said very softly.

By the time they sat down to eat, the roast meat was cold, and the wine, which had been taken out of the icebox, was warm. Uno came by and, treading softly as he had been taught by old Muga, walked along the wall lighting lamps, though it was still light out.

"This is your servant?" Kira asked.

"No, he's a free boy. A fine boy, only very stingy."

"Money doesn't grow on trees," Uno observed without turning around.

"So you still haven't bought new sheets?" asked Rumata.

"What for?" the boy asked. "The old ones will do."

"Listen, Uno," Rumata said. "I can't sleep an entire month on the same sheets."

"Ha," the boy said. "His Majesty does it for half a year without a murmur."

"And the oil," Rumata said, winking at Kira. "The oil in the lamps. What is it, free?"

Uno stopped. "But my master has a guest," he finally said firmly.

"See how he is!" said Rumata.

"He's nice," Kira said seriously. "He loves you. Let's take him with us."

"We'll see," Rumata said.

The boy asked suspiciously, "Take me where? I'm not going anywhere."

"We'll go," Kira said, "where all the people are like Don Rumata."

The boy thought for a moment and said scornfully, "What, heaven for the highborn?" Then he snorted derisively and shuffled out of the study, dragging feet in battered shoes.

"A good boy," she said. "Grumpy like a bear cub. He's a nice friend."

"All my friends are nice."

"What about Baron Pampa?"

"How do you know about him?" Rumata asked in surprise.

"You never talk about anyone else. That's all I ever hear about—Baron Pampa this and Baron Pampa that."

"Baron Pampa is a very good friend."

"How can a baron be a good friend?"

"I mean that he's a very good man. Very kind and merry. And very much in love with his wife."

"I'd like to meet him. Or are you ashamed of me?"

"No, I'm not ashamed. It's just that he's a good man, but he's still a baron."

"Oh . . ." she said.

Rumata pushed his plate away. "Do tell me why you were crying. And why you came here alone. Is this the time to be running around the streets alone?"

"I couldn't manage at home. I'll never go home. Can I be a servant here? For free."

Rumata chuckled through the lump in his throat.

"Father copies confessions every day," she continued with quiet desperation. "And the paper they are written on is all covered in blood. He gets them at the Merry Tower. Oh, why did you ever teach me to read? Every evening, every evening . . . copying transcripts of tortures—and drinking. So awful, so awful! 'You know,' he says, 'Kira, our neighbor the calligrapher taught people to write. Who do you think he is? He revealed during torture that he's a wizard and Irukanian spy. Who,' he says, 'am I supposed to believe now? I learned to write from him myself,' he says. And my brother comes home from the patrol more drunk than beer itself, hands covered in dried blood. 'We'll kill them all,' he says, 'until the twelfth generation.' He interrogates father about why he's literate . . . Today, he and his buddies dragged some man into the house. They beat him up, splattered everything with blood. He even stopped screaming. I can't live like this, I'd rather you kill me than go back!"

Rumata stood beside her, stroking her hair. She was staring fixedly into space with tearless, gleaming eyes. What could he say to her? He lifted her in his arms, carried her to the sofa, sat down beside her, and started telling her about the temples made of crystal, about the cheerful gardens that stretched for many miles without any mosquitoes, rot, or evil spirits, about enchanted tablecloths, about flying carpets, about the magical city of Leningrad, about his friends—proud, cheerful, and happy people, about the wondrous country over the seas and mountains with the strange name Earth . . . She listened quietly and attentively, clinging tighter to him when hobnailed boots—*thump, thump, thump*—stomped on the pavement beneath their windows.

She had an amazing quality—an utter and selfless belief in good. Tell such a tale to a serf—he'd grunt doubtfully, wipe off the snot with his sleeve, and keep going without saying a word, only looking back at the kind, sober, but—ah, what a pity!—crazy noble don. Start telling this to Don Tameo and Don Sera—they wouldn't let you finish: one would fall asleep, and the other would burp and say, "That's all *reeeal* noble, but how are their women?" And Don Reba would listen attentively until you were done, and having heard you out, would wink at his storm troopers, so they could bend the noble don's elbows to his shoulder blades and find out where exactly the noble don heard such dangerous tales and who he'd had the time to tell them to.

When Kira calmed down and fell asleep, he kissed her peaceful sleeping face, covered her with a fur-trimmed winter coat, and tiptoed out, closing the unpleasantly squeaking door behind him. After walking through the dark house, he went down to the servants' quarters and said, looking above the bowed heads, "I hired a housekeeper. Her name is Kira. She will stay upstairs, with me. The room behind the study should be thoroughly tidied by tomorrow. Listen to the housekeeper like you do to me." He scanned around the room: any mocking grins? No one was grinning; everyone was listening with proper deference. "And if anyone talks outside the gates, I'll rip their tongue out!"

After finishing the speech, he stood there for some time for emphasis, then turned around and went back up to his chambers. In the living room, which was hung with rusty weapons and cluttered with odd, bug-eaten furniture, he stood by the window and looked outside, leaning his forehead against the cold, dark glass. The bells chimed for the first night watch. In the windows across the way, people were lighting lamps and closing the shutters, in order not to attract evil men or evil spirits. It was quiet, except that at one point a drunk shouted in a terrible voice below—either someone was undressing him or he was trying to barge into the wrong door.

These evenings were the worst—tedious, lonely, cheerless. We thought that it'd be an endless battle, fierce and victorious. We thought that we'd always have clear ideas about good and evil, about our friends and foes. And on the whole we were right, except there was a lot we didn't take into account. For example, we couldn't have imagined these evenings, although we knew they'd exist . . .

There was a clatter of iron below—the doors were being bolted for the night. The cook was praying to Holy Míca to send her any husband at all, as long as he was independent and with a head on his shoulders. Old Muga was yawning, making circular motions with his thumb. In the kitchen, servants were finishing the evening's beer and gossiping, while

Uno, unfriendly eyes flashing, spoke like a grown-up: "Hold your tongues, tomcats."

Rumata stepped back from the window and walked around the living room. It's hopeless, he thought. There's no force strong enough to drag them out of their usual range of cares and ideas. You could give them everything. You could put them in the most modern spectroacoustic housing and teach them ionic procedures, and they'd still gather in the kitchen in the evening, playing cards and cackling about the neighbor whose wife wallops him. And there isn't a better way for them to spend their time. In that sense, Don Condor is right: Reba is nothing, a tiny speck in comparison with the enormous influence of traditions, the rules of the herd—sanctified by centuries, unshakeable, tested, accessible to the dullest of the dull, freeing one from the necessity of thinking and wondering. And Don Reba probably wouldn't even make it into a school curriculum. "A minor adventurer in the era of increasing absolutism."

Don Reba, Don Reba! Neither tall nor short, neither fat nor too skinny, neither particularly thick of hair nor anywhere near bald. Neither abrupt nor sluggish in his movements, with an unmemorable face that looks simultaneously like thousands of other faces. Polite, gallant to the ladies, an attentive conversationalist—but not notable for having any original thoughts.

He emerged out of some musty basement of the palace bureaucracy three years ago, a petty, insignificant functionary, obsequious and pallid, with an almost bluish tint to his skin. Soon the then–First Minister was suddenly arrested and executed, a number of horror-stricken and bewildered officials died during torture, and this tenacious, ruthless genius of mediocrity grew like a pale fungus on their corpses. He's no one. He's from nowhere. This is not a powerful mind underneath a weak monarch, which has been known by history; not a great and terrible man who gives his life to the idea of unifying the country in the name of autocracy. This is no money-grubbing lackey, thinking only of gold and of women, killing right and left for the sake of power, and staying in power in order to kill. People even whispered that he wasn't Don Reba at all, that Don Reba was a completely different person, and this was God-knows-who, a werewolf, a double, a changeling.

All of his schemes fell through. He instigated a fight between two influential families in the kingdom in order to weaken them and begin a broad offensive against the barony. But the families reconciled, clinked their goblets and declared an eternal union, and took a substantial chunk of land away from the king—land that had belonged to the Totzes of Arkanar since time immemorial. He declared war on Irukan, led the army to the border himself, drowned it in the swamps and lost it in the forests, left them all to fend for themselves, and fled back to Arkanar. Thanks to the efforts of Don Gug, which Don Reba of course had no idea about, he was able to make peace with the Duke of Irukan at the cost of two border towns. And after this, the king was forced to scrape out the bottom of the empty coffers in order to put down the peasant revolts that had swept the country.

For these kinds of blunders, any minister would be hung upside down by his feet at the top of the Merry Tower, but Don Reba somehow remained in power. He abolished the Ministries of Education and Welfare, established the Ministry of the Defense of the Crown, and removed the ancestral aristocrats and the few scientists from their government posts. He caused a complete economic collapse, wrote the treatise *On the Brutish Nature of the Farmer*, and finally, a year ago, organized the "protective guard"—the gray troops. The monopolies had stood behind Hitler. No one was standing behind Don Reba, and it was obvious that the storm troopers would eventually devour him like a fly. But he kept twisting and turning, piling one absurdity on top of another, writhing around as if he was trying to deceive himself, as if he knew nothing but the paranoid task of exterminating any trace of culture. Just like Waga the Wheel, he had no past. Two years ago, any aristocratic mongrel would contemptuously speak about the "worthless boor who was deceiving His Majesty," but nowadays every aristocrat you asked claimed to be related to the Minister of the Defense of the Crown through the maternal line.

And now he wants Budach, Rumata thought. Another absurdity. Another bizarre feint of some sort. Budach is a bookworm. Bookworms get sent to the gallows. With a lot of pomp and noise, so that everyone knows about it. But there's no pomp or noise. Therefore, he needs Budach alive. Why? Don Reba can't be stupid enough to hope to force Budach to work for him. Or maybe he really is stupid. Maybe Don Reba is nothing more than a stupid, lucky schemer who doesn't know what he wants himself, slyly making a fool of himself for all to see. It's funny, I've been watching him for three years, and I still don't understand what he is. Although if he'd been watching me, he wouldn't understand either. That's the curious thing—anything is possible. Basis theory only concretely specifies the psychological motivations of the principal personality types, but there are in fact as many types as there are people; any sort of person could come to power. For example, take a man who has spent his entire life annoying his neighbors. Spitting into their pots of soup, putting ground glass into their hay. Of course he'll be removed eventually, but he'll have plenty of time to spit, to chortle, to make mischief. And it doesn't matter to him that he won't make a mark on history, or that distant descendants will rack their brains as they attempt to fit his behavior into an already developed theory of historical progress.

I don't have time for theory anymore, thought Rumata. I only know one thing: man is an objective bearer of reason, and everything that gets in the way of developing this reason is evil and must be eradicated as quickly as possible and in any way possible. Any way possible? Any at all? No, probably not. Or maybe I really do mean *any*? Stop dithering! he thought to himself. I should make up my mind. Sooner or later I will have to make up my mind.

He suddenly remembered about Doña Ocana. Make up your mind, then, he thought. Start right there. If God undertakes to clean an outhouse, let him not believe that his hands will remain clean. He felt nauseated at the thought of what awaited him. But it's better than murder. Better dirt than blood. Walking on his tiptoes, so as not to wake up Kira, he went to his study and changed clothes. He turned the transmitter-circlet over in his hands, then decisively shoved it in a drawer. Then he stuck a white feather—the symbol of passionate love—into his hair behind his right ear, strapped on his swords, and put on his best cloak. When he was already downstairs, unbolting the doors, he thought, You know, if Don Reba finds out, that'll be the end of Doña Ocana. But it was already too late to go back.

# Chapter 4

The guests were already gathered, but Doña Ocana wasn't there yet. The royal guardsmen, famed for their duels and sexual escapades, were having drinks by the gilded table, covered with appetizers—preening, arching their backs, and sticking out their wiry behinds. A number of scrawny middle-aged women giggled by the fireplace; they were completely insignificant and for this reason had been chosen by Doña Ocana to be her confidantes. They were sitting on low couches side by side, and three little old men, with skinny legs in constant motion, were bustling in front of them—famous dandies from the time of the previous regency, avowed authorities on long-forgotten anecdotes. Everyone knew that without these old men a drawing room wasn't a drawing room. In the middle of the hall, his jackbooted feet apart, stood Don Ripat, a loyal and sensible agent of Rumata's, a lieutenant of a gray company of haberdashers, with a magnificent mustache and no principles whatsoever. With his big red hands stuck into his leather belt, he was listening to Don Tameo, who was giving a rambling account of his new project of suppressing the peasants in order to benefit the merchant class, and would occasionally twitch his mustache in the direction of Don Sera, who was wandering from wall to wall, probably in search of a door. In the corner, glancing around cautiously, two famous portrait painters were finishing a stew of alligator with wild garlic, and in a nearby recess sat an elderly woman in black—a duenna engaged by Don Reba to keep an eye on Doña Ocana. She was staring fixedly into space with a strict expression on her face, her whole body occasionally all of a sudden pitching forward. At some distance from the others, a royal and the secretary of the Soanian embassy were playing cards. The royal was cringing; the secretary was smiling patiently. He was the only person engaged in useful activity in the room: he was gathering material for the next embassy report.

The guardsmen by the table greeted Rumata with cheerful shouts. Rumata gave them a friendly wink and started making the rounds of the guests. He bowed to the old dandies, paid a few compliments to the confidantes, who immediately started staring at the white feather behind his ear, patted the royal's fat back, and headed toward Don Ripat and Don Tameo. As he walked by the window recess, the duenna swayed again, reeking of wine.

When he saw Rumata, Don Ripat took his hands out of his belt and clicked his heels, while Don Tameo cried softly, "Is that you, my friend? I'm so glad you came, I had already lost hope. 'Like a broken-winged swan calls wistfully to a star . . .' I was so lonely. If not for our dearest Don Ripat, I would have died of misery!" It was clear that Don Tameo had almost sobered up for dinner but still hadn't been able to stop.

"Is that how it is?" Rumata said with surprise. "We're quoting the rebel Zuren?"

Don Ripat immediately drew himself up and gave Don Tameo a predatory look.

"Er . . ." Don Tameo said, flustered. "Zuren? Is that so? Well, yes, I meant it in an ironic sense, I assure you, noble dons! After all, what is Zuren? A low, ungrateful demagogue. And I just wanted to emphasize—"

"That Doña Ocana isn't here," continued Rumata, "and that you've been lonely without her."

"That's just what I wanted to emphasize."

"By the way, where is she?"

"She should be here any minute," Don Ripat said with a bow, and walked away.

The confidantes, mouths identically agape, kept staring at the white feather. The elderly dandies snickered coyly. Don Tameo finally also noticed the feather and began to tremble. "My friend!" he whispered. "Why are you doing this? You never know when Don Reba might come by. True, he's not expected today, but still . . ."

"Let's not talk about it," said Rumata, impatiently looking around. He wanted to get it over with as quickly as possible. The guardsmen were already approaching with cups.

"You're so pale," whispered Don Tameo. "I do understand, love, passion . . . but, Holy Míca! The state is above . . . and finally, it's dangerous . . . to offend his feelings . . ."

Something changed in his face, and he began to retreat, depart, move back, bowing the entire time. Rumata was surrounded by guardsmen. Someone offered him a full cup.

"For honor and for the king!" a guardsman declared.

"And for love," another one added.

"Show them what the guardsmen are made of, noble Rumata," said a third.

Rumata took the cup and suddenly saw Doña Ocana. She was standing in the doorway, fanning herself and sensuously swaying her shoulders. Yes, she certainly was good-looking! At this distance, she was even beautiful. She wasn't at all to Rumata's taste, but she was doubtlessly good-looking, the silly, lascivious bird. Huge blue eyes without a shadow of thought or warmth, a soft and extremely experienced mouth, a gorgeous, skillfully and carefully exposed body. The guardsman behind Rumata's back apparently couldn't control himself and smacked his lips rather loudly. Rumata shoved the cup toward him without looking and took long strides toward Doña Ocana. Everyone in the room looked away from them and started assiduously talking nonsense.

"You're stunning," Rumata muttered, bowing deeply, his swords clanging. "Let me lie at your feet . . . like a greyhound lies at the feet of a nude and indifferent beauty . . ."

Doña Ocana covered herself with the fan and slyly narrowed her eyes. "You're very brave, noble don," she said. "We poor provincial women cannot hope to withstand such an assault." She had a low, husky voice. "Alas, all that remains for me is to open the castle gates and let the victor in."

Rumata, gritting his teeth from shame and rage, bowed even deeper.

Doña Ocana lowered her fan and yelled out, "Noble dons, enjoy yourselves! Don Rumata and I will be back soon! I promised to show him my new Irukanian rugs."

"Don't leave us long, enchantress!" bleated one of the old men.

"Seductress!" another old man said in a honeyed voice. "Nymph!"

The guards clattered their swords in unison. "His taste isn't bad," the royal said, too audibly. Doña Ocana grabbed Rumata by the sleeve and dragged him along. When he was already in the hallway, Rumata heard Don Sera declare in an injured tone, "I see no reason why a noble don shouldn't look at some Irukanian rugs."

At the end of the hallway, Doña Ocana came to a sudden halt, threw her arms around Rumata's neck, and with a throaty moan that was supposed to indicate a burst of passion, pressed her mouth hard against his. Rumata stopped breathing. The unwashed nymph reeked of body odor mixed with Estorian perfume. Her lips were hot, wet, and sticky from sweets. Making an effort, he attempted to return the kiss—and apparently succeeded, because Doña Ocana moaned again and fell into his arms with her eyes closed. This lasted an eternity. I'll show you, whore, thought Rumata and squeezed her in his arms. Something cracked, either her corset or her ribs, the beauty gave a plaintive squeak, opened her eyes in astonishment, and thrashed around, trying to get free. Rumata hurriedly let her go.

"Naughty boy," she said with delight, breathing heavily. "You almost broke me."

"I'm burning with love," he mumbled guiltily.

"Me too. How I've waited for you! Let's go faster."

She dragged him behind her through some cold, dark rooms. Rumata took out a handkerchief and furtively wiped his mouth. The plan now seemed completely hopeless. I should do it, he thought. But there are all sorts of things I should do! I won't get off with just talk. Holy Míca, why do they never bathe in the palace? What a temperament. If only

Don Reba would come by. She dragged him along silently and persistently, like an ant dragging a dead caterpillar. Feeling like a complete idiot, Rumata went on with some gallant nonsense about fast feet and red lips. Doña Ocana just giggled. She pushed him inside an overheated boudoir—which really was hung with rugs—flung herself onto the huge bed and, sprawling on the pillows, began looking at him with moist, protuberant eyes. Rumata stood stock-still. The boudoir smelled distinctly of bedbugs.

"You're beautiful," she whispered. "Come to me. I've waited so long!"

Rumata closed his eyes; he felt sick. Beads of sweat started to roll down his face with a repulsive tickle. I can't do it, he thought. Damn the information. A she-fox . . . a monkey . . . It's just unnatural, it's dirty. Dirt is better than blood, but *this* is much worse than dirt!

"T-To hell with this," Rumata said hoarsely.

She jumped up and ran over to him. "What is it? Are you drunk?"

"I don't know," he managed to force out. "It's stuffy."

"Should I order a basin?"

"Basin?"

"Never mind, never mind . . . It'll pass." Her fingers shaking with impatience, she began to unbutton his waistcoat. "You're beautiful," she mumbled breathlessly. "But you're as timid as a virgin. I would have never guessed. It's adorable, I swear by Holy Bara!"

He was forced to grab her hands. He was looking down at her, seeing the untidy hair shining with pomade, the round, naked shoulders dotted with clumps of powder, the small red ears. It's too bad, he thought. I can't do it. It's a pity—she must know some things. Don Reba talks in his sleep . . . He brings her to interrogations—she is very fond of interrogations . . . I can't do it.

"Well?" she said irritably.

"Your rugs are beautiful," he said loudly. "But I must go."

She didn't get it at first, then her face contorted. "How dare you?" she whispered, but he had already felt for the door with his shoulder blades, run out into the hallway, and quickly walked away. Starting tomorrow, I'm not taking any more baths, he thought. This place needs hogs, not gods!

"Eunuch!" she shouted after him. "Gelding! Old woman! To the gallows with you!"

Rumata opened a random window and jumped down into the garden. He stood underneath the tree for a while, greedily gulping the cool air. Then he remembered the idiotic white feather, pulled it out, crushed it furiously, and threw it away. Pashka wouldn't have been able to do it either, he thought. No one would have been able to. *Are you sure about that?* Yes, I'm sure. *Then you aren't worth much!* But it makes me sick! *The Experiment doesn't care about your feelings—if you can't do it, don't try.* I'm not an animal! *If the Experiment demands it, you must become an animal!* The Experiment can't demand that. *As you can see, it can.* In that case . . .

In that case what? He didn't know what. In that case . . . In that case . . . All right, let's assume that I'm a bad historian. He shrugged. I'll try to improve. We'll learn how to become pigs.

When he came home, it was about midnight. He didn't get undressed, only undid the clasps on his sword slings, collapsed onto the sofa in the living room, and slept like a log.

He was woken up by Uno's indignant cries and an amiable bass roar: "Go away, go away, cub, or I'll twist your ear off!"

"He's sleeping, I tell you!"

"Scram, don't get in the way!"

"I was ordered not to, I tell you!"

The door swung open, and Baron Pampa don Bau barged into the living room—enormous like the beast Pekh, red-cheeked, white-toothed, and with a pointy mustache. He was wearing a velvet beret cocked to the side and a splendid raspberry cloak, his copper armor shining dully underneath. Uno trailed behind him, clutching the baron's right pant leg.

"Baron!" Rumata exclaimed, swinging his legs down from the sofa. "How did you come to be in town, dear friend? Uno, leave the baron alone!"

"An extraordinarily insistent boy," rumbled the baron, approaching Rumata with open arms. "He'll turn out well. How much do you want for him? But we'll talk about that later. Let me embrace you!"

They embraced. The baron smelled deliciously of the dusty road, horse sweat, and a bouquet of various wines.

"I see that you're completely sober, my friend," he said with disappointment. "But then you're always sober. Lucky man!"

"Have a seat, my friend," said Rumata. "Uno! Bring us Estorian wine, and lots of it!"

The baron raised his huge hand. "Not a drop!"

"Not a drop of Estorian wine? Uno, don't bring Estorian wine, bring Irukanian wine!"

"No wine at all!" the baron said bitterly. "I'm not drinking."

Rumata sat down. "What happened?" he asked anxiously. "Are you not feeling well?"

"I'm as strong as an ox. But these damned family scenes . . . In short, I had a fight with the baroness—and here I am."

"A fight with the baroness! You? Come, Baron, what a strange joke!"

"If you can believe it. I'm in a daze myself. A hundred and twenty miles galloped in a daze!"

"My friend," said Rumata. "We are immediately saddling our horses and riding to Bau."

"But my horse hasn't rested yet!" objected the baron. "And anyway, I want to punish her!"

"Who?"

"The baroness, damn it! After all, am I a man or not?! She's dissatisfied with Pampa drunk, you see, so let her see what he's like sober! I'd rather rot here from drinking water than return to the castle."

Uno said gloomily, "Tell him not to twist any ears."

"Go away, cub!" the baron rumbled genially. "And bring me some beer! I've been sweating, and I need to compensate for the loss of liquid!"

The baron compensated for the loss of liquid for half an hour and became a bit tipsy. In between sips he related his troubles to Rumata. He spent some time cursing at "my drunkard neighbors, who are always in and out of the castle. They show up in the morning, supposedly to hunt, and before you know it they are drunk and chopping up the furniture. They wander all over the castle, make a horrible mess, insult the servants, injure the dogs, and set a horrible example for the young baronet. Then they go home and leave you as drunk as a lord, alone with the baroness . . ." At the end of this story the baron became completely dejected and even demanded some Estorian wine, but recollected himself and said, "Rumata, my friend, let's leave this place. Your cellar is much too well stocked! Let us ride away!"

"But where should we go?"

"It doesn't matter where! Say, the Gray Joy."

"Hmm," said Rumata. "And what will we do at the Gray Joy?"

The baron was silent for some time, fiercely tugging on his mustache. "What do you mean?" he asked finally. "What a strange question. We'll sit, we'll talk . . ."

"At the Gray Joy?" Rumata asked doubtfully.

"Yes. I see what you're saying," said the baron. "It's horrible. But we really must leave. When I'm here, I keep wanting to order Estorian wine!"

"Get me a horse," said Rumata. He went into his study to get the transmitter.

In a few minutes, they were riding side by side down a narrow, pitch-black street. The baron, who had cheered up somewhat, was loudly describing the boar hunt from the day before yesterday, the remarkable qualities of the young baronet, and the miracle in the monastery of Holy Tuca, in which the father abbot gave birth to a six-fingered boy from his hip. He also remembered to have some fun: once in a while, he'd howl like a wolf, hoot, and bang his whip on the closed shutters.

When they arrived at the Gray Joy, the baron reined in his horse and fell into deep thought. Rumata waited. The dingy inn windows shone brightly and horses pranced at the hitching post; a few painted girls were sitting side by side on a bench beneath the windows and squabbling lazily, while two servants were straining to roll a huge barrel covered in nitrate stains through the open doors.

The baron said sadly, "All alone . . . I hate to think of it— the whole night is ahead of us, and I'm all alone! And she's all alone at home."

"Don't be so upset, my friend," Rumata said. "After all, the baronet is keeping her company, and I'm here with you."

"That's completely different," said the baron. "You don't understand at all, my friend. You're too young and flighty. You probably even get pleasure out of looking at these whores."

"Well, why not?" Rumata said, looking curiously at the baron. "They seem like very nice girls."

The baron shook his head and smiled sarcastically. "The one standing up," he said loudly, "has a saggy ass. And the one brushing her hair has no ass at all. These are cows, my friend—at best these are cows. Just think of the baroness! Think of her hands, her grace! Think of her poise, my friend!"

"Yes," Rumata agreed. "The baroness is lovely. Let's leave this place."

"Where would we go?" the baron asked with melancholy. "And why?" Resolve suddenly appeared on his face. "No, my friend, I'm not leaving this place. You do what you like." He started climbing off his horse. "Although I would be very hurt if you left me here alone."

"Of course I'll stay with you," Rumata said. "But—"

"No buts," the baron said.

They threw the reins to an approaching servant, proudly walked past the girls, and entered the hall. It was stifling inside. The lamplight barely penetrated the mist of fumes, as if they were in a large and very dirty steam bath. The benches by the long tables were filled with sweaty soldiers in unbuttoned uniforms, seafaring vagrants in colorful caftans over naked bodies, women with barely covered breasts, gray storm troopers holding their axes between their knees, and craftsmen in scorched rags—all of whom were drinking, eating, cursing, laughing, crying, kissing, and bawling bawdy songs. To the left of them, you could make out a bar, behind which the owner sat at a special dais between giant barrels, managing the swarm of nimble, shifty-eyed servants. To the right of them, a bright rectangle of light shone through—the entrance to the clean half, which was reserved for noble dons, respectable merchants, and gray officers.

"Why shouldn't we have a drink, after all?" Baron Pampa inquired irritably, grabbing Rumata's sleeve and hurrying toward the bar through the narrow passage between the tables, scratching people's backs with the spikes of his armor. At the bar, he snatched the capacious ladle that the owner was using to pour wine into cups, silently drank it down, and declared that all was lost and the only thing left to do was make merry. Then he turned toward the owner and inquired thunderously whether this establishment boasted a place where noblemen could decently and modestly spend their time, without being annoyed by the presence of various tramps, scamps, and thieves. The owner assured him that this was just such an establishment.

"Excellent!" the baron said majestically. He tossed a few gold pieces at the owner. "Bring the best things in the house for myself and this don here, and let us be served by some respectable matron and not some cute little coquette!"

The owner conducted the dons into the clean half himself. There weren't many people there. In the corner, a party of gray officers was sullenly making merry—four lieutenants in tight-fitting uniforms and two captains in short cloaks with the stripes of the Ministry of the Defense of the Crown. Two young aristocrats, sour-faced from general disenchantment, were sitting looking bored by a window, behind a large narrow-necked jug. Not far from them was a cluster of impecunious dons in shabby tunics and darned cloaks. They took tiny sips of beer and constantly looked around the room with thirsty eyes.

The baron collapsed on a seat at an empty table, looked askance at the gray officers, and grumbled, "Even this place has some tramps." But then a stout woman wearing an apron brought out the first course. The baron grunted, took his dagger off his belt, and started to make merry. He silently devoured hefty chunks of roast venison, heaps of pickled clams, mountains of lobsters, tubs of salads and mayonnaise, washing it all down with waterfalls of wine, beer, or mead, or a mixture of wine, beer, and mead. The impecunious dons started to trickle over in ones and twos, and the baron would meet them with a grand wave of the hand and a guttural growl.

He suddenly stopped eating, stared at Rumata with bulging eyes, and roared in a monstrous voice, "It's been a long time since I've been in Arkanar, my noble friend! And to be honest with you, there's something I don't like around here."

"What is it, Baron?" Rumata asked with interest, sucking on a chicken wing. The faces of the impecunious dons expressed deferential attention.

"Tell me, my friend!" the baron uttered, wiping his greasy hands on the hem of his cloak. "Tell me, noble dons! Since when is it the custom in the capital of His Majesty the King for the descendants of the ancient races of the empire to be unable to take a single step without bumping into all sorts of shopkeepers and butchers?"

The impecunious dons exchanged looks and started to move away. Rumata glanced into the corner where the gray officers were sitting. They had stopped drinking and were peering at the baron.

"I'll tell you what it is, noble dons," Baron Pampa continued. "It all comes from cowardice. You tolerate them because you're scared. Yes, you, you're scared!" he bellowed at the nearest impecunious don. The man's face turned pale and he walked away with a wan smile. "Cowards!" barked the baron. His mustache stood on end.

But the impecunious dons weren't much use. They clearly didn't want to fight; they wanted to eat and drink.

Then the baron threw his legs over the bench, grabbed the right side of his mustache in his fist, and, glaring into the corner where the gray officers sat, declared, "But I'm not scared of a damn thing! I beat up the gray scum whenever I have the chance!"

"What's that beer barrel wheezing about?" a gray captain with a long face inquired loudly.

The baron gave a satisfied smile. He got up from the table with a clatter and clambered onto the bench. Rumata, raising both eyebrows, started eating a second wing.

"Hear me, gray scum!" the baron bellowed as if the officers were a mile away. "Know that three days ago, I, Baron Pampa don Bau, gave your kind a good thrashing! You see, my friend," he said to Rumata from his perch, "we were drinking with Father Cabani at my castle. Suddenly, my groom rushes in and tells me that a band of gray soldiers is tearing up the Golden Horseshoe. That's my inn, on my ancestral land! I give the order: 'Saddle the horses!'—and we're off. I swear by my spurs, there were about twenty of them there, a whole gang. They had captured some three men, then got as drunk as pigs. These shopkeepers don't know how to drink . . . so they started walloping everyone and breaking everything. I grabbed one of them by the feet—and the fun began! I chased them all the way to Heavy Swords. There was blood—you won't believe me, my friend—up to the knee, and the number of axes they dropped—"

Here the baron's tale was interrupted. The long-faced captain motioned with his hand, and a heavy throwing knife clanged against the breastplate of the baron's armor.

"About time!" said the baron. He hauled a huge two-handed sword out of its sheath.

With unexpected agility, he jumped down to the floor; the sword swept a gleaming arc through the air and cut through a ceiling beam. The baron swore. The ceiling sank, and debris rained on everyone's heads.

Everyone was now on their feet. The impecunious dons recoiled and clung to the walls. The young aristocrats climbed onto a table for a better view. The grays, holding their blades in front of them, formed a semicircle and started taking small steps toward the baron. Only Rumata remained seated, trying to gauge which side of the baron he could stand up on without getting in the way of his sword.

The wide blade was humming ominously as it described gleaming circles above the baron's head. The baron was awe inspiring. He bore an uncanny resemblance to an idling cargo helicopter.

Having surrounded him from three sides, the grays were forced to stop. One of them had carelessly stood with his back to Rumata, so Rumata bent over the table, grabbed him by the collar, flipped him onto his back into the plates with leftovers and struck him beneath the ear with the edge of his palm. The soldier closed his eyes and went still. The baron cried, "Slaughter him, noble Rumata, and I'll finish off the rest!"

He'll kill all of them, thought Rumata with displeasure. "Listen," he said to the grays. "Let's not spoil a pleasant night for each other. You can't stand against us. Lay down your weapons and leave this place."

"Hey!" said the baron. "I want to fight! Let them fight! Keep fighting, damn you!" As he spoke, he advanced on the grays, sword rotating faster and faster. The soldiers retreated, turning visibly pale. They had obviously never seen a cargo helicopter.

Rumata leapt over the table. "Wait, my friend," he said. "We have absolutely no reason to quarrel with these men. You don't like their presence here? They'll leave."

"We're not leaving without our weapons," one of the lieutenants informed them sullenly. "We'll get in trouble. I'm on patrol."

"What the hell, take your weapons," Rumata gave permission. "Sheathe your blades, hands behind your heads, single file! And none of your tricks! I'll break your bones!"

"How are we supposed to leave?" the long-faced captain said irritably. "This don is blocking the way!"

"And I'll continue to block it!" the baron said stubbornly.

The young aristocrats laughed derisively.

"All right," Rumata said. "I'll hold the baron, and you run by, and better hurry up—I won't be able to hold him long! Hey, you, in the door, out of the way! Baron," he said, hugging Pampa around his ample waist. "My friend, I think you have forgotten something important. As you know, your ancestors only used this glorious sword for noble battle, for it is said, 'Thou shalt not bare thy blade in a tavern.'"

The baron continued rotating the sword, but his face turned pensive. "But I have no other sword," he said uncertainly.

"That's even worse!" Rumata said significantly.

"You think so?" the baron still hesitated.

"You know this better than I do!"

"Yes," said the baron. "You're right." He looked up at his furiously spinning wrist. "You may not believe me, my dear Rumata, but I can keep this up for three to four hours in a row—and I wouldn't even get tired. Oh, why doesn't she see me now!"

"I'll tell her about it," Rumata promised.

The baron sighed and lowered his sword. The gray soldiers ducked and rushed past him. The baron followed them with his eyes. "I wonder, I wonder . . ." he said indecisively. "Do you think I was right not to send them off with a kick to the rear?"

"You were absolutely right," Rumata assured him.

"Well," said the baron, sheathing his sword, "since we didn't succeed in having a fight, we now finally have the right to have a bit of food and drink." He dragged the still-unconscious gray lieutenant off the table by his feet and boomed, "Hey there, kind hostess! Food and wine!"

The young aristocrats came over and politely congratulated them on the victory.

"Nonsense, nonsense," the baron said complacently. "Six miserable thugs, cowardly like all shopkeepers. I scattered two dozen of them in the Golden Horseshoe. How lucky," he turned to Rumata, "that I didn't have my fighting sword that time! I may have carelessly bared it. And even though the Golden Horseshoe isn't a tavern but only an inn—"

"That's how some say it," said Rumata. "'Thou shalt not bare thy blade in an inn.'"

The hostess brought some fresh plates of meat and jugs of wine. The baron rolled up his sleeves and dug in.

"By the way," Rumata said, "Who were the three prisoners you freed in the Golden Horseshoe?"

"Freed?" the baron stopped chewing and stared at Rumata. "But, my noble friend, I must not have expressed myself clearly! I didn't free anyone. They were under arrest—it's a matter of state. Why in the world would I free them? There was a don, probably a big coward, an elderly bookworm, and a servant." He shrugged his shoulders.

"Yes, of course," Rumata said sadly.

The blood suddenly rushed to the baron's face and he savagely rolled his eyes. "What! Again?" he roared.

Rumata looked around. Don Ripat was standing in the doorway. The baron began to get up, knocking over benches and scattering dishes. Don Ripat gave Rumata a significant look and went outside.

"I beg your pardon, Baron," said Rumata, getting up. "His Majesty's service . . ."

"Oh," said the baron in disappointment. "My sympathy. I would never join the service!"

Don Ripat was waiting just outside the door.

"What is it?" Rumata asked.

"Two hours ago," Don Ripat informed him briskly, "by the order of the Minister of the Defense of the Crown Don Reba, I arrested Doña Ocana and conveyed her to the Merry Tower."

"All right," Rumata said.

"An hour ago, Doña Ocana died, unable to withstand the trial by fire."

"All right," Rumata said.

"Officially, she was charged with espionage. But . . ." Don Ripat faltered and looked down. "I think . . . It seems to me . . ."

"I understand," Rumata said.

Don Ripat raised guilty eyes at him.

"It's none of your business," Rumata said gruffly.

Don Ripat's eyes turned opaque again. Rumata nodded to him and went back to the table. The baron was polishing off a plate of stuffed cuttlefish.

"Pour me some Estorian wine!" said Rumata. "And let them bring more food." He cleared his throat. "We'll make merry. We'll make merry, goddamn it."

When Rumata came to, he found himself standing in the middle of a large vacant lot. A gray dawn was breaking; the timekeeping roosters were shrieking in the distance. Cawing crows were densely circling over some unpleasant heap nearby; it smelled of dampness and decay. The fog in his head was quickly dissipating, the familiar state of piercingly sharp and clear sensations was setting in, and something bitter and minty was pleasantly melting on his tongue. The fingers on his right hand really smarted. Rumata brought his clenched fist to his eyes. His knuckles were raw, and he was squeezing an empty vial of casparamid in his fist. Apparently, after he had already gotten to this vacant lot, before he had turned into a complete pig, he unconsciously, almost instinctively, poured the entire contents of the vial into his mouth.

The place was familiar—the tower of the burnt-out observatory loomed in front of him, and to his left he could see the thin, minaret-like watchtowers of the royal palace through the gloom. Rumata took a deep breath of cold damp air and headed home.

Baron Pampa had really made merry last night. Accompanied by a host of impecunious dons, who were quickly losing human form, he made a gigantic tour of the bars of

Arkanar, drank away everything including his splendid belt, demolished an unbelievable quantity of food and drink, and got into at least eight fights along the way. At least, Rumata could distinctly recall eight fights he had intervened in, trying to break things up and prevent loss of life. His later memories were lost in the fog. Certain images floated up through the mist: predatory faces with knives in their teeth, the vacantly sad face of the last impecunious don, whom Baron Pampa was attempting to sell into slavery at the port, a furious hook-nosed Irukanian angrily demanding that the noble dons give back his horses . . .

Early in the night, he was still an operative. He drank as much as the baron: Irukanian wine, Estorian wine, Soanian wine, Arkanarian wine, but before each new wine he would furtively put a casparamid pill under his tongue. He still retained his judgment, and by force of habit noted the clusters of gray patrols at the intersections and bridges, and the outpost of mounted barbarians on the road to Soan, where the baron would certainly have been shot if Rumata hadn't known the barbarian tongue. He distinctly recalled being shocked by the realization that the motionless rows of strange soldiers in long black hooded cloaks, who were lined up in front of the Patriotic School, were a monastic militia. What does the church have to do with anything? he thought then. Since when does the Arkanarian church interfere in secular affairs?

It had taken him a while to get drunk, but when he did, it happened abruptly, all at once; and when in a moment of clarity he saw an oak table cut in half in a completely unfamiliar room, a drawn sword in his hand, and the applauding impecunious dons around him, he did briefly think that it was time to go home. But it was too late. A wave of fury and repulsive, obscene joy at being free from everything human had already gotten hold of him. He was still an earthling, an operative, an heir to the people of fire and iron, who didn't spare himself or others in the name of a great purpose. He couldn't become Rumata of Estor, flesh of the flesh of twenty generations of warlike ancestors, renowned for their pillaging and drunkenness. But he was no longer a communard. He no longer had responsibilities to the Experiment. He was only concerned with his responsibilities to himself. He no longer had any doubts. He was certain of everything, absolutely everything. He knew exactly whose fault everything was, and he knew exactly what he wanted: to hack them to pieces, set them on fire, hurl them down from the palace steps onto the spears and pitchforks of a roaring crowd.

Rumata started and took his swords out of their scabbards. The blades were notched but clean. He remembered fighting with someone, but whom? And how did it end?

They drank away the horses. The impecunious dons had disappeared somewhere. Rumata—he remembered this, too—had dragged the baron home with him. Pampa don Bau was full of energy, utterly sober, and completely ready to continue the merrymaking—he simply could no longer stand on his feet. Furthermore, for some reason he thought that he had just said good-bye to his beloved baroness and was now on a military campaign against his ancient enemy Baron Kaska, who had become impudent to the last degree. ("Judge for yourself, my friend—this scoundrel gave birth to a six-fingered boy from his hip and called him Pampa.") "The sun is setting," he declared, looking at a tapestry depicting a sunrise. "We could make merry the whole night, noble dons, but military feats require sleep. Not a drop of wine during the campaign. Besides, the baroness would be displeased."

"What? Go to bed? What bed is there in an open field? Our bed is a horse blanket!" With these words, he tore the unfortunate tapestry off the wall, wrapped himself up to his head in it, and collapsed under a lamp with a crash. Rumata ordered Uno to put a bucket of brine and a tub of pickles next to the baron. The boy had an irate, sleepy face. "He sure is plastered," he grumbled. "Eyes pointing in different directions."

"Quiet, fool," Rumata said then, and . . . something happened after this. Something very bad, which chased him all the way across the city to the vacant lot. Something very, very bad, unforgivable, shameful.

He remembered when he was nearly back at home, and when he remembered, he stopped.

Flinging Uno aside, he had climbed up the stairs, opened the door, and burst in on her, like her master, and in the light of the night-lamp he saw a white face, huge eyes full of terror and disgust, and in those eyes, a reflection of himself— staggering, with a drooping, slobbering lower lip, with raw knuckles, with trash-smeared clothes, an insolent and loathsome blue-blooded boor. And this look threw him backward, onto the stairs, down into the hall, out the door, into the dark street, and far, far, far away, as far away as possible . . .

Gritting his teeth and feeling all his insides freeze together, he quietly opened the door and tiptoed into the hallway. In the corner, resembling a gigantic sea mammal, the baron was slumbering peacefully, puffing in his sleep.

"Who's there?" cried Uno, who was dozing on a bench with a crossbow on his knees.

"Quiet," Rumata whispered. "Let's go to the kitchen. Bring a barrel of water, vinegar, and new clothes, quick!"

He spent a long time furiously pouring water on himself and rubbing himself down with vinegar, acutely relishing scrubbing off the night's filth. Uno, who was unusually silent, bustled around him. And only afterward, helping the don fasten a pair of idiotic purple pants with buckles on the behind, he informed him gloomily, "At night, when you took off, Kira came down and asked me if the don had been back, must have decided she dreamt it. I told her that you hadn't come back since you went off for guard duty last night."

Rumata took a deep breath, turning away. That wasn't better. It was worse.

"And I've been sitting by the baron with a crossbow all night. I was worried he'd drunkenly try to climb upstairs."

"Thanks, kid," Rumata said with difficulty.

He pulled on his shoes, went out into the hall, and spent some time in front of a dark metal mirror. The casparamid had worked beautifully. The mirror showed an elegant noble don with a face that was slightly haggard after an exhausting night shift but eminently respectable. The damp hair, clasped by the gold circlet, fell softly and beautifully around his face. Rumata automatically adjusted the lens above his nose. They got to watch some pretty scenes on Earth today, he thought grimly.

By now, the sun had risen. It was peering into the dusty windows. Shutters began to slam. Sleepy voices were calling to each other in the street. "How did you sleep, Brother Kiris?" "Soundly, praise the Lord, Brother Tika. The night is over, and thank God." "And we had someone try to break into our windows. The noble Don Rumata was partying last night, I hear." "His Lordship has a guest, they say." "There's no real partying nowadays. I remember, in the young king's time, they'd party—wouldn't notice before they burned half the city down." "What can I say, Brother Tika? Thank the Lord that we have such a don for a neighbor. If he parties once a year it's a lot."

Rumata went upstairs, knocked, and went into the study. Kira was sitting in the chair like yesterday. She looked up and gazed into his face in fear and anxiety.

"Good morning, little one," he said, came up to her, kissed her hands, and sat in a chair across from her.

She was still looking at him searchingly, then asked, "Tired?"

"Yes, a little. And I have to go out again."

"Shall I make you something?"

"No, thank you. Uno will do it. You could put perfume on my collar."

Rumata could feel a wall of lies growing between them. Thin at first, but becoming thicker and stronger. For our whole life! he thought bitterly. He sat there with his eyes closed as she carefully dabbed various perfumes onto his fluffy collar, his cheeks, his forehead, and his hair. Then she said, "You didn't even ask me how I slept."

"How did you sleep, little one?"

"I had a dream. You know, a scary, scary dream."

The wall became as thick as a castle wall. "That's how it always is in a new place," Rumata said artificially. "And the baron was probably making a ruckus downstairs."

"Should I order breakfast?" she asked.

"Please."

"And what kind of wine do you like in the morning?"

Rumata opened his eyes. "Order some water," he said. "I don't drink in the morning."

She went out, and he heard her calm, clear voice speaking to Uno. Then she came back, sat on the arm of his chair, and started to tell him her dream, and he listened, raising his eyebrows, with each minute feeling the wall become thicker and more impregnable, forever separating him from the only person truly dear to him in this hideous world.

And then he hurled his whole body at the wall. "Kira," he said. "It wasn't a dream."

And nothing in particular happened.

"My poor darling," Kira said. "Wait, let me bring you some brine . . ."

# Chapter 5

It wasn't long ago that the Arkanarian court was one of the most educated in the empire. There had been scientists at court, most of whom were, of course, charlatans, but there had also been some like Bagheer of Kissen, who had discovered the sphericity of the planet; the healer Tata, who had made the brilliant conjecture that epidemics come from tiny invisible worms, spread by wind and water; and the alchemist Sinda, who like all alchemists had been in search of a way to transform clay into gold but instead had discovered the law of conservation of matter. The Arkanarian court had also had poets, mostly foot lickers and sycophants, but some like Pepin the Glorious, the author of the historical tragedy *The March to the North*; Zuren the Truthful, who had composed more than five hundred ballads and sonnets that had been set to music by the people; and also Gur the Storyteller, who had written the first secular novel in the history of the empire—the sad story of a prince who had fallen in love with a beautiful barbarian. The court also used to have marvelous actors, dancers, and singers. Wonderful artists had covered the walls with unfading frescoes; fabulous sculptors had decorated the palace parks with their creations. You couldn't say that the Arkanarian kings had been enthusiastic supporters of education or connoisseurs of the arts. It had simply been considered the decent thing to do, like the ceremony of dressing in the morning or the presence of splendid guards by the main entrance.

Aristocratic tolerance would occasionally go so far as to allow scientists and poets to become visible cogs in the state apparatus. Thus, only half a century ago, the highly learned alchemist Botsa had occupied the now-abolished-as-unneeded position of Minister of Mineral Resources, founded a number of mines, and made Arkanar famous for its amazing alloys, the secret of which had been lost after his death. And Pepin the Glorious had been in charge of public education until very recently, when the Ministry of History and Literature, which he had headed, had been discovered to be harmful and guilty of corrupting minds.

Of course, even in years past, there had been occasions where a scientist or artist who had displeased the king's mistress—a dull and lascivious creature—was sold abroad or poisoned with arsenic, but only Don Reba had set to work in earnest. During his tenure as the all-powerful Minister of the Defense of the Crown, he had caused such devastation in the world of Arkanarian culture that he had even managed to displease some of the noble lords, who declared that court had become boring and that balls were now only good for mindless gossip.

Bagheer of Kissen, accused of lunacy bordering on treason, had been thrown in a dungeon and had only been rescued by Rumata with great difficulty. He had been sent to the metropole, but his observatory had been burned down and his surviving students had dispersed. The healer Tata, along with five other healers, had suddenly turned out to be poisoners who had been plotting against the king at the instigation of the Duke of Irukan. Tata had confessed to everything under torture and was hanged in the Royal Plaza. In the process of trying to save him, Rumata had spent seventy pounds of gold, lost four agents (noble dons who knew not what they did), and been injured during an attempt to free the prisoners, but he couldn't do a thing. It was his first defeat, after which he had finally realized that Don Reba was not a random figure. After learning a week later that the alchemist Sinda was going to be accused of concealing the philosopher's stone from the treasury, Rumata, enraged by the defeat, had organized an ambush by the alchemist's house. He wrapped a black rag around his face, disarmed the storm troopers who came to take the alchemist away, tied them up, and threw them in a cellar. He had then sent Sinda, who hadn't understood a thing, into Soan, where he shrugged his shoulders and continued to look for the philosopher's stone under the watchful eye of Don Condor.

The poet Pepin the Glorious had suddenly become a monk and retired to a secluded monastery. Zuren the Truthful, pronounced guilty of criminal innuendo and pandering to the tastes of the lower classes, had been stripped of honor and property; the poet had attempted to dispute the findings and read his now openly subversive ballads in pubs, and had twice been beaten half to death by patriotic individuals. Only then had he yielded to the entreaties of his good friend and fan Don Rumata and left for the metropole. Rumata would always remember him, bluish-white from drink, standing on the deck of a departing ship, clutching the rigging with his thin hands, and in a clear, young voice shouting his farewell sonnet: "As a wilted leaf falls on my soul . . ." As for Gur the Storyteller, after a conversation in Don Reba's office, he had realized that an Arkanarian prince couldn't have fallen in love with enemy scum and threw his own books into a fire on the Royal Plaza. And now, hunched and dead-faced, he would stand in the crowd of courtiers during the king's appearances, and at a small gesture from Don Reba would step forward with poems of ultrapatriotic content, inducing boredom and yawns.

The actors now only performed one play: *The Fall of the Barbarians, or Marshal Totz, King Pitz the First of Arkanar.* And the singers now preferred songs without lyrics, accompanied by an orchestra. The surviving artists daubed signs. However, two or three of them had managed to remain at court and painted portraits of the king with Don Reba respectfully supporting him by the elbow (originality was not encouraged: the king was always depicted as a dashing twenty-year-old in armor, and Don Reba as a man in his prime with a significant face).

Yes, the Arkanarian court had become boring. Nonetheless, lords, noble dons with nothing to do, officers of the Guard, and thoughtless beautiful doñas continued to fill the palace reception halls each morning—some out of vanity, others out of habit, still others out of fear. To be perfectly honest, many of them didn't notice any changes at all. In the concerts and poetry competitions of times past they had most of all appreciated the intermissions, during which the noble dons could debate the merits of their hunting dogs and tell jokes. They were capable of a brief discussion about the attributes of the creatures of the netherworld, but questions about the shape of the planet or the causes of epidemics were considered simply indecent. The officers of the Guard did feel somewhat dejected about the disappearance of the painters, some of whom had been masters at depicting the nude form.

Rumata got to the palace a little late. The morning reception had already begun. The halls swarmed with people, and he could hear the king's peevish voice and the melodious commands of the Minister of Ceremonies, who was in charge of dressing His Majesty. The courtiers mostly talked about last night's incident. Some criminal with Irukanian features had infiltrated the palace armed with a stiletto, killed a watchman, and burst into His Majesty's bedchamber, where he was ostensibly disarmed by Don Reba himself; he was then torn to pieces by a crowd of patriots, maddened by their devotion, on the way to the Merry Tower. This was the sixth assassination attempt over the last month, and therefore the fact of the attempt itself elicited almost no interest. Only the details were under discussion. Rumata learned that at the sight of the murderer, His Majesty had sat up in bed, shielding the beautiful Doña Midara with his body, and uttered the historic words "Get along, rascal!" The majority willingly believed in the historic words, assuming that the king took the murderer for a footman. And everyone agreed that Don Reba was, as always, on his guard and incomparable in hand-to-hand combat.

Rumata made some gracious remarks in concurrence with this opinion, and in response told a just-invented story about how Don Reba had been attacked by twelve robbers, three of whom he felled on the spot, and the rest of whom had fled. The story was listened to with great interest and approval, after which Rumata mentioned seemingly casually that the story had been told to him by Don Sera. The interested expressions immediately disappeared from the faces of those present, for they were all aware that Don Sera was a noted fool and liar. No one said a word about Doña Ocana. Either they didn't know about it yet or were pretending not to know about it.

Scattering courtesies and shaking ladies' hands, Rumata gradually moved into the front rows of the decked-out, perfumed, profusely sweating crowd. The noble gentry were chatting in low voices. "Yes, yes, that same mare. It was lame, but I'll be damned if I didn't lose it the very same night to Don Keu . . ." "As for the hips, my noble don, they are of an extraordinary shape. As it is said by Zuren . . . *umm* . . . Mountains of cool foam . . . *umm*. . . no, cool hills of foam . . . Anyway, tremendous hips . . ." "Then I gently open the window, take the dagger in my teeth, and imagine, my friend, I feel the lattice bending beneath me . . ." "I gave him a good crack on the teeth with the sword hilt, making that gray dog roll over twice. Feast your eyes on him standing there, as if he has the right . . ." "And Don Tameo barfed onto the table, slipped, and fell headfirst in the fireplace . . ." ". . . so then the monk says to her, 'Tell me your dream, beautiful.' Ha ha ha!"

What a terrible shame, thought Rumata. If I'm killed now, this colony of simpletons will be the last thing I ever see. Only the element of surprise. The element of surprise will save me. Me and Budach. Seize the moment and make a surprise attack. Catch him off his guard, don't let him open his mouth, don't let him kill me, I have absolutely no wish to die.

He made his way to the doors of the bedchamber and, holding his swords with both hands, bending his knees slightly as required by etiquette, approached the king's bed. The king's stockings were being pulled on. The Minister of Ceremonies, holding his breath, was closely watching the nimble-fingered hands of the two valets. Don Reba stood in front of the messy bed and was quietly conversing with a tall, bony man in a military uniform of gray velvet. This was Father Zupic, one of the leaders of the Arkanarian storm troopers, a colonel of the palace guards.

Don Reba was an experienced courtier. Judging by his face, the conversation was about nothing more important than the paces of a mare or the virtuous behavior of the king's niece. Father Zupic, on the other hand, as a military man and a former grocer, didn't know how to control his face. He darkened and bit his lip, his fingers on the sword hilt would clench and unclench, and he finally jerked his cheek, spun around, and, breaking every rule, left the bedchamber heading right at the crowd of courtiers, shocked into stillness by such bad manners. Don Rumata, smiling apologetically, watched him leave, and Rumata followed him with his eyes and thought, There goes another dead man. He was aware of the tensions between Don Reba and the gray leadership. The story of brownshirt leader Ernst Röhm was about to be repeated.

The stockings had been pulled on. The valets, obeying the melodious order of the Minister of Ceremonies, had reverently picked up the king's shoes with their fingertips. At this point, the king, kicking the valets away, turned toward Don Reba so abruptly that his stomach, which resembled an overstuffed sack, rolled onto one of his knees. "I'm tired of your assassinations!" he screeched hysterically. "Assassinations! Assassinations! I want to sleep at night, not fight off murderers. Why can't we make it so they do it during the day? You're a crummy minister, Reba! Another night like that and I'll give the order to strangle you!" Don Reba bowed, pressing his hand to his heart as the king continued: "Assassination attempts give me a headache!"

The king suddenly stopped and stared vacantly at his stomach. The moment was right. The valets were hesitating. First, Rumata had to draw attention to himself. He snatched the right shoe from the hand of a valet, dropped to one knee before the king, and started to respectfully place the shoe onto the pudgy, silk-covered foot. This was the ancient privilege of Rumata's family—putting on the right shoe of the crowned heads of the empire.

The king was looking at him dully. A spark of interest appeared in his eyes. "Ah, Rumata!" he said. "You're still alive? And Reba promised to strangle you!" He giggled. "He's a crummy minister, that Reba. All he does is make promises. He promised to eradicate insubordination, and insubordination keeps growing. He's stuffed the palace full of some gray bumpkins. I'm sick and he's hanged all the healers."

Rumata finished putting on the shoe and took two steps back, bowing. He noticed Don Reba eyeing him closely, and hastened to assume a haughtily vacant expression.

"I'm very sick," continued the king. "Everything hurts. I want to retire to rest. I would have long since retired to rest, but you dolts would be lost without me."

His second shoe had been put on. He stood up and immediately gasped, grimacing, and clutched his knee.

"Where are the healers?" he wailed mournfully. "Where's my good Tata? You hanged him, moron! The sound of his voice alone made me feel better! Silence, I already know he was a poisoner! And I don't give a damn! Who cares that he was a poisoner? He was a *heaaaler*! Get it, murderer? A healer. He'd poison one, heal another! And you only know how to persecute! You ought to have hanged yourself instead!" Don Reba bowed, pressing his hand to his heart, and stayed in this position. "You've hanged everyone! There are only charlatans left! And the priests, who give me holy water instead of medicine. Who'll make the potions? Who'll rub the salve into my foot?"

"Sire!" Rumata said loudly, and it seemed to him that the whole palace went still. "You only need to give the order, and the best healer in the empire will be in the palace in half an hour."

The king stared at him in bewilderment. It was an awful risk. Don Reba had only to blink . . . Rumata knew why there was a row of round black vents under the bedroom's ceiling—he could feel the number of eyes looking at him intently over the fletchings of their arrows. Don Reba was also looking at him with an expression of polite and benevolent curiosity. "What's the meaning of this?" the king inquired testily. "All right, I give the order. All right, where's your healer?"

Rumata felt his whole body tense up. It seemed to him that the arrows were already pricking his shoulder blades. "Sire," he said quickly, "order Don Reba to present the famous Doctor Budach to you!"

Apparently Don Reba really had been caught off guard. The most important thing had been said, and Rumata was still alive. The king shifted his bleary gaze to the Minister of the Defense of the Crown.

"Sire," Rumata continued, no longer in a hurry and using appropriate language. "Being aware of your truly unbearable suffering and bearing in mind the debt my family has to the Crown, I sent for the highly learned healer Doctor Budach from Irukan. However, unfortunately Doctor Budach's journey was interrupted. The gray soldiers of the honorable Don Reba captured him last week, and his further fate is known only to Don Reba. I would assume that the healer is somewhere close at hand, most likely in the Merry Tower, and I hope that Don Reba's strange aversion to healers has not yet had a fatal effect on Doctor Budach's destiny."

Rumata paused, holding his breath. Everything seemed to have gone off without a hitch. Watch out, Don Reba! He took a look at the minister—and went cold. The Minister of the Defense of the Crown had in no way been caught off his guard. He was nodding at Rumata with affectionate paternal reproach. Rumata hadn't expected this at all. Why, he's delighted, thought Rumata in bewilderment.

The king, on the other hand, was behaving as expected. "You rogue!" he screamed at Don Reba. "I'll strangle you! Where's the doctor? Where's the doctor, I ask! Silence. I'm asking, where's the doctor?"

Don Reba stepped forward, smiling pleasantly. "Your Majesty," he said, "you're a truly fortunate monarch, for you have so many loyal subjects that they occasionally interfere with each other in their efforts to serve you." The king was staring at him vacantly. "I will admit that as with everything else that happens in your country, I was aware of the noble plan of the fiery Don Rumata. I will admit that I sent our gray soldiers to meet Doctor Budach—solely for the purpose of sparing a venerable old man the trials of a long journey. I will also admit that I was in no hurry to present Budach of Irukan to your majesty."

"How dare you?" the king asked reproachfully.

"Your Majesty, Don Rumata is young and is as naive in politics as he's experienced in noble battle. He is unaware of the lows the Duke of Irukan would stoop to in his insane fury at your majesty. But you and I know this, sire, do we not?" The king nodded. "And therefore I felt it incumbent upon me to make a preliminary investigation. I would not be in a hurry, but if you, Your Majesty"—a low bow to the king—"and Don Rumata"—a nod in Rumata's direction—"so insist, then this very day after dinner Doctor Budach will appear before you, Your Majesty, to begin a course of treatment."

"You're no fool, Don Reba," the king said, thinking about it. "An investigation is a good thing. It can't hurt. Damn that Irukanian—" He howled and grabbed his knee again. "Damn this leg! So after dinner, then? We'll be waiting, we'll be waiting."

And the king, leaning on the shoulder of the Minister of Ceremonies, slowly walked toward the throne room past a stunned Rumata. As he entered the crowd of courtiers, which parted in front of him, Don Reba smiled amiably at Rumata and asked, "I believe you're on duty tonight at the prince's bedchamber? Am I not mistaken?"

Rumata silently bowed.

Rumata wandered aimlessly through the endless corridors and passages of the palace—dark, dank, and stinking of ammonia and decay. He walked past luxurious rooms decorated with rugs, past dusty studies with barred narrow windows, and past storerooms piled with junk stripped of gilding. There was almost no one here. Only the rare courtier would risk visiting this maze at the back of the palace, where the royal apartments imperceptibly became the offices of the Ministry of the Defense of the Crown. It was easy to get lost here. Everyone remembered the incident in which a patrol of the Guard, walking the perimeter of the palace, had been frightened by the heartrending wails of a man stretching his badly scratched arms through the bars of an embrasure. "Save me!" the man shouted. "I'm a gentleman of the bedchamber! I don't know how to get out! I haven't eaten for two days! Get me out of here!" (There was a lively ten-day correspondence between the Minister of Finances and the Minister of the Court, after which they did decide to break down the bars, but for the duration of these ten days the unfortunate gentleman of the bedchamber had been fed with meat and bread passed to him on the end of a pike.) Besides, it wasn't entirely safe. In these tight corridors, you could meet drunk guardsmen who were protecting the king's person, and drunk storm troopers who were protecting the ministry. These would fight tooth and nail, and when satisfied would go their separate ways, carrying away the wounded. Finally, the murdered also wandered here. Over two centuries, the palace had accumulated a lot of them.

A storm trooper on sentry duty stepped out from a deep recess in the wall, his ax at the ready. "You may not pass," he declared sullenly.

"A lot you know, fool!" Rumata said carelessly, pushing him aside.

He heard the storm trooper stomping indecisively behind him and suddenly caught himself thinking that insulting words and careless gestures now came naturally to him, that he was no longer playing the role of a highborn boor but had largely become one. He imagined himself like this on Earth and felt disgusted and ashamed. Why? What has happened to me? Where did it go, my nurtured-since-childhood respect and trust in my own kind, in man—the amazing creature called man? Nothing can help me now, he thought in horror. Because I sincerely hate and despise them. Not pity them, no—only hate and despise. I can justify the stupidity and brutality of the kid I just passed all I want—the social conditions, the appalling upbringing, anything at all—but I now clearly see that he's my enemy, the enemy of all that I love, the enemy of my friends, the enemy of what I hold most sacred. And I don't hate him theoretically, as a "typical specimen," but him as himself, him as an individual. I hate his slobbering mug, the stink of his unwashed body, his blind faith, his animosity toward everything other than sex and booze. There he goes, stomping around, the oaf, who half a year ago was still being thrashed by a fat-bellied father in a vain attempt to prepare him for selling stale flour and old jam; he's wheezing, the dumb lug, struggling to recall the paragraphs of badly crammed regulations, and he just can't figure out whether he's supposed to cut the noble don down with his ax, shout "Stop!" or just forget about it. No one will find out anyway, so he'll forget about it, go back to his recess, stuff some chewing bark into his mouth and chew it loudly, drooling and smacking his lips. And there's nothing that he wants to know, and there's nothing he wants to think about. Think! And is our eagle Don Reba any better? Yes, of course, his psychology is more intricate and his reflexes are more complicated, but his thoughts are like these palace mazes, reeking of ammonia and crime, and he himself is just foul beyond expression—a dreadful criminal and shameless spider. I came here to love people, to help them unbend, see the sky. No, I'm a bad operative, he thought remorsefully.

I'm a no-good historian. When exactly did I manage to fall into the swamp that Don Condor was talking about? Does a god have the right to feel anything other than pity?

He heard a hurried *clomp-clomp-clomp* of boots along the corridor behind him. Rumata turned around and crossed his arms, placing his hands on the hilts of his swords. He saw Don Ripat running toward him, holding on to the blade at his side. "Don Rumata! Don Rumata!" he cried from afar in a hoarse whisper. Rumata let go of his swords. When he got close, Don Ripat took a look around and in a barely audible voice said in his ear, "I've been looking for you for an entire hour. Waga the Wheel is in the palace! He's having a conversation with Don Reba in the lilac quarters."

Rumata even squeezed his eyes shut for a second. Then, cautiously moving away, he said with polite surprise, "You mean the famous robber? But he's either been executed or was invented to begin with."

The lieutenant licked his dry lips. "He's real. He's in the palace. I thought you'd like to know."

"My dearest Don Ripat," Rumata said impressively, "I'm interested in rumors. Gossip. Jokes. Life can be so boring . . . You have clearly misunderstood me." The lieutenant looked at him with wild eyes. "Judge for yourself," Rumata went on. "Why should I care about the unsavory relationships of Don Reba—who, however, I respect too much to presume to judge? Besides, I apologize, I'm in a hurry. There's a lady waiting for me."

Don Ripat licked his lips again, gave an awkward bow, and sidled away.

Rumata was suddenly struck by a happy thought. "By the way, my friend," he called out amiably, "how did you like the little intrigue that Don Reba and I carried out this morning?"

Don Ripat stopped eagerly. "We are very pleased," he said. "It was very charming, don't you think?"

"It was magnificent! The gray officers are very glad that you have finally openly taken our side. You're such an intelligent man, Don Rumata, and yet you consort with barons, with noble bastards—"

"My dear Ripat!" Rumata said haughtily, turning to walk away. "You forget that from the height of my birth I see absolutely no difference even between the king and yourself. Good-bye."

He strode through the corridors, making confident turns and silently pushing sentries aside. He wasn't sure what he was going to do, but he realized that this was a piece of astonishing, rare luck. He had to listen to the conversation between the two spiders. No wonder Don Reba had asked fourteen times as much for Waga alive than for Waga dead.

Two gray lieutenants, their blades drawn, stepped out toward him from the lilac curtains.

"Hello, friends," Don Rumata said, stopping between them. "Is the minister here?"

"The minister is busy, Don Rumata," said one of the lieutenants.

"I'll wait," Rumata said. He passed through the curtains.

It was pitch black. Rumata groped his way between the chairs, tables, and iron lamp stands. A number of times he distinctly heard someone huffing by his ear and was enveloped in a rich odor of garlic and beer. Then he saw a faint streak of light, heard honorable Waga's familiar tenor, and stopped. At that instant, the end of a spear gently poked him between the shoulder blades. "Quiet, blockhead," he said irritably but softly. "It's me, Don Rumata." The spear was removed. Rumata dragged a chair toward the streak of light, sat down, stretching his legs, and yawned loudly enough to be heard. Then he began to watch.

The spiders had met. Don Reba was sitting in a tense posture, his elbows resting on the desk and his fingers interlaced. A heavy throwing knife with a wooden handle was lying on top of a pile of papers to his right. The minister was wearing a pleasant although somewhat dazed smile. Honorable Waga was sitting on a sofa with his back to Rumata. He looked like an eccentric aged nobleman who hadn't left his country palace for the past thirty years. "The chonted will shlake," he said, "and they'll unbiggedly shump the margays with a hollow blackery. That's twenty long heapers already. It'd be marky to knork the motleners. But the heapers are bedegging redderly. This is how we'll heaten the rasten. That's our struntle."

Don Reba stroked his clean-shaven chin. "That's tooky jelly."

Waga shrugged. "This is our struntle. Denooting with us isn't rastenly for your gnawpers. It's revided?"

"It's revided," said the Minister of the Defense of the Crown decisively.

"And drink the circle," Waga said, getting up.

Rumata, who was listening to this gibberish dumbfounded, discovered a bushy mustache and a pointy gray beard on Waga's face. A true courtier from the time of the last regency.

"It was nice to talk to you," said Waga.

Don Reba also got up. "The conversation with you gave me great pleasure," he said. "I have never before seen a man as courageous as yourself, honorable . . ."

"Me too," said Waga in a bored voice. "I'm also amazed and proud of the courage of the First Minister of our kingdom."

He turned his back on Don Reba and shuffled toward the door, leaning on his staff. Don Reba, continuing to look at him pensively, absentmindedly placed his fingers on the handle of the knife. Someone behind Rumata's back immediately took an extremely deep breath, and the long brown barrel of a blowpipe squeezed past his ear toward the gap between the curtains. Don Reba remained standing for a second, as if listening, then he sat back down, opened a drawer, extracted a pile of paper, and became absorbed in his reading. The man behind Rumata's back spat on the floor; the blowpipe was removed. Everything was clear. The spiders had agreed. Rumata got up and, stepping on somebody's feet, started making his way back out from the lilac quarters.

The king dined in a huge hall with two tiers of windows. The ninety-foot table was set for a hundred people: the king himself, Don Reba, the royals (two dozen full-blooded individuals, gluttons and drunks), the Minister of the Court and the Minister of Ceremonies, a group of highborn aristocrats invited by tradition (this included Rumata), a dozen visiting barons with their ox-like baronets, and at the very end of the table various aristocratic small fry, who had somehow finagled an invitation to the royal dinner. When these last were being handed their invitations and chair numbers, they were warned, "Sit still, the king doesn't like it when people fidget. Keep your hands on the table; the king doesn't like it when people hide their hands under the table. Don't look around; the king doesn't like it when people look around." At every such dinner, vast quantities of fine food were devoured, whole lakes of ancient wines were drunk, and masses of

dishes made from the famous Estorian china were damaged
or broken. In one of his reports to the king, the Minister of
Finance bragged that just one of His Majesty's dinners costs
as much as maintaining the Soanian Academy of Science for
half a year.

While he waited for the Minister of Ceremonies to pro-
claim "To the table!" three times, accompanied by trumpets,
Rumata stood in a group of courtiers and listened for the
tenth time to Don Tameo's story about the royal dinner that
he, Don Tameo, had the honor to attend six months ago.

"... I find my seat, we stand up, the king comes in, sits
down, we also sit down. The dinner goes on as usual. And
suddenly, imagine this, my dear dons, I feel something wet
underneath me. Yes, wet! I don't dare turn around, squirm,
or feel it with my hand. However, I find an opportunity to
stick a hand underneath me—and what happens? It really is
wet! I smell my hand—it doesn't smell like anything in particular. What a fable! Meanwhile, everyone is getting up, and
as you can imagine, noble dons, I am somehow afraid to get
up. I see the king—the king himself!—walking toward me,
but I keep sitting, as if I were a bumpkin baron without any
manners. His Majesty comes up to me, smiles indulgently at
me, and puts his hand on my shoulder. 'My dear Don Tameo,'
he says, 'everyone has gotten up and is about to go to watch
the ballet, but you're still sitting down. What's wrong, did
you eat too much?' 'Your Majesty,' I say, 'chop my head off,
but something is wet underneath me.' His Majesty was so
gracious as to laugh and order me to stand up. I get up—and
what happens? Laughter all around! Noble dons, I had been
sitting on rum cake for the whole dinner! His Majesty was
so gracious as to laugh a lot. 'Reba, Reba,' he said, finally,
'these are all your jokes! Would you be so kind as to clean

the noble don up, you soiled his seat!' Don Reba, laughing uproariously, takes out a dagger and starts scraping the cake off my pants. Can you imagine my condition, noble dons? I won't deny it, I was shaking in fear at the thought that Don Reba, humiliated in front of everyone, would take revenge on me. Fortunately, nothing happened. I assure you, noble dons, this was the happiest experience of my life! How the king laughed! How His Majesty was pleased!"

The courtiers roared with laughter. In fact, such jokes were customary at the royal table. The invitees would be seated in pâtés, in chairs with sawed-off legs, on goose eggs. They'd been seated on poisoned needles too. The king liked to be amused. Rumata suddenly thought: I wonder what I would have done in this idiot's place? I'm afraid that the king would have had to look for another Minister of Defense, and the Institute would have had to send another man to Arkanar. In any case, I need to be on my guard. Like our eagle Don Reba.

The trumpets sounded, the Minister of Ceremonies bellowed melodiously, the king limped in, and everyone began to take their seats. The guardsmen on duty were standing motionless in the corners of the hall, leaning on their two-handed swords. Rumata got taciturn neighbors. On his right, the seat was filled with the quivering bulk of the sullen glutton Don Pifa, the husband of the well-known beauty, and on his left, Gur the Storyteller was staring at an empty plate. The guests paused, looking at the king. The king stuffed a grayish napkin in his collar, scanned the dishes, and grabbed a chicken leg. As soon as he sank his teeth into it, a hundred knives fell onto plates with a clatter, and a hundred hands reached for dishes. The hall became full of chomping and sucking sounds; wine started gurgling. The mustaches of the motionless guardsmen with the two-handed swords began to twitch avidly. Once upon a time, Rumata had gotten nauseated at these dinners. Now he was used to them.

Carving a shoulder of mutton with his dagger, he glanced right and immediately turned away: Don Pifa was hanging over an entire roasted wild boar, working like an excavator. He left no bones. Rumata held his breath and drained his glass of Irukanian wine in one gulp. Then he glanced left. Gur the Storyteller was listlessly picking at a small plate of salad with a spoon.

"Are you writing anything new, Father Gur?" Rumata asked in a low voice.

Gur started. "Writing? Me? I don't know . . . A lot."

"Poetry?"

"Yes . . . poetry."

"Your poetry is abominable, Father Gur." Gur looked at him strangely. "Yes, yes, you're no poet."

"No poet . . . Sometimes I wonder, who am I? And what am I afraid of? I don't know."

"Look at your plate and keep eating. I'll tell you who you are. You're a brilliant storyteller, the founder of a new literary movement—the most fruitful one there is." Gur's cheeks slowly started to glow. "In a hundred years, and maybe even earlier, dozens of storytellers will follow in your footsteps."

"God help them!" Gur blurted out.

"Now I'll tell you what you're afraid of."

"I'm afraid of the dark."

"Of the nighttime?"

"Of the nighttime too. At night we're at the mercy of spirits. But most of all I'm afraid of the dark, because in the dark everyone becomes equally gray."

"Very well put, Father Gur. By the way, is it still possible to find your book?"

"I don't know . . . And I don't want to know."

"Just in case, you should know: one copy is in the metropole, in the library of the emperor. Another is kept in the Museum of Curiosities in Soan. The third is with me."

Gur spooned some jelly onto his plate with a trembling hand. "I . . . don't know . . ." He looked at Rumata mournfully with his huge sunken eyes. "I'd like to read it . . . reread it . . ."

"I'll be happy to lend it to you."

"And then?"

"And then you'll give it back."

"And then you'll be given back!" Gur said sharply.

Rumata shook his head. "Don Reba really scared you, Father Gur."

"Scared me . . . Have you ever had to burn your own children? What do you know about fear, noble don!"

"I bow my head before what you've had to go through, Father Gur. But I wholeheartedly blame you for giving up."

Gur the Storyteller suddenly started to whisper so softly that Rumata could barely hear him over the chomping and the drone of voices. "And what is it all for? What is the truth? Prince Haar really did love the beautiful copper-skinned Yaivnivora. They had kids . . . I know their grandchildren. She really was poisoned . . . But I was told that it's a lie. I was told that truth is what currently benefits the king. Everything else is a lie and a crime. I had written lies all my life . . . And only now do I write the truth."

He suddenly stood up and loudly recited in a sing-song voice:

Great and glorious, like eternity,
Is our king, whose name is Nobility!
Infinity is in retreat,
And birthright's signaling defeat.

The king stopped chewing and stared at him vacantly. The guests pulled their heads into their shoulders. Only Don Reba smiled and gave a few silent claps. The king spit the bones onto the tablecloth and said, "Infinity? That's right. That's true, it's in retreat . . . I commend you. You may eat."

The chomping and conversations resumed.

Gur sat down. "It's so sweet and easy to tell the truth to the king's face," he croaked.

Rumata was silent. Then he said, "I'll give you a copy of your book, Father Gur. But under one condition. You will immediately start writing the next one."

"No," Gur said. "It's too late. Let Kiun write. I've been poisoned. And anyway, I'm not interested in any of it anymore. I only want one thing now—to learn to drink. And I can't. It hurts my stomach."

Another defeat, thought Rumata. I'm too late.

"Listen, Reba," the king said suddenly. "Where's the healer? You promised me the healer after dinner."

"He's here, Your Majesty," said Don Reba. "Do you order me to summon him?"

"Do I order you to? Of course! If your knee hurt like this, you'd squeal like a pig! Get him here this instant!"

Rumata leaned back in his chair and got ready to watch. Don Reba raised a hand above his head and snapped his fingers. The door opened, and a hunched old man wearing a long robe adorned with images of silver spiders, stars, and snakes entered the hall, constantly bowing. He was holding a flat, oblong bag under his arm. Rumata was puzzled: this wasn't at all how he had imagined Budach. The sage and humanist, the author of the comprehensive *Treatise on Poisons*, couldn't have such faded, darting eyes, such fearfully trembling lips, such a pathetic, ingratiating smile. But then he remembered Gur the Storyteller. The inquiry into the suspected Irukanian spy probably involved a literary conversation in Don Reba's office. Oh, to take Reba by the ear, he thought longingly. To drag him into the dungeon. To tell the torturers, "Here's an Irukanian spy, disguised as our glorious minister; the king has ordered us to extract the whereabouts of the real minister from him. Do what you do, and woe be upon you if he dies in less than a week." He put a hand in front of his face lest it betray his thoughts. What a terrible thing hatred is . . .

"Well, well, come here, healer," the king said. "You're a weakling, brother. Now squat—squat, I tell you!"

The unfortunate Budach began to squat. His face contorted in horror.

"Again, again," the king said nasally. "Once again! Again! Your knees don't hurt—you healed your own knees. Now let's see your teeth! *Hmmmm*, not bad. I should have such teeth. And the hands aren't bad, nice and strong. Nice and healthy, though you're a weakling . . . Well go on, my dear, treat me, don't just stand there."

"Y-Your Majesty . . . be so g-gracious as to show his leg . . . his leg . . ." Rumata heard the healer say. He looked up. The man was on his knees in front of the king and was carefully kneading his leg.

"Hey . . . hey!" the king said. "What are you doing? Don't paw at me! If you're going to treat me, then treat me!"

"I u-understand everything, Your Majesty," the healer mumbled. He started hurriedly digging through his bag.

The guests stopped chewing. The minor aristocrats at the end of the table even stood up and craned their necks, burning with curiosity.

Budach took a number of stone bottles from his bag, opened them, and, sniffing them one by one, lined them up along the table. Then he took the king's goblet and filled it halfway with wine. Making strange gestures over the goblet with both hands and whispering incantations, he quickly emptied all the bottles into the wine. The distinct smell of ammonia spread through the hall. The king pursed his lips, looked into the goblet, and, screwing up his nose, looked at Don Reba. The minister smiled sympathetically. The courtiers held their breath.

What is he doing? thought Rumata with surprise. The old man has gout! What is that concoction? His treatise clearly states, massage a three-day infusion of white snake venom into the swollen joints. Maybe this is the salve?

"What's this, salve?" the king asked, nervously nodding at the goblet.

"Not at all, Your Majesty," said Budach. He had already recovered a little. "This is taken orally."

"*Orally?*" The king pouted and leaned back in his chair. "I don't want anything orally. Massage it in."

"As you wish, Your Majesty," Budach said meekly. "But I must take the liberty to warn you that massaging it in will be of no use."

"For some reason, everyone else massages," the king said peevishly, "and you absolutely have to pour this stuff into me."

"Your Majesty," said Budach, proudly standing up, "this medicine is known to me alone! I used it to cure the uncle of the Duke of Irukan. As for the massagers, they certainly didn't cure you, Your Majesty."

The king looked at Don Reba. Don Reba again smiled sympathetically.

"You rascal," the king said to the healer in an unpleasant voice. "A bumpkin. A lousy weakling." He picked up the goblet. "I have half a mind to give you a good crack on the teeth with this goblet." He looked into the goblet. "And if I throw up?"

"We'd have to repeat it, Your Majesty," Budach said mournfully.

"All right, the Lord be with us!" the king said, bringing the goblet almost to his mouth—but he suddenly jerked it away so abruptly that it splashed onto the tablecloth. "Hey, you drink some first! I know you Irukanians! You sold Holy Míca to the barbarians! Drink it, I say!"

Budach took the goblet with an offended look and drank a few sips.

"Well, how is it?" said the king.

"It's bitter, Your Majesty," Budach said in a choked voice. "But you have to drink it."

"*Haaave* to, *haaave* to . . ." the king said peevishly. "I know I have to myself. Hand it over. Look at this, you polished half of it off, took your chance . . ."

He tossed off the goblet in one gulp. Sympathetic sighs sounded around the table—and suddenly everything went still. The king froze with his mouth open. Tears rained from his eyes. He slowly turned purple, then blue in the face. He stretched out a hand above the table, convulsively snapping his fingers. Don Reba hastily handed him a pickle. The king silently hurled the pickle at Don Reba and again stretched out his hand. "Wine . . ." he wheezed.

Someone dashed off and got the pitcher. The king, his eyes frantically rolling, swallowed loudly. Red rivulets were pouring down his white waistcoat. When the pitcher was empty, the king threw it at Budach but missed. "Bastard!" he said in an unexpectedly bass voice. "What did you kill me for? Haven't we hanged enough of you? Blast you!"

He stopped and touched his knee.

"It hurts!" he said in his former nasal voice. "It still hurts!"

"Your Majesty," said Budach. "For a complete cure, the potion must be taken every day for at least a week's duration—"

Something squeaked in the king's throat. "Out!" he shrieked. "Everyone get out!"

The courtiers, overturning their chairs, swarmed toward the doors.

"*Ouuut!*" the king screeched, sweeping the dishes off the table.

Rumata rushed out of the hall, then ducked behind a curtain and began to laugh. Someone else was also laughing behind the adjacent curtain—hysterically, gasping for breath, with little yelps.

# Chapter 6

his shift at the prince's bedchamber started at midnight, so Rumata decided to stop by his house to make sure everything was in order and to change clothes. The city this evening amazed him. The streets were dead silent, the taverns closed. Clusters of storm troopers with torches in their hands were standing around at the intersections, clanking their weapons. They were quiet, as if waiting for something. A number of them approached Rumata, took a good look at him, and after recognizing him, just as silently let him pass. When he was about fifty steps from his door, a group of shady characters began to trail him. Rumata stopped, clanked his scabbards against each other, and the characters fell back, but he immediately heard the sound of a crossbow being loaded in the dark. Rumata hurried onward, clinging to the walls, groped for the door, and turned his key in the lock. He remained aware of his unprotected back the entire time, and he rushed into the entrance hall with a sigh of relief.

All the servants were gathered in the entrance hall, armed as best they could be. It turned out that the door had already been tried a few times. Rumata didn't like that. Maybe I shouldn't go? he thought. To hell with him, the prince.

"Where's Baron Pampa?" he asked.

Uno, extremely agitated and with a crossbow on his shoulder, answered: "The baron woke up at midday, drank all the brine in the house, and again left to make merry." Then, lowering his voice, he informed Rumata that Kira had been very worried and had asked about the master more than once.

"All right," said Rumata. He ordered the servants to line up.

There were six servants, not counting the cook, all of them tough and used to street brawls. They wouldn't tussle with the gray soldiers, of course—they'd be afraid of the anger of the all-powerful minister—but they'd be able to withstand the tramps from Waga's night army, especially since tonight the bandits would be looking for easy prey. Two crossbows, four poleaxes, heavy butcher knives, iron hats; the doors were sturdy and bound with iron, as was the custom. Or maybe he really shouldn't go?

Rumata went upstairs and tiptoed into Kira's room. Kira was sleeping fully clothed, curled up on the still-made bed. Rumata stood over her with a lamp. To go or not to go? He really didn't want to go. He covered her with a quilt, kissed her cheek, and came back to his study. He needed to go. Whatever was happening, an operative had to be in the center of things. And it benefits the historians. He chuckled, took the circlet off, wiped the lens carefully with a soft piece of suede, and put it back on. Then he called Uno and ordered him to bring a military uniform and a polished brass helmet. Shivering from the cold, he pulled on a metalstrom shirt shaped like chain mail underneath his waistcoat, right over his undershirt. (The local chain mail offered decent protection from swords and daggers, but crossbow bolts punched right through it.) Tightening the uniform belt with the metallic buckles, he told Uno, "Listen, kid. You're the one I trust the most. Whatever happens here, Kira must remain alive and well. Let the house burn down, let all the money get stolen, but you must save Kira for me. Take her away over the rooftops, down through the cellars, whatever you like, but save her. Got it?"

"Got it," said Uno. "Maybe my master shouldn't go today."

"You listen to me. If I don't come back after three days, take Kira and bring her to the saiva, to the Hiccup Forest. Know where it is? Anyway, in the Hiccup Forest you should find the Drunken Lair—it's a hut not far back from the road. If you ask, you'll be shown the way. Just be careful who you ask. A man called Father Cabani will be there. You'll tell him everything. Got it?"

"Got it. Only maybe master shouldn't go."

"I wish I didn't have to. I do—duty calls. Well, take care."

He gently flicked the boy's nose and returned his awkward smile. Downstairs, he gave the servants a short pep talk, went out the door, and found himself in the dark again. The bars clanged shut behind him.

The prince's chambers had been poorly guarded through the ages. It's possible that was precisely why no one ever attempted to assassinate the Arkanarian princes. And there was definitely no one interested in the current prince. No one in the world needed this sickly blue-eyed boy who resembled anyone but his father. Rumata liked the boy. His education had been woefully neglected, and therefore he was smart, wasn't cruel, and—probably instinctively—couldn't stand Don Reba. He liked to sing a variety of songs set to Zuren's poetry and to play with boats. Rumata had ordered him picture books from the metropole, told him about the starry sky, and had won the boy once and for all with his tale of flying ships. For Rumata, who rarely interacted with children, the ten-year-old prince was the antithesis of every social class in this savage country. It was ordinary blue-eyed boys like this one, identical in every social class, who would grow up to be brutal, ignorant, and submissive men; and yet they, the children, showed no traces or beginnings of such rot. Sometimes Rumata thought it'd be great if all the people older than ten years of age disappeared from the planet.

The prince was already asleep. Rumata started his shift— he stood by the sleeping boy next to the departing guards- man, performing the complex motions with drawn swords required by etiquette. Then, as prescribed by tradition, he checked whether all the windows were locked, whether all the nurses were in place, and whether all the lamps were lit in all the chambers. After this, he came back to the front room, played a game of dice with the departing guardsman, and inquired how the noble don felt about what was happening in the city. The noble don, a man of great sagacity, thought very hard and conjectured that the common people were pre- paring to celebrate the Day of Holy Míca.

Left alone, Rumata pulled up a chair to the window, sat back, and began to watch the city. The prince's apartments were on a hill, and during the day, you could clearly see the entire city all the way to the sea. But now, everything was sunk in darkness, and the only things visible were scattered groups of lights—the intersections at which the storm troopers were gathered with torches, waiting for a sign. The city was asleep, or pretended to be. I wonder whether the inhabitants feel something horrible looming over them tonight? Or, like the noble don of great sagacity, did they also think that someone was preparing to celebrate the Day of Holy Míca? Two hundred thousand men and women. Two hundred thousand blacksmiths, gunsmiths, butchers, haberdashers, jewelers, housewives, prostitutes, monks, money changers, soldiers, tramps, and surviving bookworms were currently tossing in bedbug-ridden, stuffy beds; sleeping, making love, recalculating profits in their heads, crying, grinding their teeth in anger or resentment. Two hundred thousand people! To a visitor from Earth, they all had something in common. It was probably the fact that almost without exception, they were not yet humans in the modern sense of the world, but blanks, unfinished pieces, which only the bloody centuries of history could one day fashion into true men, proud and free. They were passive, greedy, and incredibly, fantastically selfish. Almost all of them had the psychology of slaves—slaves of religions, slaves of their own kind, slaves of their pathetic passions, slaves of avarice. And if the fates decreed for one of them to be born or become a master, he didn't know what to do with his freedom. He would again hurry to become a slave—a slave of wealth, a slave of outlandish excesses, a slave of his slaves. The vast majority of them weren't guilty of anything. They were too passive and too ignorant. Their slavery was the result of passivity and ignorance, and passivity and ignorance again and again breeds slavery.

If they were all identical, there would be reason to throw up your hands and lose hope. But they were still people, the bearers of the spark of reason. And here and there in their midst, the fires of the incredibly distant and inevitable future would kindle and blaze up. They would kindle despite it all. Despite all their seeming unworthiness. Despite the oppression. Despite the fact that they were being trampled with boots. Despite the fact that no one in the world needed them, and that everyone in the world was against them. Despite the fact that at best, they could expect contemptuous, puzzled pity.

They didn't know that the future was on their side, that the future was impossible without them. They didn't know that in a world belonging to the terrible ghosts of the past, they were the only manifestation of the future—that they were an enzyme, a vitamin in society's organism. If you destroy this vitamin, society will rot, and social scurvy will begin: the muscles will go weak, the eyes will lose their sharpness, the teeth will fall out. No country can develop without science—it will be destroyed by its neighbors. Without arts and general culture, the country loses its capacity for self-criticism, begins to encourage faulty tendencies, starts to constantly spawn hypocrites and scum, develops consumerism and conceit in its citizens, and eventually again becomes a victim of its more sensible neighbors. Persecute bookworms all you like, prohibit science, and destroy art, but sooner or later you'll be forced to think better of it, and with much gnashing of teeth open the way for everything that is so hated by the power-hungry dullards and blockheads.

And no matter how much the gray people in power despise knowledge, they can't do anything about historical objectivity; they can slow it down, but they can't stop it. Despising and fearing knowledge, they will nonetheless inevitably decide to promote it in order to survive. Sooner or later they will be forced to allow universities and scientific societies, to create research centers, observatories, and laboratories, and thus to create a cadre of people of thought and knowledge: people who are completely beyond their control, people with a completely different psychology and with completely different needs. And these people cannot exist and certainly cannot function in the former atmosphere of low self-interest, banal preoccupations, dull self-satisfaction, and purely carnal needs. They need a new atmosphere—an atmosphere of comprehensive and inclusive learning, permeated with creative tension; they need writers, artists, composers—and the gray people in power are forced to make this concession too. The obstinate ones will be swept aside by their more cunning opponents in the struggle for power, but those who make this concession are, inevitably and paradoxically, digging their own graves against their will. For fatal to the ignorant egoists and fanatics is the growth of a full range of culture in the people— from research in the natural sciences to the ability to marvel at great music. And then comes the associated process of the broad intellectualization of society: an era in which grayness fights its last battles with a brutality that takes humanity back to the middle ages, loses these battles, and forever disappears as an actual force.

Rumata kept looking at the city, motionless in the dark. Somewhere out there, in a stinking garret, curled up on a pathetic bed, the crippled Father Tarra was burning with fever, and Brother Nanin sat by his side at a wobbly table, drunk, cheerful, and angry—finishing his *Treatise on Rumors*, using hackneyed phrases with relish to disguise a vicious mockery of gray life. Somewhere out there, Gur the Storyteller was blindly wandering through empty luxurious apartments, realizing with horror that despite everything, some mysterious pressure caused vivid worlds full of remarkable people and extraordinary feelings to burst into his consciousness out of the depths of his torn, trampled soul. And somewhere out there, God knows how, Doctor Budach was whiling away the night—broken down, brought to his knees, tormented but alive. My brothers, thought Rumata. I'm yours, I'm the flesh of your flesh! He suddenly felt with tremendous force that he was no god, shielding the fireflies of reason with his hands, but instead a brother helping a brother, a son saving a father.

I'll kill Don Reba, he thought. *What for?* He's killing my brothers. *He knows not what he does.* He's killing the future. *It's not his fault—he's a product of his time.* So he doesn't know it's his fault? But does it matter whether he knows it? I know it's his fault. *And what will you do with Father Zupic? Father Zupic would give a lot for Don Reba to be killed . . .*

*You're silent? There are a lot of people you'd need to kill, aren't there?* I don't know, maybe there'd be a lot. One after the other. Everyone who raises a hand against the future. *That's been done already. They used poison, they threw pipe bombs. And nothing changed.* No, things did change. That's how the strategy for the revolution was created. *You don't need to create a strategy for the revolution. You just want to kill.* Yes, I do. *And are you capable of it?*

Yesterday, I killed Doña Ocana. I already knew that I was killing her when I walked toward her with a feather behind my ear. And the only thing I regret is killing her in vain. So they've almost taught me. *But that's bad. That's dangerous. Remember Sergei Kozhin? And George Lenny? And Sabine Kruger?* Rumata passed a hand over his damp forehead. You keep thinking, thinking, thinking like this—and eventually you invent gunpowder . . .

He jumped up and opened the window. The groups of lights were now in motion, dispersing, lining up, then moving forward, appearing and disappearing between the invisible houses. Some kind of noise sounded above the city—a distant many-voiced howl. Two fires broke out and illuminated the neighboring rooftops. Something blazed up at the port. Things were developing. In a few hours he would know the meaning of the alliance between the gray army and the night army, the unnatural accord between shopkeepers and highway robbers; he would learn what Don Reba was trying to do and what new provocation he had conceived. Or, to put it simply: who was being slaughtered today. Chances were that it was the beginning of a Night of the Long Knives, which would see the destruction of a gray leadership that had gone too far, accompanied by an extermination of the barons who happened to be in town and the most inconvenient of the aristocrats. I wonder how Pampa is doing, he thought. If he's not sleeping, he'll fight them off.

He didn't have the chance to finish his thought. Someone was pounding on the door with a heartrending wail of "Open up! Guardsman, open up!" Rumata threw back the bolt. A half-dressed man, blue-gray from fear, burst in, grabbed Rumata by the lapels of his waistcoat, and shrieked, trembling: "Where's the prince? Budach has poisoned the king! Irukanian spies have started a riot in the city! Save the prince!"

This was the Minister of the Court, a foolish and highly loyal man. Pushing Rumata away, he dashed into the prince's bedroom. Women screeched. Sweaty, jowly storm troopers in gray shirts were already trying to get through the door. Rumata drew his swords. "Back off!" he said coldly.

He heard a short, muffled scream in the bedroom behind him. Something's not right, thought Rumata. I don't understand a thing. He jumped into a corner and barricaded himself in with a table. Storm troopers were filling the room, breathing hard. There were about fifteen of them. A lieutenant in a tight gray uniform pushed his way to the front, his blade drawn. "Don Rumata?" he said, out of breath. "You're under arrest. Lay down your swords."

Rumata gave a derisive laugh, glancing at the window. "Take them," he said.

"Get him!" the officer barked.

Fifteen well-fed bumpkins with axes weren't too much for a man who'd mastered methods of battle that would only become known on this planet three centuries in the future. The mob pressed forward and fell back. A number of axes remained on the floor; two storm troopers were doubled over and clambering into the back rows, carefully cradling their dislocated arms. Rumata had complete mastery of the fan defense, in which attackers are faced with a solid curtain of gleaming steel, and breaking through this curtain seems impossible. The storm troopers, huffing and puffing, exchanged uncertain glances. They gave off a sharp odor of beer and onions.

Rumata pushed the table away and carefully walked to the window along the wall. Someone in the back rows threw a knife but missed. Rumata laughed again, put a foot on the windowsill, and said, "Try it again, and I'll start chopping hands off. You know me."

They knew him. They knew him extremely well, and not one of them budged, despite the cursing and prodding of the officer, who nonetheless was also behaving very cautiously. Rumata stood on the windowsill, continuing to make threatening gestures with his sword, and at that very moment a spear came out of the dark yard and hit him in the back. It was a terrible blow. It didn't pierce the metalstrom shirt, but it knocked him off the windowsill and threw him onto the floor. Rumata didn't let go of his swords, but they were now completely useless. The entire herd was immediately on top of him. Together, they probably weighed more than a ton, but they got in each other's way, and he managed to get to his feet. He slammed his fist into someone's wet lips, someone screamed like a rabbit under his arm, he kept smashing and smashing them with his elbows, fists, and shoulders (he hadn't felt this free in a long time), but he couldn't shake them off. With great difficulty, dragging a pile of bodies behind him, he walked toward the door, bending down and tearing off storm troopers who clung to his legs along the way. Then he felt a painful blow to the shoulder and fell onto his back, the crushed storm troopers flailed beneath him, but he stood up again, delivering short strikes with full force, causing the storm troopers to smack heavily into the walls, waving their arms and legs. The twisted face of the lieutenant, who was holding his unloaded crossbow in front of him, was already flickering before his eyes, but then the door opened and some new sweaty faces clambered toward him. They threw a net on him, tightened the ropes on his legs, and toppled him.

He immediately stopped struggling, conserving his strength. They trampled him with boots for some time—intently, silently, grunting avidly. Then they grabbed him by the feet and dragged him. As he was being pulled past the bedroom door, he had time to see the Minister of the Court pinned to the wall with a spear, and a heap of bloodstained sheets on the bed. So it's a coup! he thought. Poor boy . . . They started dragging him down the stairs, and then he lost consciousness.

# Chapter 7

He was lying on a grassy hillock and looking at the clouds drifting in the deep blue sky. He was calm and content, but a prickly, bony pain was sitting on an adjacent hillock. It was outside him and at the same time inside him, especially in his right side and the back of his head. Someone barked, "Did he croak or something? I'll tear your heads off!" And then a mass of ice-cold water fell from the sky. He really was lying on his back and looking at the sky, except he wasn't on a hillock but in a puddle, and the sky wasn't blue but leaden and black, illuminated with red. "Nah," said another voice. "His Lordship's alive, blinking those peepers." I'm the one who's alive, he thought. They're talking about me. I'm the one blinking my peepers. But why are they speaking funny? Have they forgotten how to talk like human beings?

Someone moved nearby and splashed heavily through the water. The black silhouette of a head wearing a pointed cap appeared in the sky. "Well, noble don, will you walk yourself or should we drag you?"

"Untie my legs," Rumata said angrily, feeling a sharp pain in his swollen lips. He felt them with his tongue. Some lips, he thought. Pancakes instead of lips.

Someone fumbled at his feet, unceremoniously yanking them and moving them around. He heard low voices around him: "You got him good."

"Had to, he almost took off . . . He must be charmed, arrows bounced off of him."

"I knew a man you could take an ax to and it didn't do nothing."

"Musta been a peasant."

"Uh-huh, he was."

"That's what did it. And this one's noble-born."

"Oh, stick a tail in it . . . Can't do nothing with these damn knots. Some light here!"

"So use a knife."

"Please, brothers, please, don't untie him. He'll start swiping at us again. He almost crushed my head as is."

"Nah, betcha he won't."

"Brothers, do what you want, but I hit him real hard with that spear. I've pierced armor like that."

An imperious voice shouted from the darkness: "Hey, you almost finished?"

Rumata felt that his legs were free, tensed his muscles, and sat up. A few squat storm troopers were silently watching him squirm in the puddle. Rumata gritted his teeth in shame and humiliation. He wriggled his shoulder blades; his hands were twisted behind his back, in such a way that he couldn't even tell his elbows from his wrists. He mustered all his strength, jerked himself up to his feet, and was immediately twisted by the terrible pain in his side. The storm troopers laughed.

"Betcha he won't run away," said one.

"Yeah, His Lordship's a bit tired, stick a tail in it."

"Come on, Don, not enjoying yourself?"

"Enough prattle," said the imperious voice from the darkness. "Come here, Don Rumata."

Rumata walked toward the voice, feeling himself tottering from side to side. A little man with a torch appeared out of somewhere and went ahead of him. Rumata recognized this place: it was one of the countless interior courtyards of the Ministry of the Defense of the Crown, somewhere near the royal stables. He quickly realized, If they take me to the right, that means the tower, the dungeon. If they take me to the left, that means the office. He shook his head. It's OK, he thought. While I'm alive, I can still fight.

They turned left. Not right away, thought Rumata. There will be a preliminary investigation. That's strange. If it comes down to an investigation, what can they accuse me of? I guess that's easy. Inviting the poisoner Budach, poisoning the king, plotting against the crown. Possibly murdering the prince. And, of course, spying for Irukan, Soan, the barbarians, the barons, the Holy Order, and so on, so forth. It's simply astonishing that I'm still alive. The pale fungus must be plotting something else.

"Over here," said the man with the imperious voice.

He opened a low door, and Rumata crouched down and entered a spacious room lit by a dozen lamps. There were tied-up, bloodied people sitting and lying down in the middle of a threadbare carpet. A few of them were either already dead or unconscious. Practically all of them were barefoot, in tattered nightshirts. Red-faced troopers, savage and self-satisfied, were standing along the walls, casually leaning on their axes and poleaxes—the champions of the night. An officer holding a sword, his hands behind his back, was pacing back and forth in front of them, wearing a gray uniform with an extremely greasy collar. Rumata's escort, a tall man in a dark cloak, approached the officer and whispered something in his ear. The officer nodded, looked curiously at Rumata, and disappeared behind the colorful curtains at the opposite end of the room.

The storm troopers were examining Rumata curiously. One of them, with an eye swollen shut, said, "A nice rock on the don!"

"That's some rock," another one agreed. "Fit for a king. And the circlet's solid gold."

"We're all kings today."

"So let's take it?"

"Enough!" the man in the black cloak said quietly.

The storm troopers stared at him, bewildered.

"Who's this come to pester us?" said the swollen-eyed storm trooper.

The man in the cloak turned around without answering, walked over to Rumata, and stood by his side.

The storm troopers looked him up and down with hostile eyes.

"A priest, huh?" the swollen-eyed storm trooper said. "Hey, Friar, your robe on fire?"

The storm troopers guffawed. The swollen-eyed storm trooper spat on his hands, tossing his ax from one hand to the other, and moved toward Rumata. He's really going to get it now, thought Rumata, slowly drawing back his right foot.

"Who I've always beaten up," the storm trooper continued, stopping in front of him and examining the man in black, "it's priests, literates of any kind, and toolsmen. Once I—"

The man in the cloak raised his hand, palm up. A loud snap came from just below the ceiling. *Bzzzz!* The swollen-eyed storm trooper dropped his ax and fell onto his back. A short, thick crossbow bolt with dense feathering protruded from the middle of his forehead. The room went quiet. The storm troopers backed away, nervously eyeing the vents beneath the ceiling. The man in the cloak lowered his hand and ordered, "Remove the carcass, quickly!"

Several storm troopers dashed forward, grabbed the dead man by his hands and feet, and dragged him away. A gray officer emerged from behind the curtains and waved invitingly.

"Let's go, Don Rumata," said the man in the cloak.

Rumata walked toward the curtains, going around the group of prisoners. I don't understand a thing, he thought. In the darkness behind the curtains they grabbed him, searched him, tore the empty scabbards off his belt, and then pushed him into the light.

Rumata immediately realized where he'd been taken. He was in Don Reba's familiar office in the lilac quarters. Don Reba was sitting in the same place and in exactly the same position, tensely upright, his elbows on the desk and his fingers interlaced. You know, the old man has hemorrhoids, Rumata suddenly thought with pity. On Don Reba's right side, Father Zupic sat in state—pompous, concentrated, with pursed lips; on his left side, there was a genially smiling fat man with captain's stripes on his gray uniform. There was no one else in the office.

When Rumata entered, Don Reba said, quietly and affectionately, "And here, my friends, is the noble Don Rumata."

Father Zupic grimaced contemptuously, while the fat man nodded graciously.

"Our old and rather constant foe," said Don Reba.

"Foes get hanged," Father Zupic rasped.

"And what is your opinion, Brother Aba?" asked Don Reba, helpfully leaning toward the fat man.

"You know . . . somehow I don't even . . ." Brother Aba gave an uncertain, childlike smile, spreading his pudgy little hands. "You know, somehow I don't care. But maybe we shouldn't hang him? Maybe we should burn him, what do you think, Don Reba?"

"Yes, probably," Don Reba said pensively.

"You see," the enchanting Brother Aba continued, smiling affectionately at Rumata, "we hang the trash, the small fry. And we must maintain the people's respect for the social classes. After all, he's a scion of an ancient family, a noted Irukanian spy—it's Irukanian, if I'm not mistaken?" He grabbed a piece of paper off the desk and peered at it with nearsighted eyes. "Oh, and Soanian too. Even more so!"

"So let's burn him," Father Zupic agreed.

"Very well," said Don Reba. "Agreed. We'll burn him."

"However, I think Don Rumata can improve his own lot," Brother Aba said. "You see what I'm saying, Don Reba?"

"I have to admit, not exactly."

"The property! My dear noble don, the property! The Rumatas are a fabulously rich family!"

"You are right, as always," Don Reba said.

Father Zupic yawned, covering his mouth with his hand, and glanced at the lilac curtains to the right of the table.

"Well, let us then begin in due form," Don Reba said with a sigh.

Father Zupic kept glancing at the lilac curtains. He was clearly waiting for something and was completely uninterested in the proceedings. What are they playing at? thought Rumata. What does this mean?

"Well, my noble don," Don Reba said, addressing Rumata, "it would be extremely gratifying to have you answer a number of questions of interest to us."

"Untie my hands," said Rumata.

Father Zupic recoiled and dubiously moved his lips. Brother Aba frantically shook his head.

"Oh?" Don Reba said and first looked at Brother Aba, then at Father Zupic. "I understand you, my friends. However, under the circumstances, which Don Rumata probably suspects . . ." He gave an expressive look at the rows of vents beneath the ceiling. "Untie his hands," he said, without raising his voice.

Someone silently came up behind him. Rumata felt someone's strangely soft, dexterous fingers touch his hands, and he heard the ropes creak as they were being cut. Brother Aba, with surprising agility for his bulk, took a huge combat crossbow out from underneath the desk and placed it on the papers in front of him. Rumata's hands dangled at his sides like whips. He almost couldn't feel them.

"Let us begin," Don Reba said briskly. "Your name, family, station?"

"Rumata, from the family of the Rumatas of Estor. A noble gentleman through twenty-two generations."

Rumata looked around, sat down on the sofa, and began to massage his wrists. Brother Aba, breathing anxiously through his nose, aimed the crossbow at him. "Your father?"

"My noble father was an imperial advisor, loyal servant, and faithful friend of the emperor."

"Is he alive?"

"He's dead."

"How long?"

"Eleven years."

"How old are you?"

Rumata didn't have the time to answer. There was a noise behind the lilac curtains. Brother Aba looked around, displeased.

Father Zupic, smiling ominously, slowly stood up. "Well, that's all, my dear sirs!" he began, cheerfully and maliciously.

Three people Rumata least expected to see here jumped out from behind the curtains. They were enormous monks in black cassocks with hoods pulled down over their eyes. They swiftly and silently ran up to Father Zupic and took him by the elbows.

"Ah . . . b-bu—" mumbled Father Zupic. His face had turned ashen. He had clearly been expecting something completely different.

"With your permission, Brother Aba?" Don Reba inquired calmly, bending down toward the fat man.

"But of course!" he replied emphatically. "Certainly!"

Don Reba made a slight motion with his hand. The monks picked up Father Zupic and, moving just as noiselessly as before, took him away behind the curtains. Rumata winced in disgust. Brother Aba rubbed his soft little paws together and said briskly, "Everything went marvelously, don't you think, Don Reba?"

"Yes, it wasn't bad," Don Reba agreed. "But let us continue. Well, how old are you, Don Rumata?"

"Thirty-five."

"When did you arrive in Arkanar?"

"Five years ago."

"From where?"

"I was previously living in Estor, at the family castle."

"And what was the purpose of your relocation?"

"Unfortunate circumstances forced me to leave Estor. I was searching for a capital that could compare in splendor to the capital of the metropole."

Fiery prickles finally started running up and down his arms. Rumata continued to patiently and persistently massage his swollen wrists. "Do tell us, what were these circumstances?" asked Don Reba.

"I killed a member of a most august family in a duel."

"Is that so? Who was it?"

"The young Duke Ekin."

"And the reason for the duel?"

"A woman," Rumata said curtly.

He began to suspect that all these questions didn't mean anything. This is a game, he thought, just like the discussion of the method of execution. I'm waiting until my hands recover. Brother Aba, the fool, is waiting for the gold from Don Rumata's ancestral treasury to pour into his lap. Don Reba is also waiting for something. But the monks, the monks! Why are there monks in the palace? Especially such skillful and energetic ones?

"The woman's name?"

The questions he asks, thought Rumata. They couldn't be any stupider. Let me try to wake them up a bit. "Doña Rita," he answered.

"I didn't expect you to answer. Much obliged."

"I'm always ready to be of service."

Don Reba bowed. "Have you ever been to Irukan?"

"No."

"Are you certain?"

"You are certain of it too."

"We want the truth!" Don Reba demanded. Brother Aba nodded. "And nothing but the truth!"

"Aha," said Rumata. "And here I thought..." He paused.

"What did you think?"

"I thought you mostly wanted to get your hands on my ancestral property. I simply can't imagine, Don Reba, in what way you hope to get it."

"What about a deed of gift? A deed of gift?" Brother Aba cried out.

Rumata laughed as derisively as possible. "You're a fool, 'Brother Aba,' if that's what you're called. I could immediately tell that you're a shopkeeper. Are you not aware that an entailed estate cannot be transferred into the hands of a stranger?"

He could see that Brother Aba was completely furious but restraining himself.

"You shouldn't speak in that tone," Don Reba said gently.

"You wanted the truth?" Rumata countered. "Here's the truth, the real truth, and nothing but the truth: Brother Aba is a nitwit and a shopkeeper."

However, Brother Aba had already regained control of himself. "I believe we've digressed," he said with a smile. "What do you think, Don Reba?"

"You are right, as always," said Don Reba. "Noble don, have you ever been to Soan?"

"I've been to Soan."

"For what purpose?"

"To visit the Academy of Science."

"A strange purpose for a man of your rank."

"A whim."

"And are you familiar with the chief justice of Soan, Don Condor?"

Rumata became wary. "He is a very old friend of my family."

"A most noble man, is he not?"

"A very respectable person."

"And are you aware that Don Condor was involved in the plot against His Majesty?"

Rumata jutted out his chin. "Get it into your head, Don Reba," he said arrogantly. "For us, the hereditary nobility of the metropole, all these Soans and Irukans, and even Arkanars, were and will always remain vassals of the imperial crown." He crossed his legs and turned away.

Don Reba was looking at him thoughtfully. "Are you rich?"

"I could buy all of Arkanar, but I'm not interested in garbage dumps."

Don Reba sighed. "My heart is bleeding," he said. "To cut down such a glorious offspring of such a glorious family! It would be a crime, if it were not brought about by the exigencies of state."

"Think less about the exigencies of state," Rumata said, "and more about your own hide."

"You're right," Don Reba said, then snapped his fingers.

Rumata quickly clenched and unclenched his muscles. His body seemed to be working. Three monks again jumped out from behind the curtains. With the same elusive speed and accuracy, indicating vast experience, they formed a circle around Brother Aba, who was still smiling sweetly, grabbed him, and bent his hands behind his back.

"Ow-ow-ow-ow!" shrieked Father Aba. His fat face contorted in pain.

"Quick, quick, hurry up!" Don Reba said with distaste.

The fat man resisted frantically as he was dragged behind the curtains. They could hear him screaming and yelping, then he suddenly shrieked in a horrible, unrecognizable voice and immediately went silent. Don Reba stood up and carefully unloaded Father Aba's crossbow. Rumata watched him, stunned.

Don Reba paced up and down the room, pensively scratching his back with a crossbow bolt. "Good, good," he mumbled almost tenderly. "Charming!" He seemed to have forgotten about Rumata. His steps kept getting quicker and quicker; he waved the bolt like a conductor's baton as he walked. Then he suddenly stopped abruptly at the desk, tossed the bolt away, gingerly sat down, and said, smiling from ear to ear: "How I got them, huh? Not a peep! They can't do that where you come from, I think."

Rumata was silent.

"*Yes* . . ." Don Reba intoned dreamily. "Good! Well, now let us talk, Don Rumata. Or maybe it's not Rumata? Maybe you're not even a don? Hmm?"

Rumata was silent, examining him curiously. Pale-skinned, with red veins on his nose, whole body shaking with excitement—he just wants to shout, clapping his hands, "I know! I know!" And you don't know a thing, you son of a bitch. And if you find out, you won't believe it. Well, go on, go on, I'm listening. "I'm listening to you," he said.

"You're not Don Rumata," Don Reba announced. "You're an impostor." He looked at Rumata, a severe expression on his face. "Rumata of Estor died five years ago and is lying in his family's vault. And the saints have long since laid to rest his rebellious and, frankly, not particularly pure soul. Well, will you confess on your own, or do you need some help?"

"I'll confess," said Rumata. "My name is Rumata of Estor, and I'm not accustomed to having my words doubted." Let me try to make you a little angry, he thought. My side hurts, or I'd lead you on a merry chase.

"I see that we will have to continue the conversation elsewhere," Don Reba said ominously.

His face was undergoing extraordinary changes. Gone was the pleasant smile, his lips had compressed into a hard line. The skin on his forehead was moving in a strange and eerie way.

Yes, thought Rumata, he really can be frightening. "Is it true that you have hemorrhoids?" Rumata asked solicitously.

Something flickered in Don Reba's eyes, but his facial expression didn't change. He pretended not to hear.

"You used Budach badly. He's a real master," Rumata said. "At least he was," he added significantly.

Something flickered in the faded eyes again.

Aha, thought Rumata, Budach must still be alive. He sat back and wrapped his arms around one knee.

"Thus, you refuse to confess," said Don Reba.

"To what?"

"To being an impostor."

"Honorable Reba," Rumata admonished, "such things need to be proved. You're insulting me!"

Don Reba's expression turned cloying. "My dear Don Rumata," he said. "Forgive me, I will keep calling you by that name for the time being. Anyway, I usually don't prove a thing. They prove things elsewhere, in the Merry Tower. For this purpose, I keep experienced, well-paid professionals, who are capable of using Holy Míca's Meat Grinder, the Greaves of Our Lord, the Gloves of the Great Martyr Pata, or, say, the Benches . . . uhhh . . . I'm sorry, the Chairs of Totz the Warrior to prove anything whatsoever. That God exists and that God doesn't exist. That people walk on their hands and people walk on their sides. Do you see what I'm saying? You may not be aware of this, but there's a whole science devoted to obtaining proofs. Judge for yourself: why would I prove what I already know? And after all, a confession isn't dangerous for you."

"It's not dangerous for me," said Rumata. "It's dangerous for you."

Don Reba pondered for some time. "All right," he said. "It appears I'll have to start after all. Let's see what Don Rumata of Estor has been observed doing in the five years of his afterlife in the Arkanarian kingdom. And then you will explain to me the meaning of it all. Agreed?"

"I don't want to make any rash promises," Rumata said, "but I'm interested in hearing you out."

Don Reba rummaged in his desk, pulled out a square of thick paper, and, raising his eyebrows, scanned it. "Let it be known to you," he said, smiling amiably, "let it be known to you that I, the Minister of the Defense of the Arkanarian Crown, undertook certain actions against the so-called bookworms, scientists, and other worthless people detrimental to the state. These actions met with some strange resistance. At the same time as the whole nation acted in concert and, remaining faithful to the king and the Arkanarian traditions, helped me in any way possible—betrayed the hidden, meted out their own justice, directed me to suspicious characters that had escaped my attention—at this same time, some unknown but highly energetic person snatched the most important, most inveterate and abominable criminals from under our noses and then sent them outside the kingdom. In this way, the following people slipped through our fingers: the godless astrologer Bagheer of Kissen; the criminal alchemist Sinda, who had been proven to have dallied with

the devil and with the Irukanian regime; the vile pamphle-
teer and disturber of the peace Zuren; and a number of others of lower rank. The crazy sorcerer and mechanic Cabani
disappeared somewhere. Someone spent a fortune in gold to
prevent the people's wrath from being carried out against the
godforsaken spies and poisoners, the former healers of His
Majesty. Under truly fantastical circumstances, forcing one to
again recall the enemy of the human race, someone liberated
the monster of depravity and corrupter of men's souls, the
leader of the peasant revolt Arata the Hunchback . . ." Don
Reba stopped and, moving the skin on his forehead, looked
at Rumata significantly. Rumata, looking up at the ceiling,
smiled dreamily. He had abducted Arata the Hunchback by
coming for him in a helicopter. This had made a stupendous
impression on the guards. On Arata, too, to be honest. That
really was well done, he thought. I have done good work.

"Let it be known to you," Don Reba continued, "that
the said Arata is now personally leading the mutinous slaves
through the eastern areas of the metropole, spilling an abun-
dance of noble blood, experiencing no shortage of either
money or weapons."

"I can easily believe it," Rumata said. "He immediately
struck me as a very determined man."

"So you confess?" Don Reba said immediately.

"To what?" Rumata asked in surprise.

They looked each other in the eye for some time.

"I will go on," said Don Reba. "The rescue of these cor-
rupters of souls cost you, Don Rumata, according to my
humble and incomplete estimates, no less than one hundred
pounds of gold. I won't mention the fact that in doing so you
have forever polluted yourself by consorting with the devil.
I also won't mention the fact that for the entirety of your

stay in the Arkanarian kingdom you haven't received a single penny from your estate in Estor, and why should you have? Why send a dead man money, even if he's family? But your gold!"

He opened a jewelry box that was buried beneath the paper on the desk and extracted from it a handful of gold coins with the profile of Pitz the Sixth.

"This gold itself would be enough to burn you at the stake!" he shrieked. "This is the devil's gold! Human hands are incapable of producing metal of such purity!"

He was glaring at Rumata. Yes, thought Rumata generously, that's well done. That's something we probably should've thought of. And he's probably the first to notice. We must take that into account.

Reba suddenly calmed down again. Sympathetic paternal notes came into his voice. "And you've always been so very imprudent, Don Rumata. This entire time, I've been so worried about you. Such a duelist, such a troublemaker! A hundred and twenty-six duels over five years! And not a single man killed. Someone could eventually draw conclusions from that. I did, for example. And I wasn't the only one. For example, tonight, Brother Aba . . . it isn't nice to speak ill of the dead, but he was a very cruel man. I found it difficult to tolerate him, I admit. Anyway, for your arrest Brother Aba chose not the most capable fighters but the fattest and the strongest. And he turned out to be right. A few dislocated arms, a few crushed necks, missing teeth are no concern . . . and here you are! And you must have known that you were fighting for your life. You're a master. You're doubtlessly the best swordsman of the empire. You have doubtlessly sold your soul to the devil, for it is only in hell that you could have learned these incredible, fabulous methods of battle.

I'm even ready to allow that you got this ability under the condition that you do not kill. Although it's hard to imagine why the devil would impose such a condition. But let our scholars figure that out—"

He was interrupted by a shrill, piglike squeal and glanced at the lilac curtains, displeased. There was a fight behind the curtains. They could hear dull blows, shrieks of "Let me go! Let me go!" and other hoarse voices, swearing, and exclamations in a strange dialect. Then a curtain snapped off and fell on the floor. Some man burst into the office, collapsing onto all fours—he was bald, with a bloodied chin and wildly bulging eyes. Huge paws reached out from behind the curtain, grabbed the man's legs, and pulled him back. Rumata recognized him as Budach. He was shrieking wildly: "You lied to me! You lied to me! It was poison! Why?"

He was dragged into the darkness. A man in black quickly picked up and hung the curtain. Silence fell, then a disgusting noise came from behind the curtains—someone was retching. Rumata understood.

"Where's Budach?" he asked sharply.

"As you can see, some misfortune seems to have befallen him," Don Reba answered, but it was evident that he was caught off guard.

"Don't even try it," said Rumata. "Where's Budach?"

"Oh, Don Rumata," Don Reba said, shaking his head. He had already recovered. "What do you want Budach for? What is he, related to you? You've never even seen him."

"Listen, Reba!" Rumata said furiously. "I'm not kidding around! If anything happens to Budach, you'll die like a dog. I'll crush you."

"You won't have enough time," Don Reba said quickly. He was very pale.

"You're a fool, Reba. You're an experienced schemer, but you don't understand a thing. Never in your life have you played a game as dangerous as this one. And you don't even know it."

Don Reba cowered behind the desk, his eyes glowing like embers. Rumata felt that he had also never been this close to death. They were laying their cards on the table. Soon they would know who was to be the master in this game. Rumata tensed his muscles, getting ready to leap.

No weapon, neither spear nor arrow, kills instantly—you could clearly read this thought on Don Reba's face. The hemorrhoidal old man wanted to live. "Now, don't be like that," he whined. "We were just sitting around, talking . . . Your Budach's alive, don't worry, alive and well. He was still going to treat me. No need to overreact."

"Where's Budach?"

"In the Merry Tower."

"I need him."

"I need him, too, Don Rumata."

"Listen, Reba," Rumata said. "Don't make me angry. And stop pretending. You're afraid of me. And rightly so. Budach belongs to me, understand? To me!"

They had now both stood up. Reba was terrible. He had turned blue, his lips were twitching convulsively, he was mumbling and sputtering. "Whippersnapper!" he hissed. "I'm not afraid of anyone. I'm the one who could crush you like a bug!"

He suddenly turned around and pulled back a tapestry hanging behind his back. There was a wide window behind it.

"Look!"

Rumata went to the window. It faced the square in front of the palace. Dawn was approaching. The smoke from the fires rose into the gray sky. The square was littered with corpses. And a motionless black rectangle stood at its center. Rumata looked closer. These were horsemen, standing in an improbably precise formation—in long black cloaks, black hoods hiding their eyes, with black triangular shields on their left hands and long pikes in their right hands.

"I present to you!" Don Reba said in a clanging voice. His whole body was shaking. "The humble men of our Lord, the cavalry of the Holy Order. They landed tonight at the Port of Arkanar to suppress the barbaric rebellion of the night tramps of Waga the Wheel, in league with some swollen-headed shopkeepers! The rebellion has been suppressed. The Holy Order now has control of the city and country, which will henceforth be known as the Arkanarian Region of the Order."

Rumata involuntarily scratched his head. I'll be damned, he thought. So that's who the unhappy shopkeepers were paving the way for. Quite the provocation! Don Reba was grinning triumphantly.

"We have not met yet," he continued in the same clanging voice. "Let me introduce to you the Holy Order's governor for the Arkanarian Region, bishop and battle master, the servant of God, Reba!"

You know, I could have guessed, thought Rumata. Wherever grayness triumphs, black robes come to power. Oh, historians, stick a tail in all of you . . . But he put his hands behind his back and rocked from toe to heel. "Right now I'm tired," he said disdainfully. "I want to sleep. I want to take a hot bath and wash off the blood and saliva of your thugs. Tomorrow . . . actually, today . . . let's say an hour after sunrise, I'll come back to your office. By this time, the order for Budach's release should be ready."

"There are twenty thousand of them!" Don Reba shouted, pointing at the window.

Rumata winced. "A little quieter, please," he said. "And remember, Reba, I know very well that you're no bishop. You're just a filthy traitor and an incompetent petty schemer." Don Reba licked his lips, his eyes glazed over. Rumata continued. "I have no mercy. Any vile thing you do to me or my friends will cost you your head. Bear in mind, I hate you. I am willing to put up with you, but you will have to learn how to get out of my way in time. Do you understand me?"

Don Reba said hurriedly, with a pleading smile, "I want only one thing. I want you to be on my side, Don Rumata. I can't kill you. I don't know why, but I can't."

"You're afraid," said Rumata.

"I'm afraid," Don Reba agreed. "Maybe you're the devil. Maybe you're the son of God. Who knows? Or maybe you're a man from the powerful countries overseas—they say those do exist. I don't even try to gaze into the abyss that brought you forth. My head spins and I fall into heresy. But I can kill you too. Any time. Right now. Tomorrow. Yesterday. Do you understand that?"

"I'm not interested in that," Rumata said.

"Then what? What are you interested in?"

"I'm not interested in anything in particular," Rumata said. "I'm having a good time. I'm neither the devil nor God, I'm Rumata of Estor, a merry noble gentleman, burdened with various whims and prejudices, and accustomed to freedom in every way. Can you remember that?"

Don Reba had already regained his composure. He wiped his face with a handkerchief and smiled pleasantly. "I value your determination," he said. "After all, you also aspire to certain ideals. And I respect these ideals, even though I don't understand them. I'm very glad that we've had this talk. It's possible that some day, you will describe your views to me, and it's entirely possible that you will force me to reconsider my own. People are prone to making mistakes. Perhaps I'm wrong and the goals I aspire to are not the ones worthy of the diligent and selfless work I've been doing. I'm an open-minded man, and I can easily imagine that one day I will work with you side by side."

"We'll see," Rumata said, then walked toward the door. What a slug! he thought. Some colleague. Side by side . . .

The city had been stricken by intolerable terror. The reddish morning sun shone down grimly on the empty streets, smoldering ruins, torn-off shutters, and broken-down doors. Shards of glass glittered in the dust, crimson from the dawn. Hordes of uncountable crows had descended on the city as if on an empty field. Groups of two and three horsemen in black hung around the squares and intersections—slowly turning their whole bodies in the saddle, peering through the slits in the hoods pulled low over their eyes. Charred bodies were hanging from hastily erected posts over extinguished coals. It was as if there was no one left alive in the city—only the shrieking crows and the businesslike murderers in black.

Half the time, Rumata was walking with his eyes closed. He was suffocating, his battered body aching painfully. Are they people or are they not? Is there anything human about them? Some get slaughtered in the streets, while others sit at home and meekly wait their turn. And everyone is thinking, *Let it be anyone but me.* The cold-blooded brutality of those

who slaughter, and the cold-blooded meekness of those
who are slaughtered. The cold-bloodedness, that's the worst
thing. Ten people stand around, transfixed with horror, and
meekly wait, while another one comes by, picks his victim,
and cold-bloodedly slaughters him. These people's souls are
full of rot, and each hour of meek waiting contaminates them
even more. This very moment, these silent houses are invis-
ibly breeding rascals, informers, and murderers, thousands
of people who will remain stricken by fear their whole lives,
and who will mercilessly teach fear to their children and the
children of their children. A little longer and I'll go insane
and become just like them; a little longer and I'll no longer
have any idea what I'm doing here. I need to rest, get away
from all this, calm down . . .

*At the end of the Year of Water—such and such a year
by the new calendar—the centrifugal processes in the ancient
empire became relevant. Taking advantage of this, the Holy
Order, essentially representing the interests of the most reactionary groups of feudal society, who desired to stop the disin-
tegration by any means necessary . . .* And do you know how
the burning corpses on the posts smell? And have you ever
seen a naked woman with her stomach ripped open lying in
the dust of the street? And have you seen a city in which all
the men are silent, and only the crows scream? You, the still
unborn boys and girls in front of the educational stereovisor
in the schools of the Arkanarian Communist Republic?

He bumped into something hard and sharp with his chest.
A black-robed horseman was in front of him. A long spear
with a broad, carefully serrated blade was resting against
Rumata's torso. The horseman was silently looking at him
from the dark recesses of his hood. The only thing visible
under the hood was a thin-lipped mouth with a small chin.

I have to do something, thought Rumata. But what? Knock him off his horse? No. The horseman started slowly drawing back the spear to strike. Oh, yes! Rumata listlessly raised his left hand and pulled back his sleeve, showing the iron bracelet he was given when he left the palace. The horseman looked closer, raised his spear, and rode past. "In the name of the Lord," he said in a muffled voice with a strange accent.

"In His name," Rumata muttered and kept going, walking past another horseman, who was trying to use his spear to reach an expertly carved wooden figure of a merry imp sticking out below the eaves of the roof. A horror-stricken fat face flickered behind the partially torn off shutter on the second floor—this must have been one of the shopkeepers who only three days ago were rapturously shouting "Hurray for Don Reba" over their beer and listening to the *thump, thump, thump* of the hobnailed boots on the pavement with delight. Oh, the grayness, the grayness . . . Rumata turned away.

And how are things at home? he suddenly wondered. He quickened his pace, almost running the entire last block. The house was still standing. Two monks were sitting on the front steps; they had thrown their hoods back and were showing their carelessly shaved heads to the sun. They stood up when they saw him. "In the name of the Lord," they said in unison.

"In His name," responded Rumata. "What is your business here?"

The monks bowed, crossing their arms on their stomachs. "You're here, so we're leaving," one of them said. They walked down the steps and slowly plodded away, hunching and stuffing their hands into their sleeves. Rumata followed them with his eyes and remembered the thousands of times he had seen these meek figures in long black robes in the streets.

Only before, they didn't have the scabbards of extremely heavy swords dragging behind them in the dust. We messed up, oh, how we messed up! he thought. It had been quite the sport for the noble dons—sidling up to a monk who was plodding alone, and telling each other naughty stories over his head. And I, the idiot, would pretend to be drunk and trail behind them, roaring with laughter, and was so happy that the empire was at least not prone to religious fanaticism. But what could we have done? Yes, *what could we have done?*

"Who's there?" a quavering voice asked.

"Open up, Muga, it's me," Rumata said softly.

The bars rattled, the door cracked open, and Rumata squeezed into the entrance hall. Everything here was as usual, and Rumata gave a sigh of relief. Old, gray-haired Muga, nodding his head, reached for Rumata's helmet and swords with his usual deference.

"How's Kira?" Rumata asked.

"Kira's upstairs," said Muga. "She fine."

"Excellent," Rumata said, stepping out of his sword slings. "And where's Uno? Why isn't he greeting me?"

Muga took the sword. "Uno was killed," he said calmly. "He lies in the servants' quarters."

Rumata closed his eyes. "Uno was killed . . ." he repeated. "Who killed him?"

Without waiting for an answer, he went into the servants' quarters. Uno was lying on the table, a sheet covering him up to his waist; his arms were folded across his chest, his eyes were wide open, and his mouth was twisted in a grimace. Downcast servants were standing around the table and listening to a monk mumbling in the corner. The cook was sobbing. Rumata, not taking his eyes off the boy's face, started unbuttoning the collar of his waistcoat with clumsy fingers.

"Bastards," he said. "Everyone is such a bastard!"

He tottered, came closer to the table, looked into the dead eyes, lifted the sheet, and immediately put it back down.

"Yes, it's too late," he said. "Too late . . . It's hopeless. Oh, those bastards! Who killed him? The monks?"

He turned toward the monk, yanked him up and bent over his face.

"Who killed him?" he demanded. "Was it you? Tell me!"

"It wasn't the monks," Muga said quietly behind his back. "It was the gray soldiers."

Rumata spent a while longer peering into the monk's thin face, into his slowly expanding pupils. "In the name of the Lord . . ." wheezed the monk. Rumata let him go, sat down on the bench at Uno's feet, and started to cry. He cried, covering his face with his hands, and listened to Muga's quavering, indifferent voice. Muga was telling him how after the second night watch, someone knocked on the door in the name of the king, and Uno shouted not to let them in, but then they did have to let them in, because the grays were threatening to burn down the house. They burst into the hall, beat up the servants and tied them up, and then started climbing the stairs. Uno, who was standing by the entrance to his chambers, started firing his crossbows. He had two crossbows, and he managed to fire twice, but he missed once. The gray soldiers threw their knives, and Uno fell. They dragged him downstairs and started trampling him with their feet and beating him with their axes, but then the black monks entered the house. They hacked the two gray soldiers to death and disarmed the rest, put nooses around their necks, and dragged them out onto the street.

Muga's voice fell silent, but Rumata kept sitting there for a long time, resting his elbows on the table at Uno's feet.

Then he rose heavily, wiped off the tears stuck in his two-day stubble with his sleeve, kissed the boy's icy forehead, and, barely able to move his legs, plodded upstairs.

He was half-dead from shock and exhaustion. After somehow managing to clamber up the stairs, he walked through the living room, made his way to the bed, and with a moan, collapsed facedown into the pillows. Kira came running. Rumata was so worn out that he didn't even help her undress him. She pulled off his boots, then, crying over his swollen face, tore off his tattered coat and metalstrom shirt, then cried some more over his battered body. Only now did he feel that all his bones hurt, like after high-gravity training. Kira was rubbing him down with a vinegar-soaked sponge and he, without opening his eyes, hissed through closed lips and muttered, "And I could have killed him . . . I was right next to him . . . Could have squashed him with two fingers . . . Is this life, Kira? Let's leave this place . . . This Experiment is on me, not on them." He didn't even notice that he spoke Russian. Kira kept looking at him fearfully, with eyes that were glassy from tears, and only silently kissed his cheeks. Then she covered him with threadbare sheets—Uno never did manage to buy new ones—and ran downstairs to make him some mulled wine. He crawled out of bed and, groaning from the all-consuming pain, shuffled barefoot into his study, opened a secret drawer in his desk, rummaged in the first-aid kit, and took a few sporamin pills. When Kira came back with a steaming teapot on a heavy silver tray, he was lying on his back and listening to the pain receding, the noise quieting down in his head, and his body filling with renewed strength and vigor. After finishing the teapot, he felt completely well, called Muga, and ordered him to prepare his clothes.

"Don't go, Rumata," Kira said. "Don't go. Stay home."

"I have to, little one."

"I'm scared. Please stay. They'll kill you."

"Now, now. Why in the world would they kill me? They are all afraid of me."

She began to weep again. She was weeping quietly, timidly, as if she was afraid he'd be angry. Rumata sat her down on his knees and started stroking her hair.

"The worst is over," he said. "And when this is all done, we'll leave this place."

She quieted down, clinging to him. Muga, nodding his head, stood nearby, looking indifferent, holding the master's pants with little gold bells at the ready.

"But first, there's a lot to do here," continued Rumata. "There were many killed last night. I need to find out who survived and who was killed. And I need to help save the ones they are planning to kill."

"And who will help you?"

"Happy is the man who thinks of others. Besides, you and I are being helped by powerful men."

"I can't think of others," she said. "You came back barely alive. I can tell you were beaten. And they killed Uno outright. What were your powerful men doing? Why didn't they stop the killing? I don't believe you. I don't believe you."

She tried to get away, but he held her tight. "What can we do?" he asked. "This time they were a little late. But they are now watching us and protecting us again. Why don't you believe me today? You've always believed me before. You've seen it yourself: I came back barely alive, and look at me now!"

"I don't want to look," she said, hiding her face. "I don't want to cry again."

"There! Just a few scratches! It's nothing. The worst is over. At least for you and me. But there are very good, wonderful people for whom this horror hasn't ended yet. And I have to save them."

Kira took a deep breath, kissed Rumata's neck, and gently freed herself. "Come back tonight," she said. "Please come back?"

"Of course!" he said fervently. "I'll come back earlier, probably not alone. Expect me for dinner."

She stepped aside, sat down in a chair, and putting her hands in her lap, watched him get dressed. Rumata, mumbling Russian words, pulled on the pants with the little bells (Muga immediately crouched down in front of him and started to fasten the numerous buckles and buttons), put the now-blessed chain mail over a clean undershirt, and finally said in despair, "Little one, please understand, I have to go — what can I do? I have no choice!"

Kira suddenly said pensively, "Sometimes I can't understand why you don't hit me."

Rumata froze in the middle of buttoning up a shirt with a frilly ruff. "What do you mean, why I don't hit you?" he asked, bewildered. "How could I hit you?"

"You're not just a good, kind man," she continued, not listening. "You're also a very strange man. You're like an archangel. When you're with me, I become brave. Right now I'm brave. Someday, I'll definitely have to ask you about one thing. Will you — not right now, but later, when it's all done — tell me about yourself?"

Rumata was silent for a long time. Muga handed him an orange waistcoat with striped red bows. Rumata pulled it on with disgust and tightened his belt. "Yes," he finally said. "Someday I'll tell you everything, little one."

"I'll wait," she said seriously. "And now go, and pay no attention to me."

Rumata came close to her, kissed her lips with his swollen lips, then took an iron bracelet off his arm and gave it to her. "Put it on your left arm," he said. "No one else should come to the house today, but if they do—show them this."

She was watching him go, and he knew exactly what she was thinking. She was thinking, *I don't know if you're the devil or the son of God or a man from the fabulous countries overseas, but if you don't come back, I'll die.* And because she was silent, he was infinitely grateful to her, because leaving was incredibly difficult—like diving headfirst from a sunny emerald shore into a rancid pool.

# Chapter 8

Rumata took the back roads to the office of the Bishop of Arkanar. He crept through the residents' small yards, getting tangled in old clothes hung out to dry; climbed through holes in fences, leaving splendid bows and bits of precious Soanian lace on rusty nails; and hastily crawled between potato patches. But he still couldn't evade the watchful eye of the black army. When he climbed out into the narrow, crooked alley that led to the dump, he bumped into two gloomy, tipsy monks.

Rumata tried to go around them—the monks drew their swords and blocked the way. Rumata grabbed the hilts of his swords—the monks gave a three-fingered whistle, calling for help. Rumata started to retreat toward the hole he had just climbed out of, but a nimble little man with an insignificant face suddenly jumped out toward him into the alley. Jostling Rumata with his shoulder, he ran up to the monks and said something to them, after which the monks picked their cassocks up over their long, purple-clad legs and trotted away, disappearing behind the houses. The little man shuffled after them without turning around.

Got it, thought Rumata. A spy-bodyguard. And he isn't even bothering to hide much. The Bishop of Arkanar is being prudent. I wonder what he's most worried about—what I'll do, or what they'll do to me? Following the spy with his eyes, he headed toward the dump. The dump led to the back of the offices of the former Ministry of the Defense of the Crown and was, he hoped, not patrolled.

The alley was empty, but he could already hear shutters softly creaking, an infant crying, and people whispering cautiously. A gaunt, thin face, black from baked-in soot, warily poked out from behind a half-rotted fence. Fearful, hollow eyes stared at Rumata.

"I beg your pardon, noble don, and beg your pardon again. Won't the noble don tell me what's happening in the city? I'm the blacksmith Kikus, nicknamed Limpy, and I need to go to the smithy, but I'm scared."

"Don't go," Rumata advised. "The monks aren't kidding around. There's no more king. The man in charge now is Don Reba, the Bishop of the Holy Order. So sit tight."

The blacksmith hastily nodded after each word, and his eyes filled with anguish and despair. "The Order, huh," he muttered. "Oh, cholera . . . Beg your pardon, noble don. So it's now the Order. Are they grays or what?"

"Nah," Rumata said, eyeing him with curiosity. "The grays might be finished. These are monks."

"Oh, wow!" said the blacksmith. "So they got the grays too. That's some Order! The grays are finished—that's good, of course. But what about us, noble don, what does Your Lordship think? Will we adapt, eh? Under the Order, eh?"

"Why not?" said Rumata. "The Order needs to eat and drink too. You'll adapt."

The blacksmith perked up. "That's what I figure—we'll adapt. The way I figure it, the most important thing's not to bother anyone, then no one will bother you, eh?"

Rumata shook his head. "Oh, no," he said. "The ones who don't bother anyone get slaughtered first."

"That's true," the blacksmith sighed. "But what can you do? All alone in the world, with eight brats clutching my pants. Oh, Holy Mother, I hope they at least slaughtered my master! He was a gray officer. What does Your Lordship think? Could they have slaughtered him, noble don? I owed him five gold pieces."

"I don't know," Rumata said. "They might have slaughtered him. Here's something else for you to ponder, blacksmith. You're all alone in the world, but there are ten thousand of you in the city."

"So?" said the blacksmith.

"Think about it," Rumata said irritably, and kept walking.

The hell he'll think of anything. It's too early for him to think. And it seems so simple: ten thousand hammerers like that, in a rage, could crush anyone to a pulp. Except rage is what they don't have yet. Only fear. Everyone for himself, only God for all.

The elder bushes at the end of the block suddenly rustled, and Don Tameo crawled into the alley. Seeing Rumata, he cried out in joy, jumped up, and, tottering wildly, moved in his direction, reaching his mud-smeared hands toward him. "My noble don!" he cried. "I'm so glad! I see you're also going to the office?"

"Of course, my noble don," Rumata answered, skillfully avoiding the embrace.

"May I join you, noble don?"

"I'd be honored, noble don."

They bowed to each other. It was clear that Don Tameo had started yesterday and hadn't yet been able to stop. He extracted a finely made glass flask from a pair of extremely wide yellow pants. "Would you like some, noble don?" he offered courteously.

"Thank you," Rumata said.

"It's rum!" declared Don Tameo. "Real rum from the metropole. I paid a gold piece for it."

They went down to the dump and, holding their noses, began to walk between piles of garbage, corpses of dogs, and reeking puddles swarming with white worms. The continuous hum of myriad emerald flies was in the air.

"How strange," Don Tameo said, closing the flask, "I've never been here before."

Rumata didn't say anything.

"Don Reba has always amazed me," said Don Tameo. "I was convinced that he would eventually overthrow our worthless monarch, pave new roads, and open shining prospects for us." With that, his foot slipped into a yellow-green puddle, splattering him heavily, and he grabbed Rumata in order not to fall down. "Yes!" he continued when they reached solid ground. "We, the young aristocracy, will always stand behind Don Reba! The desired relaxation has finally come. Judge for yourself, Don Rumata. I've been walking the alleys and kitchen gardens for an hour but I haven't met a single gray. We've swept the gray scum off the face of the earth, and how sweet and easy it is to breathe in the reborn Arkanar. Instead of the coarse shopkeepers, those insolent boors, and the peasants, the streets are full of the servants of God. I've seen it myself: some noblemen are now openly strolling in front of their houses. They no longer need to fear that some imbecile in a dung-covered apron will splatter them with his filthy cart. And we now no longer have to fight our way through yesterday's butchers and haberdashers. Blessed by the great Holy Order, for which I have always had the utmost respect and, I will not conceal, heartfelt affection, we will arrive at a state of unprecedented prosperity—in which not a single peasant will dare raise his eyes at a nobleman without a permit signed by the district inspector of the Order. I'm bringing a memorandum about this right now."

"What a horrible stench," Rumata said with feeling.

"Yes, it's awful," Don Tameo agreed, closing the flask. "But how easy it is to breathe in the reborn Arkanar! And the price of wine has fallen by half."

By the end of their walk, Don Tameo had drained the flask to the very bottom and hurled it away, and had become extraordinarily excited. He fell twice, the second time refusing to clean himself off, declaring that he was sinful and unclean by nature and wished to present himself in that state. He kept reciting his memorandum at the top of his lungs: "How forcefully put!" he exclaimed. "Take this passage, for example, noble dons: 'Lest the reeking peasants . . .' Hmm? What a thought!" When they got to the courtyard behind the office, he collapsed onto the first monk he saw and, bursting into tears, started begging for absolution. The half-suffocated monk fought back fiercely, tried to whistle for help, but Don Tameo clutched his cassock and they both tumbled into a garbage heap. Rumata left them behind, and for a long time, as he was going away, kept hearing the plaintive intermittent whistling and exclamations: "'Lest the reeking peasants'! *Bleeessings!* With all my heart! I felt affection, affection, you get it, peasant face?"

A detachment of monks on foot, armed with fearsome-looking knotted clubs, was standing in the square by the entrance, in the shadow of the Merry Tower. The corpses had been removed. The morning wind was swirling yellow columns of dust around the square. Crows were screaming and quarreling beneath the wide conical roof of the tower—there, as always, the bodies of the hanged swung upside down from the exposed beams. The tower had been built about two hundred years ago by an ancestor of the late king for military purposes. It had been built on top of a solid three-story foundation, which was once used to store reserves of food in case of a siege. The tower was later turned into a prison. But then an earthquake had collapsed all the interior walls, and the prison had to be moved to the basement. In her time, some Arkanarian queen had complained to her king that the wails of the tortured resounding through the neighborhood interfered with her amusements. Her august husband ordered a military band to play in the tower from morning to night. That was how the tower had gotten its current name. It had long been an empty stone shell—the investigation chambers had long been relocated to the newly excavated, very lowest floors of the foundation—and it had been a long time since a band had played there, but the residents still called it Merry.

The square near the Merry Tower was usually deserted. But today the place was bustling with activity. People were being led, pulled, and dragged along the ground toward the tower—storm troopers in torn gray uniforms, lice-ridden vagabonds in rags, half-dressed city residents covered in goose bumps from fear, hysterically screaming girls, and whole gangs of sullenly staring tramps from the night army. And at the same time, corpses were being removed from the tower, hauled out with hooks through some hidden passageways, stacked onto carts, and driven out of the city. The tail of an extremely long line of noblemen and wealthy citizens, which extended out of the open doors of the ministry office, watched this appalling commotion in fear and confusion.

They allowed everyone into the office, even bringing some people in under escort. Rumata pushed his way in. It was as stuffy here as at the dump. An official with a yellow-gray face and a big goose feather stuck behind his protruding ear was sitting at a wide table surrounded by lists. The next applicant, the noble Don Keu, gave his name, arrogantly fluffing his mustache.

"Take off your hat," the official said in a colorless voice, without looking up from his papers.

"The privilege of the family of Keu is to wear a hat in the presence of the king himself," Don Keu proclaimed proudly.

"No one has any privileges before the Order," the official said in the same colorless voice.

Don Keu huffed, turning livid, but took the hat off.

The official ran a long yellow nail along the list. "Don Keu . . . Don Keu . . ." he muttered, "Don Keu . . . Royal Street, Building Twelve?"

"Yes," Don Keu said in an irritated bass voice.

"Number four hundred eighty-five, Brother Tibak."

The heavyset Brother Tibak, who was sitting at the adjacent table, crimson from the stuffy air, searched through the papers, wiped the sweat off his bald head, stood up, and read out monotonously, "Number four hundred eighty-five, Don

Keu. Royal, Twelve, for the defamation of the name of His
Grace the Bishop of Arkanar Don Reba, which took place at
the palace ball the year before last, shall receive three dozen
lashes on his bared buttocks, and shall kiss His Grace's boot."

Brother Tibak sat down.

"Down that corridor," said the official in a colorless
voice, "the lashes on the right, the boot on the left. Next."

To Rumata's complete astonishment, Don Keu did not
protest. He had apparently already seen a lot in line. He just
grunted, adjusted his mustache with dignity, and departed
for the corridor. The next in line, the giant Don Pifa, quivering with fat, had already taken off his hat.

"Don Pifa . . . Don Pifa . . ." the official droned, running
a finger along the list. "Milkmen Street, Building Two."

Don Pifa made a guttural noise.

"Number five hundred and four, Brother Tibak."

Brother Tibak again wiped his head and stood up.
"Number five hundred and four, Don Pifa, Milkmen, Two,
not known to be guilty of anything toward His Grace—con-
sequently clean."

"Don Pifa," the official said, "take your symbol of purification." He bent down, pulled an iron bracelet from a chest
next to the chair, and handed it to noble Pifa. "Wear it on
your left arm, produce it as soon as a soldier from the Order
demands it. Next."

Don Pifa made a guttural noise and walked away, examining the bracelet. The official was already droning the next
name. Rumata took a look at the line. There were many
familiar faces here. A few were dressed in their customary
rich fashion, others were clearly attempting to appear poor,
but all were thoroughly smeared with mud. Somewhere from
the middle of the line, loud enough for everyone to hear, Don

Sera declared for the third time in five minutes, "I see no reason why even a noble don shouldn't receive a couple lashes
in the name of His Grace!"

Rumata waited until the next person was directed down
the corridor (it was a well-known fishmonger, who had been
given five lashes but no kiss for unenthusiastic ways of thinking), pushed his way through to the table, and brusquely put
a hand on the papers lying in front of the official. "Pardon
me," he said. "I need the order for the release of Doctor
Budach. I'm Don Rumata."

The official didn't raise his head.

"Don Rumata . . . Don Rumata . . ." he muttered and,
shoving Rumata's hand away, ran his nail along the list.

"What are you doing, you old inkwell?" said Rumata. "I
need the order for the release!"

"Don Rumata . . . Don Rumata . . ." Apparently this
automaton was impossible to stop. "Boilermakers Street,
Building Eight. Number sixteen, Brother Tibak."

Rumata felt everyone behind his back hold their breath.
And he had to admit he also felt a bit uneasy. The sweaty,
crimson Brother Tibak stood up: "Number sixteen, Don
Rumata, Boilermakers, Eight, for special services to the
Order has earned the particular gratitude of His Grace and
will kindly receive an order for the release of Doctor Budach,
with whom he will do whatever he pleases—see sheet six seventeen eleven."

The official immediately pulled this sheet from underneath the lists and handed it to Rumata. "Through the yellow door, up to the second floor, room six, down the hall, go
right then left," he said. "Next."

Rumata scanned the sheet. It wasn't the order for
Budach's release. It was the justification for his receiving a

pass into the fifth, special department of the office, where he was supposed to receive instructions to take to the secretariat of secret affairs.

"What did you give me, blockhead?" asked Rumata. "Where's the order?"

"Through the yellow door, up to the second floor, room six, down the hall, go right then left," the official repeated.

"I'm asking, where's the order?" Rumata barked.

"I don't know. I don't know. Next!"

Rumata heard heavy breathing by his ear, and something soft and hot pressed up against his back. He moved away. Don Pifa squeezed up to the table again. "It doesn't fit," he squeaked.

The official looked dully at him. "Name? Rank?" he asked.

"It doesn't fit," Don Pifa said again, tugging on the bracelet, which barely fit over three fat fingers.

"It doesn't fit . . . It doesn't fit . . ." the official mumbled and suddenly jerked a thick book lying on the table to his right toward him. The book had an evil look—the binding was black and greasy. Don Pifa looked at it dumbfounded for a couple of seconds, then suddenly recoiled and, without saying a word, rushed toward the door. The people in line shouted, "Hurry up, get a move on!" Rumata also walked away from the table. What a quagmire, he thought. I'll show you . . . The official started droning into space: "If the indicated symbol of purification does not fit onto the left wrist of the purified or if the purified has no left wrist as such . . ." Rumata walked around the table, stuck both hands into the chest with the bracelets, grabbed as many as he could and walked off.

"Hey, hey," the official called without any expression in his voice. "Your justification!"

"In the name of the Lord," Rumata said significantly, looking over his shoulder. The official and Brother Tibak stood up together and dissonantly replied, "In His name." The people in line watched Rumata leave with envy and admiration.

Coming out of the office, Rumata slowly walked toward the Merry Tower, clasping the bracelets onto his left arm along the way. It turned out that there were nine bracelets, and only five of them fit on his left arm. The remaining four Rumata stuck on his right arm. The Bishop of Arkanar is trying to wear me out, he thought. It won't work. The bracelets clinked with each step, and Rumata was holding an impressive-looking paper in his hand—sheet six seventeen eleven, adorned with multicolored seals. Every monk he met, both on foot and on horseback, quickly got out of his way. The insignificant spy-bodyguard kept appearing then disappearing in the crowd, keeping a respectful distance. Rumata, mercilessly bashing the dawdlers with his scabbards, made his way to the gates, barked menacingly at a guard who tried to butt in, walked through the courtyard, and descended the slimy, weathered stairs into a semidarkness lit by smoking torches. This was the where the holy of the holies of the former Ministry of the Defense of the Crown began—the royal prison and investigation chambers.

In the vaulted corridor, smoking torches stuck out of rusty sockets in the wall at intervals of ten feet. A black door was visible in a cavernous alcove beneath each torch. These were the entrances to the prison cells, locked from the outside by heavy iron bolts. The corridors were full of people. They were shoving, running, shouting, and giving orders. Bolts were creaking and doors were slamming; someone was being beaten and he wailed; someone was being dragged and he resisted; someone was being pushed into a cell that was already packed to full capacity; someone was being unsuccessfully dragged out of a cell, screaming hysterically, "Not me, not me!" and clutching his neighbors. The faces of the passing monks were businesslike to the point of severity. Every one of them was in a hurry; every one of them was involved in affairs of importance to the state. Rumata, trying to find his way, slowly walked through corridor after corridor, descending lower and lower. Things were calmer in the lower floors. Here, judging by the conversations, the graduates of the Patriotic School were taking their examinations. Half-naked, broad-chested young oafs in leather aprons were standing in clusters by the doors of the torture chambers, flipping through their greasy instruction manuals, occasionally walking over to a large tank with a cup chained to it to drink some water. Horrible screams and sounds of blows were coming from the chambers, and there was a thick burning smell. And oh, the conversations, the conversations!

"The bone-crusher has this screw-on top, and it broke. That my fault? He kicked me out. 'You dumb lug,' he says, 'go get five lashes on your buttocks and come back.'"

"We oughta find out who's doing the flogging, maybe it's one of us students. So you could arrange it in advance, collect five coins a head and pay 'em off."

"When there's a lot of fat, no point in heating up the prong, it'll cool off in the fat anyway. You should take the tweezers and tear a bit of lard off."

"So the Greaves of Our Lord are for the legs, they are wider and have spikes, and the Gloves of the Great Martyr, they have screws—that's specifically for the hand, got it?"

"Funny thing, brothers! I go inside and see—you know who's in chains? Fika the Red, the butcher from our street, used to slap me around when drunk. You better watch out, I think, I'm gonna have some fun."

"Pekora the Lip hasn't been back since the monks dragged him off this morning. And he didn't come to the exam."

"Ugh, I shoulda used the meat grinder, but I stupidly bashed his sides with a crowbar, so, you know, I broke a rib. So Father Kin grabs my head and kicks me square in the tailbone, and brothers, I gotta tell you—I saw stars, it hurt so bad. 'What are you doing,' he says, 'spoiling my goods?'"

Look, my friends, look, thought Rumata, slowly turning his head from side to side. This isn't theory. This is something no one has ever seen. Watch, listen, videograph this . . . and appreciate and love your age, damn it, and bow to the memory of those who went through this! Take a good look at these mugs—young, dumb, indifferent, used to all sorts of brutality—and don't turn up your noses at it, either. Your own ancestors were no better.

They saw him. Two dozen eyes who'd seen it all stared at him.

"Hey, there's a don. His Lordship's so white."

"Heh . . . Everyone knows nobles ain't used to it."

"You're supposed to give water in these cases, I hear, but the cup's chain is too short—we couldn't reach him."

"No need, the don will come around."

"I hope I get that kind . . . With that kind, you ask them a question and they answer it."

"Quiet, brothers, before His Lordship starts slashing at us. Look at all those rings . . . and the paper."

"See how he's staring at us. Let's get out of harm's way, brothers."

They moved away together, retreating to the shadows, their cautious spider eyes gleaming at him from the gloom.

That's enough of that, thought Rumata. He was about to grab some passing monk by the cassock, but then he noticed three of them at once, not scurrying around but doing their work. They were beating one of the tower's torturers with sticks, probably for negligence.

Rumata approached them. "In the name of the Lord," he said quietly, clanking the rings.

The monks lowered their sticks and took a good look. "In His name," the tallest one said.

"Now, Fathers," Rumata said, "please take me to the floor attendant."

The monks exchanged glances. The torturer nimbly crawled away and hid behind the tank. "What do you need him for?" asked the tall monk.

Rumata silently raised the paper to his face, held it there for a bit, and lowered it.

"Aha," the monk said. "So right now I'm the floor attendant."

"Excellent," said Rumata. He rolled the paper into a tube. "I'm Don Rumata. His Grace has given me Doctor Budach. Go and fetch him."

The monk stuck his hand under his hood and loudly scratched himself. "Budach?" he said meditatively. "Which one's Budach? The child molester?"

"Nah," another monk said. "The child molester—that's Rudach. He was already released last night. Father Kin unchained him himself and took him out. And I—"

"Nonsense, nonsense!" Rumata said impatiently, slapping his hip with the paper. "Budach. The king's poisoner."

"Ah," the attendant said. "I know him. But he's probably already been hanged. Brother Paca, go to twelve, take a look. Why, are you going to take him away?" he addressed Rumata.

"Naturally," said Rumata. "He's mine."

"Then hand that paper over. The paper's for the file."

Rumata gave him the paper.

The attendant turned it over in his hands, inspected the seals, and then said in admiration: "They sure can write! Don, you stand aside for a bit, we have work to do. Hey, where did he go?"

The monks started to look around, searching for the delinquent torturer. Rumata moved away. They dragged the torturer out from behind the tank, laid him down on the floor once again, and started giving him a businesslike thrashing, not being excessively cruel. Five minutes later, the dispatched monk appeared from beyond the turn, dragging a thin, completely gray-haired old man wearing dark clothes on a rope behind him.

"Here he is, your Budach!" he shouted happily from a distance. "Not hanged at all, Budach's alive, he's healthy! A bit weak, though, must have been sitting hungry for a while, I guess."

Rumata stepped toward them, tore the rope from the monk's hands, and took the noose off the old man's neck. "You're Budach of Irukan?" he asked.

"I am," the old man said, looking at him from beneath his brows.

"I'm Rumata; follow me and stay close." Rumata turned toward the monks. "In the name of the Lord," he said.

The attendant straightened his back and, lowering his stick, answered, a little out of breath, "In His name."

Rumata looked at Budach and saw that the old man was holding on to the wall and could hardly stand. "I don't feel well," he said with a sickly smile. "I apologize, noble don."

Rumata took him by the arm and led him away. When the monks were out of sight, he stopped, took a sporamin pill from the vial, and handed it to Budach. Budach looked at it quizzically. "Take it," Rumata said, "You'll immediately feel better."

Budach, still holding on to the wall, took the pill, examined it, sniffed it, raised his shaggy eyebrows, then carefully put it on his tongue and smacked his lips.

"Swallow it, swallow it," Rumata said with a smile.

"*Mm-m-m* . . ." he said. "I had assumed that I knew everything about medicines." He paused, noting his sensations. "*Mmmm!*" he said "Curious! The dried spleen of the boar Y? Although, no, the flavor isn't putrid."

"Let's go," said Rumata.

They walked along the corridor, went up the stairs, went down another corridor, and climbed another staircase. And then Rumata stopped in his tracks. A familiar deep roar was resounding through the prison arches. Somewhere in the bowels of the prison, bellowing at the top of his lungs, spouting monstrous curses, raging against God, the saints, hell, the Holy Order, Don Reba, and who knows what else, was the friend of his heart Baron Pampa don Bau de Suruga de Gutta de Arkanar. The baron got caught after all, thought Rumata with remorse. I had completely forgotten about him. And he wouldn't have forgotten about me.

Rumata hurriedly took two bracelets off his hand, put them on Doctor Budach's thin wrists, and said, "Go up, but don't go through the gates. Wait off to the side somewhere. If someone bothers you, show them the bracelets and act impudent."

Baron Pampa roared like a nuclear ship in the polar fog. The echo resounded through the arches. The people in the hallways froze, reverently listening with mouths open. Many of them were making circular motions with their thumbs, warding off the devil. Rumata rushed down two staircases, knocking the monks going the other way off their feet, laid himself a path through the crowd of graduates with his scabbards, and kicked open the door of the chamber, which was warping from the baron's roars. In the flickering torchlight he saw his friend Pampa: the mighty baron had been chained to a cross, naked and upside down. His face had darkened from the blood flow. A stooped official sat behind a crooked table, covering his ears, and the torturer, glossy with sweat and somehow resembling a dentist, was sorting through clanking instruments in an iron basin.

Rumata gently closed the door behind him, walked up to the torturer from behind, and hit him on the back of the head with the hilt of his sword. The torturer turned around, wrapped his arms around his head, and sat down in the basin. Rumata pulled his sword from its scabbard and struck the paper-covered table at which the official was sitting, cutting it in half. Everything was now in order. The torturer was sitting in the basin, hiccuping softly, and the official had very nimbly crawled away into the corner and lay down there. Rumata came up to the baron, who had been looking at him upside down with cheerful curiosity, grabbed the chains that held the baron's feet, and ripped them out of the wall with two jerks. Then he carefully put the baron's feet on the floor. The baron went silent, froze in the strange position, then gave a hard tug and freed his hands.

"Is it possible," he thundered again, rotating his bloodshot eyes, "that it's you, my noble friend? At last I've found you!"

"Yes, it's me," Rumata said. "Let's go, my friend, this is no place for you."

"Beer!" said the baron. "There was beer somewhere around here." He walked around the chamber, dragging the broken links of his chains and continuing to rumble. "I've been running around town for half the night! Goddamn it, I was told that you were arrested, and I beat up a ton of people! I was certain that I'd find you in this prison! Ah, there it is!"

He walked over to the torturer and flicked him off like dust, along with the basin. There turned out to be a barrel beneath the basin. The baron knocked the top out with his fist, lifted the barrel, and turned it upside down over himself, throwing his head back. The stream of beer rushed toward his throat with a gurgle. How lovely, thought Rumata, looking tenderly at the baron. You'd think this is an ox, a brainless ox, but he was looking for me, wanted to save me—he probably came to this prison to find me, by himself. No, there are people in this world, let it be damned . . . But how well things turned out!

Baron Pampa drained the barrel and hurled it into the corner, where the official was shaking noisily. A squeak came from that direction.

"There we go," the baron said, wiping his beard with his hand. "Now I'm ready to follow you. Is it all right that I'm naked?"

Rumata looked around, walked over to the torturer, and shook him out of his apron. "Take this for now," he said.

"You're right," the baron said, tying the apron around his loins. "It would be awkward to come to the baroness naked."

They came out of the chamber. Not a single person dared get in their way—the corridor kept emptying out for twenty paces in front of them.

"I'll destroy them all!" the baron roared. "They occupied my castle! And they stuck some Father Arima there! I don't know whose father he is, but I swear by God, his children will soon be orphans. Damn it, my friend, don't you find that they have amazingly low ceilings? My head is all scratched up."

They came out of the tower. The spy-bodyguard flashed in front their eyes and ducked back into the crowd. Rumata gave Budach the sign to follow him. The crowd by the gates parted as if split by a sword. You could hear some people shouting that an important state criminal had escaped, and others that "here he is, the Naked Devil, the famous Estorian torturer and mutilator."

The baron went out onto the middle of the square and stopped, squinting from the sunlight. They had to hurry. Rumata quickly looked around.

"My horse was around here somewhere," the baron said. "Hey, you there! A horse!"

There was a commotion at the hitching post where the Order's horses were tied up.

"Not that one!" barked the baron. "The other one—the dapple gray!"

"In the name of the Lord!" Rumata called out belatedly. He started pulling the sling with his right sword over his head.

A scared little monk in a soiled cassock brought the baron the horse.

"Give him something, Don Rumata," the baron said, climbing heavily into the saddle.

There were shouts of "Stop, stop!" by the tower. Monks were running across the square, brandishing clubs. Rumata thrust his sword at the baron.

"Hurry up, Baron," he said.

"Yes," said Pampa. "I must hurry. This Arima will plunder my cellar. I'm waiting for you tomorrow or the day after, my friend. What should I convey to the baroness?"

"Kiss her hand for me," Rumata said. The monks were already very close. "Faster, faster, Baron!"

"But you are safe?" the baron asked anxiously.

"Yes, damn it, yes! Onward!"

The baron urged his horse into a gallop, aiming right at the crowd of monks. Someone fell down and rolled, someone squealed, there was a cloud of dust and a clatter of hooves on the flagstones—and the baron was gone. Rumata was looking into the alley where some passersby who had been knocked off their feet were sitting, dazedly shaking their heads, when an insinuating voice said in his ear, "My noble don, don't you think that you're allowing yourself too much?"

Rumata turned around. Don Reba, smiling somewhat tensely, was looking narrowly at him.

"Too much?" Rumata repeated. "I don't know the meaning of these words—'too much.'" He suddenly remembered Don Sera. "And anyway, I see no reason why one noble don can't help another one in trouble."

Riders with their pikes at the ready galloped past them heavily—in pursuit. Something changed in Don Reba's face. "All right," he said. "Let's not talk about that . . . Oh, I see the highly learned Doctor Budach is here. You look wonderful, Doctor. I'm going to have to inspect my prison. State criminals, even ones who have been released, shouldn't walk out of prison—they should be carried out."

Doctor Budach lunged at Don Reba, as if blinded by hatred. Rumata quickly stood between them. "By the way, Don Reba," he said, "what's your opinion of Father Arima?"

"Father Arima?" Don Reba raised his eyebrows high. "An excellent soldier. Occupies a prominent position in my diocese. Why, what about him?"

"As a loyal servant of Your Grace," Rumata said with an acute malicious joy, bowing, "I hasten to inform you that you should consider this prominent position vacant."

"But why?"

Rumata looked into the alley, where the yellow dust hadn't yet dissipated. Don Reba also looked in that direction. A worried expression appeared on his face.

It was long after midday when Kira invited her noble lord and his highly learned friend to the table. Doctor Budach, after bathing, changing into clean clothes, and carefully shaving, looked very impressive. His movements turned out to be slow and dignified; his intelligent gray eyes peered out benevolently and even indulgently. First of all, he apologized to Rumata about his outburst at the square. "But you have to understand," he said. "This is a terrible man. A werewolf who only came into this world by an oversight of God. I'm a doctor, but I'm not ashamed to admit that if I had the chance I would have gladly put him to death. I have heard that the king was poisoned. And now I understand what he was poisoned with." Rumata pricked up his ears. "This Reba showed up in my chamber and demanded that I make up a poison for him that worked in the course of a few hours. Naturally, I refused. He threatened me with torture—I laughed in his face. Then the villain called to the torturers, and they brought in a dozen boys and girls no older than ten years of age from the street. He lined them up in front of me, opened my potion bag, and declared that he would try all the potions on those children in a row until he found the right one. That's how the king was poisoned, Don Rumata."

Budach's lips began to twitch, but he managed to control himself. Rumata, tactfully turning away, nodded. I understand, he thought. I understand everything. The king wouldn't have even taken a pickle from his minister's hands. So the scoundrel snuck in some charlatan to the king, promising him the title of healer for curing the king. And I understand why Reba was so thrilled when I exposed him in the king's bedchamber: it's hard to think of a more convenient way to sneak in the false Budach to the king. All the responsibility fell on Rumata of Estor, the Irukanian spy and conspirator. We're babes in arms, he thought. The Institute should introduce a course dealing specifically with feudal intrigue. And proficiency should be measured in rebas. Better yet, in decirebas. Although even that's too much.

Apparently, Doctor Budach was very hungry. However, he gently but firmly refused animal products and devoted his attention only to the salads and the tarts with jam. He drank a glass of the Estorian wine; his eyes brightened and a healthy glow appeared on his cheeks. Rumata couldn't eat. Crimson torches crackled and smoked in front of his eyes, everything smelled of burnt meat, and there was a lump in his throat the size of a fist. So while he waited for his guest to eat his fill, he stood by the window, keeping the conversation polite, quiet, and unhurried, so as not to interfere with his guest's chewing.

The city was gradually coming to life. People appeared on the street, voices became louder and louder, hammers were pounding and wood was cracking—pagan images were being knocked off the roofs and walls. A bald, fat shopkeeper was pushing a cart with a barrel, off to sell beer at the square for two coins a cup. The residents were adapting. In the entrance across the way, the little spy-bodyguard was picking his nose and chatting with the skinny mistress of the house. Then wagons filled all the way up to the second story drove by the windows. At first, Rumata didn't understand what these wagons were, then he saw the blue and black arms and legs sticking out from beneath the burlap and hurriedly walked over to the table.

"The essence of man," Budach said, chewing slowly, "lies in his astonishing ability to get used to anything. There's nothing in nature that man could not learn to live with. Neither horse nor dog nor mouse has this property. Probably God, as he was creating man, guessed the torments he was condemning him to and gave him an enormous reserve of strength and patience. It is difficult to say whether this is good or bad. If man didn't have such patience and endurance, all good people would have long since perished, and only the wicked and soulless would be left in this world. On the other hand, the habit of enduring and adapting turns people into dumb beasts, who differ from the animals in nothing except anatomy, and who only exceed them in helplessness. And each new day gives rise to a new horror of evil and violence."

Rumata looked over at Kira. She sat across from Budach and listened without looking away, propping up her cheek on her little fist. Her eyes were sad; she was clearly very sorry for humankind. "You're probably right, honorable Budach," said Rumata. "But take me, for example. Here I am, a simple noble don." Budach's high forehead creased, his eyes opened wide with surprise and merriment. "I have tremendous love for learned men—that is, gentility of the soul. And I cannot figure out why you, the keepers and only holders of high knowledge, are so hopelessly passive. Why do you meekly allow yourself to be despised, thrown in jails, burned at the stake? Why do you separate the meaning of your life, the pursuit of knowledge—from the practical requirements of life, the struggle against evil?"

Budach pushed away the empty plate of tarts. "You ask strange questions, Don Rumata," he said. "It's funny, I was asked the same questions by Don Gug, the chamberlain of our duke. Are you acquainted with him? I thought so. The struggle against evil! But what is evil? Everyone is free to understand this in his own way. For us scholars, evil is in ignorance, but the church teaches that ignorance is a blessing and that all evil comes from knowledge. For the plowman evil is taxes and drought, and for the bread-seller droughts are good. For a slave, evil is a drunk and cruel master; for a craftsman, a greedy moneylender. So what is this evil against which we must struggle, Don Rumata?" He looked sadly at his listeners. "Evil is ineradicable. No man is able to decrease its quantity in the world. He can improve his own fate somewhat, but it is always at the expense of the fate of others. And there will always be kings, some more cruel and some less, and barons, some more violent and some less, and there will always be the ignorant masses, who admire their oppressors and loathe their liberators. And it's all because a slave has a much better understanding of his master, however brutal, than his liberator, for each slave can easily imagine himself in his master's place, but few can imagine themselves in the place of a selfless liberator. That's how people are, Don Rumata, and that's how our world is."

"The world is constantly changing, Doctor Budach," said Rumata. "We know of a time when there were no kings."

"The world cannot keep changing forever," Budach disagreed, "for nothing lasts forever, even change. We don't know the laws of perfection, but perfection will be achieved sooner or later. Consider, for example, the order of our society. How pleasing to the eye is this precise, geometrically correct system! At the bottom are the peasants and artisans, above them is the gentry, then comes the clergy, and then, finally, the king. What careful planning, what stability, what harmonious order! Why would we want to change this polished crystal, made by the hands of the jeweler in the sky? No structure is more stable than the pyramid—any knowledgeable architect will tell you that." He raised a lecturing finger. "Grain spilled from a sack doesn't settle in an even layer, but forms a so-called conical pyramid. Each seed clings to the next, in an effort not to roll down. So it is with humanity. If it wants to be an entity of its own, people must cling to one another, inevitably forming a pyramid."

"Do you sincerely consider this world perfect?" Rumata asked with surprise. "After meeting Don Reba, after prison . . ."

"My young friend, yes, of course! There's much I don't like in the world, much I would like to be different. But what can one do? Perfection looks different in the eyes of a higher power than in mine. There is no sense in a tree lamenting that it cannot move, though it would probably be glad to flee from the lumberjack's ax."

"And what if you could change the divine decrees?"

"Only a higher power is capable of this."

"But still, imagine that you're God . . ."

Budach laughed. "If I could imagine myself as God, I'd become him!"

"Well, what if you had the chance to advise God?"

"You have a rich imagination," Budach said with pleasure. "That's good! Are you literate? Wonderful! I would enjoy working with you."

"You flatter me . . . Still, what advice would you give to the Almighty? What, in your opinion, should the Almighty do, in order for you to say, 'Now the world is good and kind'?"

Budach, smiling approvingly, leaned back in his chair and folded his hands on his stomach. Kira was looking at him eagerly. "All right," he said, "if you wish. I'd tell the Almighty: 'Creator, I don't know your plans. Maybe you never intended to make people kind and happy. Then start wishing it! It would be so easy to achieve. Give people plenty of bread, meat, and wine, give them clothing and shelter. Let hunger and need disappear, and with them, all that divides people would be gone too.'"

"Is that it?" Rumata asked.

"You think that is not enough?"

Rumata shook his head. "God would answer you: 'This would not benefit man. For the strong of your world would take from the weak that which I have given them, and the weak would still remain poor.'"

"I would ask God to shield the weak. 'Enlighten the cruel princes,' I would say."

"Cruelty is power. Having lost their cruelty, the princes would lose their power, and other cruel men would replace them."

Budach stopped smiling. "Punish the cruel," he said firmly, "so that it would become unseemly for the strong to be cruel to the weak."

"Man is born weak. He becomes strong when there's no one stronger around him. When the cruel of the strong will be punished, their place will be taken by the strongest of the weak. Who will also be cruel. Then everyone will have to be chastised, and this I do not desire."

"You know best, Almighty. Then just make it so that people have all they need, and do not take away from each other that which you gave them."

"Even this will not benefit people," Rumata sighed, "for when they get everything for free, without working for it, from my hands, they will forget how to work, lose their zest for life, and will become my pets, whom I will henceforth be forced to feed and clothe for all eternity."

"Don't give it all at once!" Budach said fervently. "Give it to them gradually, little by little!"

"People will gradually take what they need themselves."

Budach gave an awkward laugh. "Yes, I see, it's not that simple," he said. "Somehow I've never thought about these things before. We seem to have considered everything. Although," he leaned forward, "here's another possibility. Make it so that people love work and knowledge more than anything, so that work and knowledge are the only meanings of their existence!"

Yes, that's another thing we were planning to try, thought Rumata. Mass hypnoinduction, positive remoralization. Hypnoemitters on three equatorial satellites. "I could do this, too," he said. "But should we deprive mankind of its history? Should we exchange one mankind for another? Would it not be the same thing as wiping mankind off the face of the planet and creating a new mankind in its place?"

Budach, crinkling his brow, pondered silently. Rumata waited. The melancholy sound of creaking wagons sounded outside the window again. Budach said quietly, "Then, Lord, wipe us off the face of the planet and create us anew in a more perfect form . . . Or, even better, leave us be and let us go our own way."

"My heart is full of pity," Rumata said slowly. "I cannot do that."

And then he saw Kira's eyes. She was looking at him with horror and hope.

# Chapter 9

having put Budach down to sleep before his long journey, Rumata headed to his study. The effects of the sporamin were wearing off; he again felt tired and shattered, his bruises ached, and his rope-mangled wrists were swelling again. I should get some sleep, he thought. I should definitely get some sleep. And I should contact Don Condor. And I should contact the patrol airship, let them report to the Base. And I need to think about what we should do next, and whether we can do anything, and how to act if there's nothing else to do.

A black-robed monk with his hood pulled low over his eyes was sitting in the study behind the desk, hunching in the chair, hands resting on the high armrests. Clever, thought Rumata. "Who are you?" he asked wearily. "Who let you in?"

"Good afternoon, noble Don Rumata," the monk said, throwing back his hood.

Rumata shook his head. "Clever!" he said. "Good afternoon, worthy Arata. Why are you here? What happened?"

"Everything is as usual," said Arata. "The army has dispersed, they are all dividing up the land, no one wants to go south. The duke is rounding up the ones he hasn't killed yet and will soon hang my peasants upside down along the Estorian tract. Everything is as usual," he repeated.

"I understand," Rumata said.

He collapsed onto the couch, put his hands behind his head, and started looking at Arata. Twenty years ago, when Anton was building model weapons and playing William Tell, this man was called Arata the Beautiful, and he was then probably completely different from how he was now.

The magnificent high forehead of Arata the Beautiful didn't have that ugly purple brand—it got there after the revolt of the Soanian shipwrights, when three thousand naked slave craftsmen, who had been driven to the Soanian shipyards from all parts of the empire and tormented until they had almost lost their instinct of self-preservation, had broken out of the port one stormy night. They rolled through Soan, leaving corpses and fires behind them, and were met in the outlying districts by the imperial infantry, encased in armor.

And of course, Arata the Beautiful had both his eyes. His right eye had popped out of its socket after a heavy strike by a baronial mace when the peasant army, twenty thousand strong, that had been chasing the baronial militias across the metropole collided in an open field with an Imperial Guard regiment five thousand strong and was cut in half with lightning speed, surrounded, and trampled under the spiked hooves of the military camels.

And Arata the Beautiful had probably been as straight as a pillar. He earned the hump and the new nickname after the Villanian War in the Duchy of Uban two seas from here. This was when, after seven years of plague and drought, four hundred thousand living skeletons massacred the noblemen with their pitchforks and poles and laid siege to the Duke of Uban—and the duke, whose weak mind had been sharpened by unbearable terror, pardoned his subjects, lowered the price of alcoholic beverages fivefold, and promised to free them all. And Arata, already seeing that everything was finished, pleaded, demanded, and implored them not to succumb to the deception but was captured by the leaders, who wanted to leave well enough alone, then beaten with iron rods and left for dead in a cesspool.

The massive iron ring on his right wrist, on the other hand, was probably already there when he was still called Beautiful. The ring had been chained to an oar of a pirate galley, but Arata broke the chain, hit Captain Egu the Seducer in the temple with it, commandeered the ship and then the entire pirate armada, and tried to create a free republic on the water. And this undertaking ended as a bloody drunken disgrace, because Arata had been young, didn't know how to hate, and believed that freedom alone would be enough to turn a slave into a god.

This was a professional rebel, an avenger by divine grace, a figure quite rare in medieval societies. Such pikes are occasionally produced by historical evolution and released into social deep waters, so that the fat carps feeding on the bottom plankton can't doze . . . Arata was the only person here for whom Rumata felt neither hatred nor pity, and in his earthling's dreams—the feverish dreams of a man who had lived for five years surrounded by stench and blood—he often imagined himself as such an Arata, having received the high right to murder the murderers, torture the torturers, and betray the traitors for having passed through all the hells of the universe.

"Sometimes I think," said Arata, "that we're all powerless. I'm the eternal rebel leader, and I know that my power comes from my extraordinary survivability. But this power doesn't change my powerlessness. My victories magically turn into defeats. My friends in battle turn to enemies—the most courageous ones flee, the most loyal ones turn traitor or die. And I have nothing but my bare hands, and I can't reach the gilded idols behind fortified walls with my bare hands."

"How did you get to Arkanar?" Rumata asked.

"I sailed with the monks."

"Have you gone insane? You're so recognizable."

"But not in a crowd of monks. Half of the officers of the Order are simpleminded, or maimed like me. Cripples are pleasing to the Lord." He chuckled, looking Rumata in the face.

"And what do you intend to do?" Rumata asked, lowering his eyes.

"The usual. I know what the Holy Order is; in less than a year, the people of Arkanar will start pouring out of their holes with axes to fight in the street. And I will lead them, so that they fight those they should, instead of each other and everyone around them."

"Will you need money?" Rumata asked.

"Yes, as usual. And weapons." He paused, then said silkily, "Don Rumata, do you remember how disappointed I was when I found out who you are? I hate priests, and it was very bitter to me that their false fairy tales turned out to be true. But a poor rebel must draw benefit from whatever circumstances he encounters. The priests say that the gods have lightning. Don Rumata, I really need lightning to break down the fortified walls."

Rumata gave a deep sigh. After the miraculous helicopter rescue, Arata had insisted on an explanation. Rumata tried to explain about himself; he even pointed out Earth's sun in the night sky—a tiny, barely visible star. But the rebel only understood one thing: the damned priests were right and there were gods living behind the firmament who were all-good and all-powerful. And since then, he steered each of his conversations with Rumata to one thing: God, since you exist, give me your power, for it is the best thing that you can do.

And each time Rumata kept quiet or changed the subject.

"Don Rumata," the rebel asked, "why don't you want to help us?"

"Wait a minute," Rumata said. "I beg your pardon, but I would like to know how you got into the house."

"That doesn't matter. No one but me knows the way. Don't try to evade the question, Don Rumata. Why don't you want to give us your power?"

"Let's not talk about it."

"No, we will talk about it. I didn't summon you. I've never prayed to anyone. You came to me yourself. Or did you just decide to have some fun?"

It's hard to be a god, thought Rumata. He said patiently, "You wouldn't understand. I tried to explain to you twenty times that I'm not a god—you never believe me. And you wouldn't believe me if I told you why I can't help you with weapons."

"You have lightning?"

"I can't give you lightning."

"I've already heard that twenty times," said Arata. "Now I want to know: why?"

"I repeat, you wouldn't understand."

"Try me."

"What do you plan to do with the lightning?"

"I will incinerate every single one of the gilded bastards like bugs, destroying their whole damn race until the twelfth generation. I'll wipe their fortresses off the face of the earth. I'll incinerate their armies and all who defend and support them. You don't need to worry—your lightning will only be used for good, and when only the freed slaves are left on the earth and peace reigns, I will give you back your lightning and never ask you for it again."

Arata stopped, breathing heavily. His face had turned dark from the rush of blood. He probably already saw the duchies and kingdoms engulfed in flames, and the piles of charred bodies amongst the ruins, and the huge armies of victors, ecstatically roaring, "Freedom! Freedom!"

"No," said Rumata, "I will not give you lightning. It would be a mistake. Try to believe me. I can see further than you." Arata was listening, his head sunk on his chest. Rumata clenched his hand. "I will only give you one reason. It pales in comparison with the primary reason, but you will actually understand it. You are very good at surviving, worthy Arata, but you too are mortal; and if you die, if the lightning passes into other hands that are not as pure as yours, then I shudder to even think of the consequences."

They were silent for a long time. Then Rumata got a pitcher of Estorian wine and some food from the cellar and put it in front of his guest. Arata, without lifting his eyes, started to break the bread and drink the wine. Rumata felt a strange sense of painful ambivalence. He knew that he was right, yet in some strange way, this rightness lowered him before Arata. Arata was clearly somehow superior to him— and not only to him but to all those who had come to this planet uninvited and who, full of helpless pity, watched the tumultuous bustling of its life from the rarefied heights of dry hypotheses and alien morality. And for the first time Rumata thought, There is no gain without a loss. We're infinitely stronger than Arata in our kingdom of good and infinitely weaker than Arata in his kingdom of evil.

"You shouldn't have come down from the sky," Arata said suddenly. "Go back to where you came from. You're only doing us harm."

"That's not so," Rumata said gently. "At any rate, we do not harm anyone."

"No, you do. You inspire groundless hopes."

"In whom?"

"In me. You have weakened my will, Don Rumata. I used to only rely on myself, and now you've made me feel your power behind me. I used to lead every battle as if it were my last. And now I've noticed that I save myself for other battles, which will be decisive because you will stand beside me. Leave this place, Don Rumata. Go back to the sky and never come back. Either give us your lightning, or at least your iron bird, or even simply draw your swords and lead us."

Arata stopped talking and reached for the bread again. Rumata kept looking at his fingers, which no longer had any nails. The nails had been torn out with a special device two years ago by Don Reba himself. You still don't know everything, thought Rumata. You still believe that you are the only one doomed to be defeated. You still don't know how hopeless your cause itself is. You still don't know that the enemy isn't so much outside your soldiers as within them. You might still overthrow the Order—the wave of peasant rebellion will throw you onto the throne of Arkanar, you will level the castles of the noblemen, you'll drown the barons in the Strait, and the insurgents will honor you as the great liberator. And you will be kind and wise—the only kind and wise person in your kingdom. And along the way, you will begin to give away land to your associates, and what will your associates do with land without serfs? And the wheel will start spinning the other direction. And you'll be lucky if you manage to pass away before the new counts and barons emerge out of yesterday's loyal fighters. That has already happened, my worthy Arata, both on Earth and on this planet.

"No response?" asked Arata. He pushed his plate away and swept the crumbs off the table with the sleeve of his cassock. "Once I had a friend," he said. "You've probably heard of him—Waga the Wheel. We had begun together. Then he became a bandit, the king of the night. I didn't forgive him for his treason, and he knew it. He had helped me a lot—out of fear and self-interest—but he never did want to come back. He had his own goals. Two years ago his people gave me up to Don Reba." He looked at his fingers and curled them into a fist. "And today I found him in the Port of Arkanar. In our business, there's no such thing as half a friend. Half a friend—that's always half an enemy." He got up and pulled the hood over his eyes. "Is the gold in its usual place, Don Rumata?"

"Yes," Rumata said slowly, "it's in its usual place."

"Then I will go. Thank you, Don Rumata."

He silently walked through the study and disappeared through the door. The bolt clanged softly in the entrance hall below.

Here's one more thing to worry about, thought Rumata. How in the world did he get into the house?

# Chapter 10

The Drunken Lair was relatively clean. The floor was carefully swept, the table was scrubbed to whiteness, and there were bundles of forest grass and twigs in the corner for fragrance. Father Cabani was primly sitting on a bench in the corner, sober and quiet, his clean hands folded in his lap. As they waited for Budach to fall asleep, they talked about nothing in particular. Budach, sitting at the table next to Rumata, listened to the mindless chatter of the noble dons with a benevolent smile and from time to time would give a start, dozing off. His hollow cheeks were burning from a vast dose of tetraluminal that had been discreetly mixed into his drink. The old man was very excited and was having trouble falling asleep. The impatient Don Gug was bending and unbending a camel shoe underneath the table, managing, however, to keep an expression of cheerful ease on his face. Rumata was crumbling bread and watching with tired interest as Don Condor slowly filled with bile: the Keeper of the Great Seals was nervous, because he was late for the emergency night session of the Conference of the Twelve Merchants dedicated to the revolution in Arkanar, at which he was supposed to preside.

"My noble friends!" Doctor Budach finally said in a ringing voice, stood up, and fell on Rumata.

Rumata gently put an arm around his shoulders.

"Is he done?" asked Don Condor.

"He won't wake up until the morning," Rumata said. He lifted Budach in his arms and carried him to Father Cabani's bed.

Father Cabani said enviously, "So the doctor can indulge, huh, and Father Cabani can't? It's bad for him, huh? That's not fair!"

"I have a quarter of an hour," Don Condor said in Russian.

"I'll only need five minutes," answered Rumata, barely managing to control his irritation. "I've told you so much about it before that I might only need a minute. In full accordance with the basis theory of feudalism," he furiously looked Don Condor in the eye, "this commonplace rebellion of the citizens against the barony," he shifted his gaze to Don Gug, "turned into a provocative intrigue by the Holy Order and resulted in the transformation of Arkanar into a base of feudal-fascist aggression. We've been racking our brains, vainly trying to squeeze the complicated, contradictory, enigmatic figure of our eagle Don Reba into the ranks of Richelieu, Necker, Tokugawa Ieyasu, and Monck, and he turned out to be a petty hoodlum and an idiot! He betrayed and sold out everyone he could, got tangled up in his own schemes, got scared to death, and ran to the Holy Order to be saved. In half a year he'll be slaughtered, and the Order will remain. The consequences of this for the Land Beyond the Strait, and then for the empire as a whole, I shudder to think about. In any case, the entire twenty years of work within the empire has gone down the drain. There will be no room to maneuver under the Holy Order. Budach is probably the last man I'll save. There will be no one left. I'm done."

Don Gug finally broke the camel shoe and threw the halves into a corner. "Yes, we dropped the ball," he said. "Maybe it's not that bad, Anton?"

Rumata just looked at him.

"You should have removed Don Reba," Don Condor said suddenly.

"What do you mean, 'removed'?"

Don Condor's face broke out in red spots. "Physically!" he said sharply.

Rumata sat down. "You mean killed?"

"Yes. Yes! *Yes!* Killed! Kidnapped! Replaced! Imprisoned! You should have acted. Not sought the advice of two idiots who didn't understand a damn thing about what was going on."

"I didn't understand a damn thing either."

"At least you felt something."

Everyone was silent.

"Was it like the Barkan massacre?" Don Condor asked in a low voice, looking to the side.

"Yes, approximately. But more organized."

Don Condor bit his lip. "It's now too late to remove him?" he asked.

"It's pointless," said Rumata. "First of all, he'll be removed without us, and second of all, it's not even necessary. He, at least, is under my control."

"How so?"

"He's afraid of me. He guesses that there's power behind me. He's already even offered to cooperate."

"Yes?" Don Condor grumbled. "Then there's no need."

Don Gug asked, stammering a little, "Come on, comrades, are you serious?"

"About what?" asked Don Condor.

"Well, all of this. Killing, physically removing . . . Come on, have you gone insane?"

"The noble don has been struck in the heel," Rumata said very quietly.

Don Condor said slowly and emphatically, "Extraordinary circumstances call for extraordinary measures."

Don Gug, moving his lips, looked back and forth between them. "D-Do you . . . Do you know what this could come to?" he asked. "D-Do you understand what this could come to, huh?"

"Calm down, please," Don Condor said. "Nothing is going to happen. Enough about that for now. What are we going to do about the Order? I propose a blockade of the Arkanarian region. Your opinion, comrades? And be quick, I'm in a hurry."

"I have no opinion yet," Rumata insisted. "And there's no way Pashka has one. We need to get advice from the Base. We need to look around. Let's meet in a week and decide."

"Agreed," Don Condor said and got up. "Let's go."

Rumata slung Budach over his shoulder and went out of the hut. Don Condor was shining a flashlight for him. They approached the helicopter, and Rumata laid Budach on the backseat. Don Condor, rattling his sword and getting tangled in his cloak, climbed into the pilot's seat.

"Will you drop me off at home?" Rumata asked. "I want to finally get some sleep."

"I'll drop you off," grumbled Don Condor. "Just be quick, please."

"I'll be right back," Rumata said. He ran back into the hut.

Don Gug was still sitting at the table, staring fixedly in front of himself and rubbing his chin. Father Cabani was standing next to him, saying, "That's how it always is, my friend. You try to make things better and they just get worse."

Rumata scooped up the swords and slings into his arms. "Bye, Pashka," he said. "Don't get upset, we're all just tired and irritated."

Don Gug shook his head. "Be careful, Anton," he said. "Oh, be careful! I'm not talking about Uncle Sasha out there; he's been here a long time, it's not our place to teach him. But you . . ."

"I just want to sleep," said Rumata. "Father Cabani, could you be so good as to take my horses to Baron Pampa? I'll be there in a day or two."

Propeller blades whirred softly outside. Rumata waved and ran out of the hut. The bright glare of the helicopter's headlights made the thickets of giant ferns and white tree trunks look strange and eerie. Rumata clambered into the cabin and slammed the door.

The cabin smelled of ozone, organic paneling, and cologne. Don Condor lifted the machine and guided it confidently over the Arkanarian road. I couldn't do that now, thought Rumata with a touch of envy. Old Budach was peacefully smacking his lips in his sleep behind them.

"Anton," Don Condor said, "I wouldn't . . . uh . . . want to be tactless, and don't think that I . . . uh . . . am interfering in your private affairs."

"I'm listening," Rumata said. He immediately guessed what he was going to say.

"We're all operatives," said Don Condor. "And all that is precious to us must be either far away on Earth or inside us. So that no one can take it away and use it as a hostage."

"You're talking about Kira?" Rumata asked.

"Yes, my boy. If all I know about Don Reba is true, keeping him under control is a difficult and dangerous task. You see what I'm trying to say."

"Yes, I see," Rumata said. "I'll try to think of something."

They were lying in the dark, holding hands. The city was quiet, except for the horses that would occasionally thrash and whinny angrily somewhere nearby. From time to time, Rumata would doze off and then immediately wake up again, because Kira would hold her breath—in his sleep, he would squeeze her hand very hard.

"You probably really want to sleep," Kira said in a whisper. "You should sleep."

"No, no, tell me, I'm listening."

"You keep falling asleep."

"I'm still listening. I feel very tired, it's true, but I miss you even more. I'm sorry to sleep. You tell me, I'm very interested."

She gratefully rubbed her nose against his shoulder and kissed his cheek and started telling him again about the neighbor's boy who came that night from her father. Her father was laid up. He had been kicked out of his office and beaten severely with sticks as a farewell. Lately he hadn't been eating anything at all, only drinking—he'd become all blue and shaky. The boy also said that her brother had turned up—wounded, but cheerful and drunk, in a new uniform. He gave money to his father, drank with him, and was once again threatening that his boys would roll over everyone. He was now a lieutenant in some special squad; he'd taken the oath of allegiance to the Order and was about to be ordained. Father asked that she not come home under any circumstances. Her brother was threatening to settle scores with her for getting mixed up with a noble, the red-haired bitch.

Yes, thought Rumata, she definitely shouldn't go home. And it's absolutely certain that she can't stay here, either. If anything happens to her . . . He imagined something bad happening to her and felt himself turn to stone.

"Are you asleep?" Kira asked.

He woke up and opened his hand. "No, no . . . And what else did you do?"

"And I also tidied up your rooms. It was really a mess in here. I found one book, Father Gur's work. The one that's about a noble prince who fell in love with a beautiful but wild girl from the other side of the mountains. She was completely wild and thought that he was God, but she still really loved him. Then they were separated, and she died of grief."

"It's a wonderful book," said Rumata.

"I even cried. I kept feeling that it was about you and me."

"Yes, it's about you and me. And just about any people who love each other. Only we won't be separated."

You'd be safest on Earth, he thought. But how would you manage without me? And how will I manage here alone? I could ask Anka to be a friend to you there. But how will I manage here without you? No, we will fly to Earth together. I'll pilot the ship myself, and you will sit next to me, and I'll explain everything to you. So you won't be afraid of anything. So you'll never regret your terrible home. Because this is not your home. Because your home has rejected you. Because you were born a thousand years ahead of your time. Kind, loyal, unselfish, self-sacrificing. Those like you have been born in every age throughout the bloody histories of our planets. Bright, pure souls who don't know hatred, who reject cruelty. Victims. Pointless victims. Much more pointless than Gur the Storyteller or Galileo. Because those like you aren't even fighters. To be a fighter, you must know how to hate, and that is precisely what you don't know how to do. Just like us nowadays . . .

Rumata dozed off again and immediately saw Kira standing on the flat roof of the Council with a degravitator on her belt, and a cheerful sardonic Anka impatiently pushing her into the mile-deep abyss.

"Rumata," Kira said, "I'm afraid."

"Of what, little one?"

"You just keep being silent. I'm scared."

Rumata pulled her close. "All right," he said. "Now I will talk, and you will listen carefully to me. Far, far away, on the other side of the saiva, there is a formidable, impregnable castle. In this castle lives the merry, kind, and funny Baron Pampa, the kindest baron in Arkanar. He has a wife, a beautiful, loving woman, who really loves Pampa sober and can't stand Pampa drunk . . ."

He paused, listening. He heard the clatter of numerous hooves along the street and the noisy breathing of many men and horses. "This the place?" asked a coarse voice at the window. "Seems to be." "*Stop!*" Heels clattered on the front steps and several fists immediately started rapping on the door. Kira flinched and clung to Rumata.

"Wait, little one," he said, throwing back the blanket.

"They've come for me," Kira said in a whisper. "I knew it!"

Rumata freed himself from Kira's arms with difficulty and ran to the window. "In the name of the Lord!" roared below. "Open up! If we have to break in, you'll be sorry!" Rumata pulled back the curtain, and the room was flooded with the familiar dancing torchlight. There were numerous riders outside—sullen men in black with pointed hoods.

Rumata looked down for a couple of seconds, then examined the window frame. As was customary here, the frame had been firmly embedded in the window opening. Rumata groped for his sword in the dark and smashed the glass with the hilt. Shards of glass tinkled down. "Hey, you!" he barked. "Tired of being alive?"

The banging on the door stopped.

"They always mess things up," someone said softly downstairs. "The master's at home."

"What's that matter to us?"

"It matters because he's the best swordsman in the world."

"And they also said that he left and won't come back till morning."

"Scared?"

"We're not scared, except there are no orders about him. If we have to kill him . . ."

"We'll tie him up. Maim him and tie him up. Hey, who has the crossbows?"

"As long as he doesn't maim us . . ."

"Nah, he won't maim us. Everyone knows he's taken a vow not to kill."

"I'll massacre you like dogs," Rumata said in a terrible voice.

Kira was clinging to his back. He could hear the wild beating of her heart. Someone downstairs ordered in a raspy voice, "Break down the door, brothers! In the name of the Lord!" Rumata turned around and looked at Kira's face. She was looking at him with horror and hope, like earlier. Reflections of torches danced in her tearless eyes.

"Come on, little one," he said tenderly. "Are you scared? Are you actually scared of this trash? Go get dressed. We have nothing else to do here." He hurriedly pulled on the metalstrom armor. "I'll drive them away, and we'll leave. We'll leave for Pampa's."

She was standing by the window, looking down. Red flashes ran across her face. Rumata felt a pang in his heart from pity and tenderness. I'll drive them away like dogs, he thought. He bent over, looking for his second sword, and when he stood up again, Kira was no longer standing by the window. She was slowly sinking to the floor, clutching the curtain.

"Kira!" he cried.

One crossbow bolt had pierced her throat. Another was sticking out of her chest. He lifted her in his arms and carried her to the bed. "Kira . . ." he called. She sobbed and stretched out. "Kira . . ." he said. She didn't answer. He stood over her for a bit, then picked up his swords, slowly descended the stairs, and started waiting for the door to fall . . .

# Epilogue

"And then?" Anka asked.

Pashka looked away, slapped his knee a few times, bent down, and reached for the wild strawberries by his feet. Anka waited. "Then . . ." he muttered. "No one really knows what happened then, Anka. He left the transmitter at home, and when the house started burning, the patrol airship realized that something was wrong and they immediately landed in Arkanar. They dropped grenades of sleeping gas on the city just in case. The house had almost burned down. At first they were taken aback, weren't sure where to look for him, but then they saw . . ." He looked uncomfortable. "Anyway, it was obvious which way he went." Pashka stopped talking and started tossing berries into his mouth one by one.

"Well?" Anka said very quietly.

"They came to the palace. That's where they found him."

"How did they find him?"

"Well . . . he was asleep. And everyone around him . . . they were also . . . lying down. Some were asleep and some, well . . . They found Don Reba there too." Pashka took a quick look at Anka and averted his eyes again. "They took him away—I mean Anton—brought him to the Base. You see, Anka, he hasn't told us anything about it. He doesn't talk much at all anymore."

Anka sat very pale and upright and looked over Pashka's head at the meadow by the little house. Pine trees were rustling, swaying gently. Puffy clouds slowly drifted through the blue sky. "And what happened to the girl?" she asked.

"I don't know," Pashka said harshly.

"Listen, Pasha," said Anka. "Maybe I shouldn't have come here."

"No, don't be silly! I think he'll be happy to see you."

"And I keep thinking that he's hiding somewhere in the bushes, looking at us and waiting for me to leave."

Pashka chuckled. "No way," he said. "Anton wouldn't sit in bushes. He's probably fishing somewhere, as usual."

"And how is he with you?"

"He isn't anything. He tolerates me. But it's different with you."

They were quiet.

"Anka," Pashka said. "Do you remember the anisotropic highway?"

Anka frowned. "What highway?"

"Anisotropic. The one with the do-not-enter sign. Remember, the three of us went there?"

"I remember. It was Anton who said that it was anisotropic."

"That was the time Anton went through the sign, and when he came back, he said that he found a blown-up bridge and the skeleton of a fascist chained to a machine gun."

"I don't remember that," said Anka. "So what?"

"I often think about that highway nowadays," said Pashka. "Like there's some connection. The highway was anisotropic, like history. You weren't supposed to go back. But he did go back. And stumbled on a chained skeleton."

"I don't understand you. What does the chained skeleton have to do with it?"

"I don't know," Pashka admitted. "It just makes sense to me."

Anka said, "Don't let him think too much. You should always talk to him about something. Any kind of nonsense. So he'll argue with you."

Pashka sighed. "I know that. Except what does he care about my nonsense? He'll listen, smile, and say, 'Why don't you just sit here, Pasha? I'll go wander.' And off he goes. And I sit there. At first, I was discreetly following him, like an idiot, but now I just sit and wait. But if you—"

Anka suddenly stood up. Pashka looked around and also stood up. Anka watched, holding her breath, as Anton walked toward them across the clearing—huge, broad, with a pale, untanned face. He hadn't changed much; he had always been a bit gloomy.

She walked toward him.

"Anka," he said tenderly. "Anka, my friend . . ."

He stretched his huge hands toward her. She timidly reached for him and immediately shrank back. On his fingers . . .

But it wasn't blood—only strawberry juice.

# Afterword

by Boris Strugatsky

Can this novel be considered a work about a "bright future"? To some extent, definitely. But only to a very small extent.

As a matter of fact, while my brother and I worked on it, it underwent substantial changes. It began in the planning stages as a fun adventure story in the spirit of *The Three Musketeers*, as indicated in this excerpt from one of my brother's letters:

> 01/02/62—AS: . . . I'm sorry, but I inserted *Seventh Heaven* [into the Detgiz (an acronym for the State Publishing House for Children's Literature) plan for 1964], the novel about our spy on the feudal alien planet with two kinds of intelligent creatures. I've sketched out a plan, it's going to be an exciting story, might be very funny, full of jokes and adventures, with pirates, conquistadores and so on, maybe even the Inquisition. . . .

The actual idea of "our spy on an alien planet" had emerged back when we were writing *Escape Attempt*. That book briefly mentions a certain Benny Durov, who was exactly such a spy on the planet Tagora. The idea flashed across our minds; we didn't have the time for it, but it didn't vanish without a trace. Now it was its turn, although we still didn't fully understand all the opportunities and perspectives that would arise here.

The title *Seventh Heaven* had been taken away from an unwritten novel about wizards that eventually became *Monday Starts on Saturday*. Why it was given to a similarly unwritten novel about "our spy" becomes clear from Arkady's letter. I can't resist reproducing a long excerpt from it here, so that the reader can see through concrete example how much the authors' initial plans and outlines can differ from an idea's final realization.

> Somewhere there exists a planet, a precise replica of Earth, possibly with minor deviations, currently in the era immediately before the great geographical discoveries. Absolutism, merry drunk musketeers, a cardinal, a king, rebellious princes, the Inquisition, sailors' taverns, galleons and frigates, beauties, rope ladders, serenades, etc. And this is the country (a cross between France and Spain, or Russia and Spain) where our earthmen, long since absolute communists, "plant" someone—a young, strapping, good-looking guy with a huge fist, an excellent fencer, etc. Actually, not all earthmen plant him there, but, say, the Moscow Historical Society. One day, they approach the cardinal and tell him, "Here's how it is: you wouldn't understand, but we're leaving this kid here; you'll protect him from any intrigues; here's a sack of gold, and if anything happens to him,

we'll skin you alive." The cardinal agrees, the boys leave a broadcasting satellite by the planet, the guy wears a gold circlet around his head, as is the local fashion — except with a camera built into it instead of a diamond, which communicates with the satellite, which then in turn communicates pictures of the society to Earth. The guy is left alone on the planet, rents an apartment from Monsieur Bonacieux, and occupies himself in sauntering around the city, milling about the noblemen's anterooms, drinking in pubs, sword-fighting (but he never kills anyone, he even becomes famous for it), chasing girls, etc. This part would be very well written, fun, and amusing. When he climbs up the rope ladders, he modestly covers the lens with a plumed hat.

Then the era of geographical discoveries begins. The local Columbus returns and reports that he discovered America, a country as beautiful as Seventh Heaven, but there's no way to stay there: he was beset by beasts unseen on this side of the ocean. Then the cardinal summons our historian, and tells him, help us, you are capable of a lot, let's avoid unnecessary victims. The rest is clear. He calls for help from Earth — a high-powered tank and ten of his buddies with blasters, assigns a rendezvous with them on the other shore, and sails there on the galleons with the soldiers. They arrive, war begins, and then it's discovered that these animals are also intelligent creatures. The historians are humiliated, called up to the World Council and given a good dressing down for their mischief.

This can be written in a really fun and interesting way, like *The Three Musketeers*, only with medieval piss and filth — how women smell there, how the wine is full of dead flies. And there would be the implicit idea that a communist who found himself in such an environment would slowly but surely become a petty bourgeois, although for the reader he would remain a sweet and kind kid.

That's almost *it*, isn't it? But at the same time it's not quite *it*—and in a certain sense it's definitely *not it*. We used to call these kinds of plans "sturdy substantial skeletons." The existence of such a skeleton was a necessary (although not sufficient) condition for beginning real work. At least in those times. Later, another extremely important condition appeared: we absolutely had to know what would "soothe our souls"—what would be the ending of the planned work, the final landmark in the direction of which we were supposed to be dragging the plotline. But at the beginning of the 1960s, we still didn't understand how important that was, and therefore we would often take a risk and be forced to change the entire plot along the way. Which is exactly what happened with *Seventh Heaven*.

The "sturdy substantial skeleton" of the novel Arkady suggested was without a doubt good and promised us some wonderful work. But apparently, even at an early stage of the discussions, some differences in approach between the coauthors appeared; we hadn't even sat down at the table to begin the work when there was already a debate, the details of which I certainly do not remember, but its general course can be traced through other excerpts from Arkady's letters. (My own letters through the year 1963 were lost—alas!—irretrievably.)

> 03/17/1963—AS: . . . the entire program which you outlined can be completed in five days. But first I'd like to tell you, my pale flabby brother, that I'm for a light kind of thing—I'm talking about *Seventh Heaven*. So

women would cry, walls would laugh, and five hundred
villains would shout, "Get him! Get him!"—and they
wouldn't be able to do a thing with one communist.

The last phrase is a slightly modified quotation from our
beloved Dumas trilogy, and we're apparently talking about
the vein in which to write the new novel.

I had my own views on that subject. What they were
exactly can be guessed from my brother's comments in this
next excerpt:

03/22/1963: . . . About *The Observer* (that's what I've
renamed *Seventh Heaven*). If you're interested in a rush
of tumultuous life, then you will have a full opportunity to spill your guts in *Days of Kraken* and *The Magi-
cians*. But what I'd like to do is to write a novel about
abstract nobility, honor, and joy, like Dumas. And don't
you dare argue. Just one story without modern problems in naked form. I'm begging on my knees, bastard!
My sword, my sword! Cardinals! Port taverns!

This entire exchange was happening against a very interesting political backdrop. In the middle of December 1962
(I don't remember the exact date), Nikita Khrushchev saw
an exhibition of contemporary art at the Moscow Manege.
Goaded (according to rumors) by Leonid Ilichev, then the
head of the ideological commission of the Central Committee,
the furious chief—a renowned expert in the areas of painting
and all fine arts, you understand—ran through the exhibition
halls (again according to rumors), shouting, "Assholes! Who
do you work for? Whose bread do you eat? Motherfuck-
ers! Who did you daub this for, daubers?" He stamped his
feet, blood rushed to his face, and he showered spittle for
two yards around him. (This was precisely the origin of the

famous anecdote in which Nikita the Corn Man, staring at
a certain ugly image in a frame, yells in a voice not his own,
"And what's this butt with ears?" And is answered with fear
and trembling: "That's a mirror, Nikita Sergeyevich.")

All mass media without exception immediately descended
on abstraction and formalism in art, as if for the last ten years
they had been preparing just for this, collecting materials and
only waiting for permission to speak about this burning topic.

And that was only the beginning. "On December 17, at
the Reception House on Lenin Hills, there was a meeting
of the leaders of the Communist Party and the Soviet government with the writers and artists." Brezhnev, Voronov,
Kirilenko, Kozlov, Kosygin, Mikoyan, Polyansky, Suslov,
Khrushchev, and various other prominent plainclothes literary and art critics gathered in one place in order to "make
comments and suggestions on the development of literature
and art."

Observations were made. The press was no longer roar-
ing, it was literally howling: THERE CAN BE NO COMPROMISE;
THE RESPONSIBILITY OF THE ARTIST; THE LIGHT OF CLAR-
ITY; THE WORRY THAT GIVES US WINGS; ART AND PSEUDO-
ART; TOGETHER WITH THE PEOPLE; OUR STRENGTH AND
WEAPON; THIS IS OUR PARTY, THIS IS OUR ART!; DOING IT
LENIN'S WAY; ALIEN VOICES . . . It was as if an ancient abscess
had burst. Bad blood and pus overflowed from the newspaper pages. All those who during the years of the "thaw"
had gone quiet (it seemed to us), who had flattened their ears
and only looked around like hunted animals, as if waiting
for the inconceivable, impossible, improbable retribution
for the past; all these monstrous offspring of Stalinism and
Beria-ism, who were up to the elbows in the blood of inno-
cent victims, all these covert and overt informers, ideological

operators and moronic do-gooders—they all instantly sprang out of their hiding places; they all turned out to be right on the spot, energetic, agile, able hyenas of the pen, alligators of the typewriter. *Go to it!*

But that wasn't all. On March 7, 1963, the "exchange of opinions on literature and art" was continued. The experts were joined by a number of other connoisseurs of the fine arts—Podgorny, Grishin, and Mazurov. The exchange of opinions lasted two days. The newspaper howls intensified, even though you'd think that was impossible. THE GREATNESS OF TRUE ART; DOING IT LENIN'S WAY! (seen before, but now with an exclamation mark); THE PHILOSOPHY OF WESTERN ART: EMPTINESS, DECAY, DEATH; HIGH IDEALS AND ARTISTIC SKILL: THE GREAT POWER OF SOVIET LITERATURE AND ART; THERE'S NO "THIRD" IDEOLOGY!; CREATING IN THE NAME OF COMMUNISM; GLORIFYING, PRAISING, CULTIVATING HEROISM; HOLD STEADY! (the number of exclamation marks is definitely increasing); PURSUITS IN POETRY, TRUE AND FALSE; LOOKING AHEAD!

> The sun is out, but no warmth—no matter.
> There's a flood, flowing floodwater.
> All cattle join in joyous song,
> A thaw has come, but it's all wrong!

That was Yuliy Kim instantly responding—as always, poisonously and with perfect precision:

> Flood water, spring water,
> Turbid, wanton, dissolute water . . .
> Grab your nets and toss them quick,
> Brothers, you will have your pick!
> *Go to it!*

All the record players in all the intellectuals' kitchens were ringing with his verses, performed in a deliberately cloying and even tender voice.

> Oh, what a time! A dream of a time!
> How the Kochets crow and crow!
> The kind of singing I hear outside,
> Even the "October" never did know!

"Kochets" doubtlessly refers here to the colleagues and associates of V. Kochetov, the then–chief editor of the pro-Stalin journal *October*, an inveterate Stalinist, anti-Semite, and reactionary who was even occasionally reprimanded by the authorities in order to maintain decorum "in the eyes of the international labor movement."

They started with the modern artists: Falk, Sidur, Ernst Neizvestny, and then, before anyone knew it, they went after Ilya Ehrenburg, Viktor Nekrasov, Andrei Voznesensky, Alexander Yashin, and the movie *I Am Twenty*. And of course, anyone who felt like it walked all over Aksenov, Yevtushenko, Sosnora, Ahmadulina, and even—but politely, bowing the whole time!—Solzhenitsyn. (Solzhenitsyn still remained in favor with the Man. But the rest of the entourage, how they all hated and feared him! In favor with the king, out of favor with his huntsmen.)

In good time, the purulent wave reached even our outskirts, our quiet science fiction shop. On March 26, 1963, there was an expanded meeting of the science fiction and adventure section of the Moscow Writers' Organization. The following people were present: Georgiy Tushkan (the chairman of the section, the author of several adventure stories and the science fiction novel *Black Whirlwind*), A. P. Kazantsev, Georgy Gurevich, Anatoly Dneprov, Roman Kim (the author of the stories "The Notebook Found in Suncheon," "The Girl from Hiroshima," and "Burn After Reading"), Sergei Zemaitis (the head of the science fiction editorship at the Young Guard publishing house), Yevgeny Pavlovich Brandis, and many others. Here's a characteristic passage from Arkady's detailed report about it:

> And that's when the worst began. Kazantsev spoke. The first half of his speech was entirely devoted to Altov and Zhuravleva. The second half I didn't listen to, because I was agonizing, not knowing what to do. Here are the theses of what he was saying. The Altov direction in science fiction had, thank God, never gotten developed. And that's not surprising, because Soviet science fiction writers as a whole are people of principle. At the 1958 meeting, Altov accused "Dneprov and I" of clinging to a single topic which everyone was sick of: the collision of two worlds. No, Comrade Altov, we are not sick of this topic, and you are an unprincipled person. (The stenographers were frantically recording everything. In general, everything was recorded in shorthand.) In the *Star River Test*, Altov takes a stand against Einstein's postulate about the speed of light. But in the '30s, fascists tortured and persecuted Einstein for precisely this postulate. All of Altov's writing in one way or another plays into the hands of fascism. (The stenographers keep recording! Don't worry, I'm not exaggerating, I thought I must be dreaming myself.) Not only that, but all of Altov's writing is so far removed from life, so empty and devoid of vital content, that we can safely call him an abstract literary artist, and therefore a dauber and a slanderer, and so on.

> I didn't listen any further. I broke out in a cold sweat. Everyone sat there, still as death, staring at the table, no one was making a sound, and that's when I

realized that for the first time in my life I was faced with
His Majesty the Avenging Idiot, with what had happened in 1937 and 1949. Should I protest? And what
if they don't support me? How do I know what they
have up their sleeve? And what if this had already been
approved and agreed upon? A terrible cowardice seized
me, and it wasn't for no reason; I was also afraid for you.
And then I got so enraged that the cowardice vanished.
And when Kazantsev finished, I yelled, "Allow me!"
Tushkan, looking at me with displeasure, said, "Now,
now, go on then." "With all due respect to Alexander
Petrovich, I strongly protest. It's possible to like Altov
or not to like Altov. I don't like him that much myself,
but think about what you're saying. Altov—a fascist!
That's a label, this is being recorded in shorthand, we're
not sitting in a pub, this is God knows what, this is simply indecent!" (I remember this much, but I then kept
babbling for another five minutes or so.)

A second of dead silence. Then Tolya Dneprov's
steely voice: "For my part, I must state that I haven't
heard Altov accusing me of a predilection for the subject of the struggle between two worlds. He accused me
of having characters that are not people, but ideas and
machines." Kim: "And he's no abstractionist. On the
contrary, when he visited me and saw so and so's picture, he criticized it severely."

Then everyone started clamoring, talking, Kazantsev began to explain what he wanted to say, and I was
shaking with anger and couldn't hear anything else.
And when it was all over, I got up, cursed (using strong
language, I think), and told Golubev, "Let's leave this
place, they are handing out labels." I said it loudly. We
went downstairs to the pub, and guzzled down a bottle
of some liqueur.

So now it seemed like absolutely everyone got what was coming to them.

However, no one was arrested. No one was even kicked out of the Writers' Union. Moreover, in the midst of the purulent stream we were even allowed to put together two or three articles containing careful objections and an outline of our (and not the party's) point of view. These objections were immediately trampled and crushed, but the fact of their appearance already meant that the authorities were not aiming to kill.

And already, the reigning Soviet playwright Anatoly Sofronov (a real piece of work, I'm sorry to say), was arrogantly soothing the frightened: "Some are now expressing concerns: that there might be excesses, that someone might be 'suppressed,' etc. Don't worry, they won't 'suppress' us, no need to fear. Our Soviet regime is kind, our party is kind and humane. We must do honest, good work, then everything will be all right."

But we weren't as much afraid as disgusted. Everything felt vile and repulsive, like rotten meat. No one really knew what had caused this rapid return to the abscess. It was possible that the authorities were upset about the very recent painful flick on the nose they had received during the Cuban Missile Crisis and were taking out their anger on their own people. It was possible that the agricultural situation had deteriorated even further, and shortages of bread were already being predicted for the near future (they did occur in 1963). It was possible that it was simply the time to show the swollen-headed "intelligoosia" who's the master of this house and who he stands with—not your Ehrenburgs, not your Ernst Neizvestnys, not your suspicious Nekrasovs—but with the good old guard, tried and true, long since bought, cowed, and reliable.

One could pick any of these versions or all of them at once. But one thing became, as they say, painfully clear. We shouldn't have illusions. We shouldn't have hopes for a brighter future. We were being governed by goons and enemies of culture. They will never be with us. They will always be against us. They will never let us say what we believe is right, because what they believe is right is something completely different. And if for us communism is a world of freedom and creativity, for them communism is a society where the people immediately and with pleasure perform all the prescriptions of the party and government.

The realization of these simple—although then far from obvious for us—truths was painful, like the realization of any truth, but beneficial at the same time. New ideas appeared and strongly demanded their immediate implementation. The "fun story in the spirit of *The Three Musketeers*" that we had thought up began to appear in an entirely different light, and I didn't need long speeches to convince Arkady that they needed to make a substantial ideological adjustment in *The Observer*. The time of "light things," the time of "swords and cardinals" seemed to have passed. Or maybe it simply hadn't come yet. The adventure story had to, was obliged to, become a story about the fate of the intelligentsia, submerged in the twilight of the Middle Ages.

From Arkady's journal:

. . . 12–16 (April 1963) was in Leningrad. . . . Made a decent sketch of *The Observer* (formerly *Seventh Heaven*) . . .

08/13/1963— . . . Wrote *Hard to Be a God* in June. Now hesitating, unsure what to do with it. Detgiz won't take it. Maybe we should try *Novy Mir*?

We never did try *Novy Mir*, but we did try the thick journal *Moskva*. To no avail. The manuscript was returned with
a condescendingly negative review—apparently *Moskva*
didn't print science fiction.

In general, the novel inspired contradictory reactions
from the reading public. Our editors were especially puzzled. Everything in this novel was unusual to them, and
a lot of requests (quite friendly, by the way, and not at all
meanly critical) were made. On the advice of I. A. Efremov,
we renamed the Minister of the Defense of the Crown Don
Reba (he had previously been Don Rebia—an overly simple
anagram, in the opinion of Ivan Antonovich.) Moreover, we
had to do a lot of work on the text and add an entire big
scene where Arata the Hunchback demands lightning from
the hero and doesn't receive it.

It's amazing that this novel went through all the hurdles
of censorship without any particular difficulties. Either the
liberalism of the then-leaders of the Young Guard played a
role, or the careful maneuvers of our wonderful editor, Bela
Grigorevna Klyueva, or maybe it was actually just that there
was a certain retreat after the recent ideological hysteria—
our enemies were catching their breath and complacently
looking around the newly captured lands and beachheads.

Although on the book's release, a reaction of a certain
sort followed immediately. This might have been the first
time that the Strugatskys were attacked by the big guns.
The academic of the Academy of Sciences of the USSR
Y. Frantsev accused the authors of abstractionism and surrealism, while his venerable fellow writer V. Nemtsov accused
us of pornography. Fortunately, that was still a time when
it was permissible to respond to the attacks, and I. Efremov
stood up for us in his brilliant article "Billions of Facets of

the Future." And the political temperature outside had by then gone down. In short, nothing happened. (The ideological mutts would still occasionally bark at this novel from their yards, but then we got around to publishing *Tale of the Troika*, *The Final Circle of Paradise*, *The Snail on the Slope*— and against that background, the novel *Hard to Be a God*, to the surprise of the authors, even became a work to emulate. The Strugatskys were already being scolded: what's this, look at *Hard to Be a God*—you know what to do when you feel like it, why don't you keep working in that vein?)

The novel, we must admit, was a success. Some readers found in it adventures reminiscent of *The Three Musketeers*, others cool science fiction. Teenagers liked the exciting plot; the intelligentsia the dissident ideas and attacks on totalitarianism. Over the course of a dozen years, the polls all showed that the novel shared the first and second place in the ratings with our *Monday Starts on Saturday*. As of October 1997, it had a circulation of 2.6 million in Russian, and that's not counting the Soviet publications in foreign languages and the languages of the peoples of the USSR. And among foreign publications, it occupies a solid second place immediately after *Roadside Picnic*. According to my information, it has been published in forty-nine editions in twenty-one countries, including Germany (eight editions), Bulgaria (five), Spain (five), Poland (four), France (four), the Czech Republic (three), etc.